FAMILIAR

FAMILIAR

A Novel

J. Robert Lennon

Graywolf Press

This publication is made possible in part by a grant provided by the
Minnesota State Arts Board, through an appropriation by the Minnesota
State Legislature from the Minnesota general fund and its arts and cultural
heritage fund with money from the vote of the people of Minnesota on
November 4, 2008, and a grant from the Wells Fargo Foundation Minnesota.
Significant support has also been provided by the National Endowment for the
Arts; Target; the McKnight Foundation; and other generous contributions
from foundations, corporations, and individuals. To these organizations
and individuals we offer our heartfelt thanks.

Published by Graywolf Press
250 Third Avenue North, Suite 600
Minneapolis, Minnesota 55401

8 3 9 8

www.graywolfpress.org

Published in the United States of America

ISBN 978-1-55597-625-5

2 4 6 8 9 7 5 3 1
First Graywolf Printing, 2012

Library of Congress Control Number: 2012936386

Cover design: Kyle G. Hunter

Cover photo: Lauri Rotko/Folio Images/Getty Images

After the death of his mother, he had spent five years in the house of his brother. It was not from what he said but from the way he said it that his enormous animosity toward the domineering, cold, and unfriendly nature of his brother became evident.

Then, in short, not very pregnant sentences, he related that he had a friend now who very much loved and admired him. Following this communication, there was a prolonged silence. A few days later he reported a dream: *he saw himself in a strange city with his friend, except that the face of his friend was different.*

—Wilhelm Reich, *Character Analysis*

FAMILIAR

PART ONE

I.

She's driving. A Monday morning in July, hot outside, the windows of her Honda are down and the highway air is rushing in. It's the sixth hour of a daylong trip from the town where her dead son is buried to the town where she lives now with her husband and living son.

Her name is Elisa Macalaster Brown. She makes this trip once a year: drives to Wisconsin, stays in a motel, drinks coffee and reads magazines in the places she used to go, when both boys were alive and they all lived there together. She visits the grave, never for long. She watches television in her room. She remembers people from when she lived there, and if she sees them she says hello, but she never seeks them out. They know why she's there and they don't want to talk about it. When she's finished she gets back into her car and goes home, and that's what she's doing now.

Interstate 90 is a dull gray strap laid over brown land. There's a drought here and everything is dead. Somewhere in Ohio. Other cars can be seen far ahead and far behind, but nobody passes anybody else. Soon she'll have to stop for lunch, but for now she is content being hungry.

She likes to drive this car—she's had it for a dozen years. Silas and Sam used to ride in back, on the way to soccer practice or music lessons, in the days when they could be persuaded to care about such things. There was a dog for a while, Derek's dog from before they married, but it died. The car still smells a little like dog, but all traces of Silas are gone. Sam borrows the car sometimes, filling the ashtray with his cigarette butts and leaving them there for Elisa to clean up. No, that's not fair—it has nothing to do with her. He just forgets. He's twenty-five, a year older than his brother would be.

But for now Elisa is alone. Solitude is something she learned how to love, and now she loves it better than almost anything. She loves it at home, in her filthy little studio at the back of the house, with her radio and paints, where she goes on her day off when Derek is at work. But she is most alone in a car, on a trip, this trip, with the windows down and the wind and highway in her ears. Or in a storm, windows shut, defogger roaring, the rain thudding against the metal and glass. She doesn't listen to the radio. It's too easy to get invested in something, only to hear it fade away. Not that there's much on the radio to capture her interest. She doesn't like the news. Politics are meaningless to her. She didn't care who won the 2008 election—this disgusted people she knew. But they forgave her because her son was dead and they figured that had something to do with it.

She believes that Silas's death makes people feel superior to her. They decided at some point that it was probably her fault. In any event, her days of worrying about other people's opinions of her are long over.

Everything's going to change in a couple of minutes.

2.

The Honda has a crack in the windshield that runs from the lower left-hand corner to a spot at eye level on the passenger side. She is looking at the crack, or rather through the crack, to the white line on the roadside that it parallels. This is a habit of hers that she is now indulging, keeping the crack aligned with the line.

When she was a teenager and her father took her out to the suburbs to teach her to drive, he recommended that, in order to stay on the road, she should keep the hood ornament aligned in her vision with the white line. It was one of four stations, as he put it, for the eye to visit: side mirror, rearview mirror, speedometer, hood ornament. Even the shortest journey should consist of a constant cycling among the four. He was methodical that way. When her mother drank or grew depressed, and Elisa ended up in tears in her bedroom with the radio turned up, her father's knock was never far behind; he would sit at the foot of her bed, ostentatiously not touching her, and offer tried and tested methods for "dealing with" her mother: never look directly into her eyes when she is in "a state"; never tell her that she reminds you of *her* mother; always offer audible feedback to indicate you're listening; frequently use the phrase "of course you're right." As though the woman were a problem to be solved.

Which in some ways she was. Which in some ways Elisa is, as she is painfully aware. Derek, to his credit, doesn't try. He lets her wend her unthinking way through her life, making only the subtlest suggestions, usually coiled up inside the phrase "You're a scientist, you figure it out." A reminder of what she gave up. An unasked question of why.

The problem, of course, with her father's driving method is that it leaves out actually looking where you're going. In truth it is not necessary to align anything with anything, in order to drive. You just focus on a point in the distance and move toward it. Here on the highway, Elisa feels proud to have overcome this limitation in her technique; gazing through the crack is just a tic. But outside the car, in her life, this has long been, and remains, a problem. There is only what lies directly in front of her, and she is afraid to look away from it. She is resourceful; tough, she hopes; able to cope with whatever she finds immediately before her. But she doesn't want to look up and see the future.

A shrink told her that once, about herself. Facile nonsense, she told Derek. Derek nodded in the way he nodded when he thought she was wrong.

She is feeling the feeling of being hungry and thinking about what food she will settle for, when she finally decides it's time to eat. A spring inside the driver's seat is worrying at her back. One cloud is in the sky, its bottom edge just visible in the tinted area running along the top of the windshield. Sunlight has slashed the dashboard in two and she can see her fingerprints in the dust, from where she braced herself several days ago, at a rest stop on the outbound leg of the trip, while she was picking some money up off the passenger-side floor.

Everything is so clear and vivid, she is almost moved.

3.

She married at twenty-one. Derek was in law school—he was twenty-five, wore a tie; he took her out and drank one bottle of beer and they had sex in his room. He was consistent in everything, the things he said, the ways he touched her: it flattered her, that he should care enough to do the things he knew would please her. She took him home to Chicago, and her parents embarrassed her, with their sagging bookcases and thick eyeglasses and Oriental rugs worn through to the boards. Growing up, she had been smuggled into jazz clubs, she read fantasy novels in the back row of Marxist lectures, inhaled pot smoke on her way to bed. Blacks and gays came to the house and she sat on their knees. Cops broke up her parents' parties. Karl Popper once took her to a Cubs game.

But Derek managed to impress them, laughing at their jokes, pretending to sympathize with their politics. When they told him he was welcome to sleep with Elisa in her room he said no thanks, the couch was fine. During the night she went to him.

"Sorry," she whispered.

"They're all right."

"They're not."

"They love you."

"They love themselves."

Derek gazed at her levelly. "We aren't any different," he said, and she said, "Fuck you, Derek!" just loud enough to be sure her parents would hear.

This was a part of him she professed to dislike—the thing they would fight about, when they fought. The way he would challenge her, reflexively, as though, because she was younger, because she was a woman, because she was less advanced in her studies, because her parents were bohemians, she lacked rigor, lacked the ability to see herself clearly. She fought against his patronizing tone, shouted at him, cursed, pushed him hard in the chest with both hands. His amusement at her rage enraged her further still.

But of course this was what attracted them, too. She liked his immovability, his physical solidity and unswerving beliefs, the way she could fling herself against him until she was exhausted. He liked her volatility, her war against the genetic and cultural heritage she ultimately had no hope of overcoming (and perhaps, at least at times, secretly loved).

And so why, when they got married and she got pregnant, did she give in? She'd been working on a master's in plant biology at UW, in Madison. Derek told her she didn't have to quit, she shouldn't, but she surprised herself by wanting to. And as soon as she did, she felt a profound relief. She drank coffee (until her growing body developed an aversion) and read, and decided that she was going to love motherhood. She made a careful study of parenting books and tallied up their shortcomings in her head even before she'd reached her third trimester; they seemed to her like bad science. When both births went smoothly, when she appeared happy, Derek professed to be pleased. If he missed her old intensity, he didn't say so. In any event, the only advice her parents could give her now was parenting advice, and they wouldn't dare. They were proud of their inexpertise. "The shittiest parents in Chicago," Elisa's mother used to boast to her friends. Her parents approved wholeheartedly of her early marriage, her abandonment of her studies, seeming to delight in having raised someone so different from themselves, someone who turned out to be conventional after all. Or perhaps Elisa was happy, and they saw this, and it pleased them? Surely it couldn't be that simple?

No, of course not. But by now it was time to stop caring about what they thought or why they thought it. She had her own life to live. Her own children to confuse.

She raised the boys, talked on the phone with friends, listened to the morning therapist on the radio and laughed at people's problems. Derek always worked late but it was all right. He didn't have anybody on the side. He was just busy. He specialized in maritime law as it applied to the Great Lakes. When she began to feel that perhaps she had thrown her youth away, she got a part-time job as a technician at the lab where she had once interned, before she met Derek. It was all right. She kept doing it. They spent most of a decade like this, turning into Wisconsinites. She was happy enough with Derek, with her lab. This is what she told herself.

Years later, when Derek accepted the job at SUNY Reevesport, Elisa considered not going with him. Keeping Sam and staying in Madison. Or even giving up Sam for a little while, staying there alone. Derek didn't understand. He had actually been offered the job the previous year—it was what they wanted then, a change, maybe a way to break the pattern of Silas's bad behavior. But then Silas died, and he had to turn it down. Now the college had called and offered it to him again—the other guy hadn't worked out. He hounded Elisa until she told him—this came to her without forethought—that it was Silas's grave, she didn't want to leave Silas's grave.

"That's it?" he said.

It wasn't, but she said, "Yes."

"But that's ridiculous."

"Leaving our son behind?"

"But you're willing to leave our living son behind."

She said nothing.

"A grave can be moved," he said.

He was right—it embarrassed her not to have thought of that.

"That's not what I want," she said.

"Then what do you want?"

This was the question Derek could always use to end an argument, because it was the question she could never seem to answer. Even when she did know what she wanted, she often found it difficult to articulate. Where to go, what to do. Should we spend this money on the house, or on a vacation? Do you want to go back to school? Do you want to go out to eat? Should Silas's friends, the ones who led him wrong, be invited to the funeral, or barred from it? Does Sam need counseling, do we all need counseling? What do you want to do for the rest of your life? What have you ever wanted to do?

The only thing she always knew she wanted was love, was Derek, was her boys, but then even that went wrong, and she didn't want anything at all. And so she began to feel as though there was no want, there was no you.

What do you want?

They moved to Reevesport together, and the grave stayed behind, an unresolved conflict between them. An artifact. It is still there, and that's why she's on the road today, five years later, July 23, 2012. That's why she has her job waiting for her in Reevesport, in another lab, managing it this time. That's why she has her art studio and her love of solitude, and an affair she's been having with a man in the town, the man who runs the frame shop. That's why she's where she is now, poised to apprehend the inexplicable thing that's about to happen.

                                        4.

Her initial method of coping was to ignore everything. To obliterate her usual mode of attention. She didn't let her eyes or mind rest. She kept moving, doing things of little or no importance. This was in Madison. She didn't answer the phone or return messages. She threw most mail away. Derek paid the bills, talked to Elisa's mother on the phone, took Sam to the shrink. She got thinner and no longer drank for pleasure, or for any reason at all. She stopped having sex, while Derek carried on, semi-openly and without evident pleasure, with a colleague. She rarely spoke and didn't look people in the eye when she did. She did not feel alive.

Then, about a year in, she made a discovery. If she managed to focus on something very small, she could enter into a state of deep concentration that her body registered as satisfaction. Embroidery. She had a kit: a long-forgotten gift from Derek's mother that she had almost thrown out. Now she spent three months doing almost nothing else. Her eyes were red and tired from incessant close focus. Her fingertips were callused from pricking. She would finish a project—flowers, ducks, it didn't matter—set it aside, pick up another. This is what she did while they prepared for the move, while Derek packed boxes, marked boxes, hauled boxes.

As she worked she would talk. In her head, she thought. The first time was with the memory of a college roommate, a sullen, lachrymose girl named Naomi with flat damp eyes and a long chin, who had stayed in Elisa's dorm for only a semester before transferring. She had worn flannel pajamas printed with a pattern of ivy not unlike the one Elisa was embroidering now. The two of them were not friends. They argued over petty things—water in the soap dish, moldy food. These were the kinds of fights they had now, in Elisa's head, but with a wild and violent intensity: the two of them facing off in the narrow vestibule of their dorm room, shoving each other against the walls, screaming and spitting in each other's faces. There was something deeply satisfying and fascinating about these fantasies; daily, Elisa took up her needlework with excitement and dread, like a junkie.

At some point the arguments with Naomi left the hallway and moved to the bedroom, where, in predawn light, Elisa could make out the ivy pajamas discarded on the floor, and in the bed, her roommate's thick stubbled ankles crossed over a man's tight and clenching ass: Derek, her husband, fucking the horsey Naomi!

The women shoved and shouted while Derek cowered, half-covered by the bedclothes. Elisa could feel the rough synthetic carpet underneath her feet, she could smell deodorant and sweaty bras and the funk of sex.

You don't go to bed without washing your fucking dinner dishes! And your fucking hair in the shower drain! And that's my husband, get your hands off my husband! Before dismissing Naomi, poor shy unhappy Naomi, from her thoughts, Elisa got her libido back, made Derek screw her, told him to give up the woman from work, *You're mine,* she told him, *you're mine.*

In the days that followed, in her head, she found herself in a pseudo-intellectual standoff with an old philosophy professor; embroiled in a religious debate with an Orthodox rabbi, the father of an old friend; in the checkout aisle of the supermarket, demanding to see the manager.

And then Silas, the nonexistent adult Silas, in the hospital waiting area, the two of them separated by twenty feet of linoleum, shouting at one another, their fingers gripping the soft and soiled arms of their chairs. She could smell the stale coffee in the little café beyond the reception desk; she could see nurses hurrying by, white moths at the edges of her vision. This was the hospital where they were told to go after the accident; this is where the doctor told them he was dead. Indeed, in this fantasy, the doctor was waiting just offstage, invisible but present; Elisa warded him off with an outstretched hand.

Here, Silas was tall—he was still growing when he died—and stooped, around twenty-five, though he seemed to have aged further. Sullen, as in life, but sadder now. Angry, but a new kind of anger. Calculated, precise. She was afraid of him, not afraid of what he might do, but that whatever he said, it might be right.

You always thought you were so smart! You thought you were smarter than everyone else! But look at you now!

He raised his face to reply, and his mouth moved and sounds came out of it. They frightened her, though they had not yet coalesced into sense. Any second now, they might.

What are you doing here? she shouted, *Why did you make us come here?* (Though Derek wasn't there in this fantasy, only Elisa; she needed Silas to think his father was present to back her up, though it wasn't clear why this was important.)

He was pointing at her now, as he spoke, pointing first at Elisa and then down the hall, where his own dead body lay, and his eyes were blazing and his lips were white with spit. He stood up, accusing her of something, she didn't know what. The twenty feet between them seemed to collapse into ten, then five.

There is nothing else I could have done, she was saying, *I would have had to become someone else.*

And now he was right there, she could feel the heat from his enraged face and she understood him now, *That's what I wanted!* he shouted, *That's what I wanted!*

(And all the while she poked and pulled at the embroidery hoop, a toad seated on a mushroom, blades of grass springing up on either side, I HEAR IT'S SPRING! was the caption, and her lips moved, muttered sounds came out, and later Sam would say he paused outside the open door calling *Mom, Mom!* and she didn't answer.)

She stops for gas and food at the first place she sees when she can no longer stand not eating. It's a sprawling rest stop, with separate parking lots for cars and big rigs, and multiple pavilions under which gas can be pumped. She chooses one, fills her tank with the wind blowing her hair into her face, then goes inside and eats something so bland and generic she isn't even aware of what it is while she's eating it. She is reminded of every other highway journey she has undertaken, every other undistinguished meal. She thinks they stopped here when they moved from Wisconsin—here or someplace exactly like it. They sat in a silent cluster, chewing their food and staring into space.

They never did find a rhythm, the three of them. A way for them to fit together without Silas. They would get along, life would be peaceful in their new home, but they had no sense of purpose. The house in Reevesport was quiet; it had more rooms, for fewer people. One of them was a studio for Elisa in which, presumably, she would find something to do. She loaded all her embroidery into it, sat there for a few days, then threw it all away.

A few weeks later, Sam said to her, "That stuff was fucking you up. You should paint." This was a habit that Sam had begun, gradually and then with increasing confidence, to indulge: treating his mother like a casual acquaintance, another teenager. He swore. He let her see his cigarettes, spilling out of the military-surplus canvas satchel on which he had Sharpied an anarchy symbol. This is something his brother might once have mocked. Sam was seventeen then, but at times seemed much younger.

Elisa said, "I don't paint."

"So?" he said. He himself was into drawing. He was trying to start a band. "It doesn't matter," he said to her. "Just paint."

She did what he said. A few months later, it was almost all she did. For a long time she tried to paint particular subjects—she bought some watercolors and an easel and went out in nature and made terrible pictures of things. But she preferred to be in the studio. So she switched to still lifes. Then she took up acrylics because the watercolors were so thin as to seem to consist of nothing at all. She liked the acrylics so much, the rich pastes in their metal tubes, that she stopped caring about what she was painting and just put the paint onto the canvas right out of the tube. Then she gave up on canvas and just slathered the paint around using a palette knife on squares of plywood she cut to size in the shed. When she broke the palette knife trying to open a frozen door lock, she switched to a heavy-duty paint scraper from the hardware store.

She did not talk to herself or to anyone else, real or imaginary, while she was painting. At first it was an effort not to. This was a thing her mind craved. But she silenced the voices and tried to appreciate the integrity of the materials before her, and as the voices went away so did her subject matter, until she was left with pure form. She tried to make her mind mirror the paintings, to render the slurry of memory and impulse as colored fields, complementary blanknesses connected by line and hue. This became the new project, doomed to failure. Which is part of why she liked it.

All of this took a year. She was working again, at the new lab. She worked, and made these paint-covered squares, in perfect contentment. The paintings weren't art. They weren't for other people. They were just a thing she was doing.

But Derek told her she should go out and find a gallery to hang them in. She believed that he was growing weary of her cadaverous presence in the house, her sexual appetite (which had not been quelled by its regular satisfaction), her newly rediscovered intensity and sobriety that appeared, once and for all, to have nothing of substance behind it. So she took a couple of the most obscure-looking paintings out to get framed, and the man at the frame shop looked at them and said, "They don't need much. They don't really need frames at all, do they?" A few weeks after that, she went to bed with him.

She gets back on the road, and again she is driving, and the windows are down and the air is rushing in. This stretch of highway is both different and exactly the same. They made it to be consistent. So that wherever you go it looks like the American highway. And the highways of Ohio, she has often thought, are the precise average of all the other highways in America. When people say "the open highway" they are thinking of Wyoming, Colorado, northern California, but if you are driving a car in America, chances are you're someplace that looks a lot like this. Elisa is surprised that more people don't fall asleep and crash.

Two cars and a pickup are approaching from the east. They are still a great distance away. Behind her, equally distant, is something that looks like a minivan. Far out in front of her is a white sports car that entered the highway ten minutes ago and accelerated quickly away. She expected it would continue to outrace her, to disappear, but it slowed down and is still visible.

The guardrail beyond the white line is gently bowed, as though a giant paused there for a rest. Underneath it grows an unfamiliar weed, some kind of fern, and beside the fern lies a perfect undented aluminum can.

5.

The crack in the windshield disappears. She tries to blink it back into place because at first she thinks that her vision has blurred, but blinking doesn't bring it back, and now she is noticing other things. The sound inside the car has changed. It's quiet. The window is closed. The window's closed and the air-conditioning is on, the dashboard isn't dusty anymore, and the taste of mint gum is in her mouth. In fact the gum is there, she has gum in her mouth right now. She pushes it out with her tongue and it falls into her lap.

The gum lands not on her cutoff jeans, but on a gray cotton skirt draped over a pair of stockings. These aren't her clothes—she doesn't have clothes like these. She's wearing an ivory silk blouse and there's a sticker

on the blouse that reads HELLO! MY NAME IS, then in her own block printing, ELISA MACALASTER BROWN.

She notices that the spring in the seat is no longer bothering her, and
that she is wearing an uncomfortable bra.

Elisa looks up at the road. Only a second, less than a second, has
passed, and the road has grown. It's wider, the sky is taller. And it's cloudy
now, partly cloudy, many small clouds, as though the single cloud has
spawned. No—it isn't the road that's wider, it's the windshield, the windshield is larger.

She glances around her, at the interior of the car, and it isn't her car.

She signals and pulls over. The shoulder here is wide, and she comes
to a stop as close to the guardrail as she dares. Another car passes her
from behind, startling her, because it wasn't there before. She shifts into
park and leaves it running: there are her hands on the wheel, her familiar
hands. One of them reaches into her lap and picks up the gum; the other
reaches for the window crank. But this car has power windows. Okay. The
switch, then. The window rolls down and out goes the gum.

After a moment, she opens the door and gets out herself. When she
tries to stand up she nearly falls over. It's her shoes. She's wearing pumps
with low heels. Not sneakers. Right. She slips off the shoes and stands
on the hot pavement in her stockings. Stockings! In the summer! But of
course the car is air-conditioned, why not?

She turns and gets a good look at this car. It's American. A Dodge
Intrepid, sort of copper-colored.

An eighteen-wheeler passes, roiling the air, and she squints. Maybe
I should find a doctor, she thinks.

Instead she gets back into the idling car, closes the window, and sits
very still for a few minutes. She peels the name tag off her blouse and folds
it over, onto itself, and sets it in the drink holder. (Drink holder!) Beside
her, on the passenger seat, is a thick plastic three-ring binder. There's a
label stuck to it, bearing her name—laser-printed, this time—under the
title 6TH ANNUAL CONFERENCE OF ACADEMIC ADMINISTRATORS. She opens
it. A schedule, presentation agendas, handouts. *New networked software
applications offer statistics-driven space management models for research and
pedagogical purposes.* Has she attended this? It doesn't seem possible. She
thumbs through the pages until she arrives at the plastic pocket in the

back of the binder. There are several printed-out e-mails, hotel reservations, maps. An envelope marked RECEIPTS in her own handwriting. She chooses an e-mail at random. It consists of an exchange between, apparently, herself and a conference organizer. Supported by a small forest of carets is a boilerplate sig line: Elisa Macalaster Brown, Graduate Studies Coordinator, Levinson Biotech Center, SUNY Reevesport. And a phone number.

This is not her job.

There's a handbag on the passenger side floor, and she reaches over and picks it up. The movement is familiar to her, she performed it just the other day, picking up that change. But it feels more effortful now, for reasons that are not yet clear. The bag is familiar too—it's her bag. Inside it is a cell phone, not one she recognizes, but no matter—the bag interior looks right, it contains the same mass of scribbled notes and receipts and ticket stubs and dead ballpoint pens she is accustomed to. Okay then. She turns on the phone and there's a photo of Derek on the screen. It looks recent—he is groomed and relaxed, smiling in the shade of a tree.

She hesitates for a moment, and in that moment feels the world trembling, as though it might implode. An involuntary gasp. Have to do something. She casts her gaze around the interior of the car, settles on the printed e-mail, picks it up. She opens the phone and calls the number in her own sig line.

She expects voicemail. But: "Levinson Center."

"Ah . . . hello?"

There's a pause. Then, "Lisa?"

She laughs. She's got to admit, it's funny! She laughs and the voice on the other end laughs and says "Are you at the conference?" and Elisa says "Yes, no, I mean I'm on the road, sorry, I meant to call Derek" and the voice laughs again, says "See you tomorrow."

Elisa ends the call.

If there's a time to panic, this is it, while she's alone. She takes several deep breaths and rests her head on the wheel. All right, she thinks, this is very unusual, this is frightening. Or it should be frightening. But she isn't afraid, not really. Instead, she is intensely aware.

She is reminded of times in her life when everything felt different, all the time. When the small changes in her social circles, her patterns of thought, the texture of her emotions, would register as tectonic shifts, altering utterly the landscape of her life. College, grad school. The early days with Derek. Often she would stop what she was doing, close her eyes, take stock, and it would feel as though her life of just a week before, even of the previous day, was thoroughly, inalienably over, and that everything was starting again, beginning with now. And there were times when she would apprehend the impending extinction of the present moment. Out walking around the lake, or in bio lab, the sweat beading on her forehead and trickling down into her safety glasses. She would think, this moment was just born, and soon it will be gone. She would meet it, fall in love with it, mourn it, all at once. She cried more in those days. Almost daily, and often in public: silently, unobtrusively. The brutal immediacy of thoughts and emotions. This is what she has forgotten. It is here now. Her throat is tight and her jaw trembles.

Something must be wrong with her. Yet she doesn't feel dizzy or lightheaded. She only feels different. Her body is different. Jesus, this bra.

She lets out breath. Leans back in the seat and unbuttons her blouse. Quickly strips it off, unclasps the bra and removes that too. She tosses the bra onto the open binder and puts the blouse back on. Then, after a moment's thought, she lifts the blouse and looks at her stomach. It is definitely different. Fatter. She's what, ten pounds heavier? Fifteen? Suddenly she can feel her thighs chafing.

But I'm thin, she thinks. I walk to work.

To her lab, that is. Maybe she doesn't walk to the Levinson Biotech Center at SUNY Reevesport. Maybe she drives this car, not her Honda. Maybe she picks up a box of doughnuts on the way.

This is fucked up.

From inside her bag comes the sound of electronically rendered mariachi music.

She reaches in and takes out the phone. There's the picture of Derek again, and the screen tells her it's him who's calling. She isn't sure if she wants to hear his voice right now. But perhaps something is wrong. Maybe it's Sam, something's wrong with Sam. Why would he call her when he knew she was driving? He doesn't ever call her. If he needs her, he just waits for her to appear.

The music is awful. She answers.

"Hi, it's me! You got on the road okay?"

She doesn't speak.

"Lisa?"

"I'm here. Yes, I'm fine, I'm on the road."

"How far are you?"

"I don't know. I'm in Ohio."

After a silence, he says, "Are you all right?"

"Sure." He sounds different. So must she.

"You're sure?"

"I'll be home soon."

"Should I have dinner ready?"

Dinner. This isn't something he does.

"Yes, okay."

"Will do," he says.

"Okay."

"Love you."

"Okay," she says. She draws another breath, then hangs up. She sits and stares at nothing for a moment then figures out how to turn the phone off entirely. Hands trembling, she drops it back into the bag.

Now she is frightened. That voice that both is and is not Derek's. The presence of love where there is supposed to be none, or at least a different kind: habitual, practical, inert. A bulwark. Whereas the voice—even in the early days, when he whispered to her in the narrow apartment bed, when their love was a force field around them, buzzing like a short circuit in the energy of the world, it was not like that. Derek was never sweet. This wasn't a thing she thought she ever wanted. Her father was sweet. No, Elisa wanted a serious man.

The Derek who just called her was not anyone she recognized. He didn't sound like her husband impersonating somebody else. He sounded like somebody else.

There is something reassuring, isn't there, about the absence of love. This is what she has often told herself. The only real marriage is the marriage of the body and the mind. Until death do us part: a romantic lie. People can indeed be parted. Love can end, and the body and mind soldier on. To pick up the phone and find that love is gone, that's something a person can understand. That's a thing that happens. To pick up the phone and find that love is here, where it doesn't belong: well.

She has felt this before. The imminence of something enormous and terrible, bearing down. Not knowing. The last time, she was not ready. She should have been, of course; all the signs were there, she should have seen it coming. She might have turned and faced it, stood in its path and stared it down. Instead she let it crush her.

Another big rig roars past. The car shakes. She grips the wheel with both hands and lowers her head to it. All the air seems to be leaving the car. She thinks of the last thing she saw before everything changed, the soda can at the side of the road, and she sees it imploding, some invisible force crumpling it, it folds and twists in on itself, a death rattle escapes it. The steering wheel presses its fake leather texture into her forehead and blood rushes to the spot, and it is the heat from the blood and from the friction of her skin against the plastic that keeps her steady as the moment passes, the car inhales, the air around her cools.

Elisa sits very still, opening and closing her fingers on the wheel, breathing deeply. She feels a cloud pass over the sun, then disappear; her vision behind her closed eyes goes black and then red. After an interval she sits up.

She could look through her bag right now. It would tell her things, no doubt. Maybe it would prepare her better for her arrival at home. She considers, then decides to check one thing only. She feels around in the bag for her wallet, which is as she remembers, and takes a look at her driver's license. It isn't the same: her photo is unfamiliar. But the address is the same. She closes the wallet, shoves it into the bag, and pushes the bag onto the floor.

A minute later she's back on the highway, again heading home. At least she knows where it is.

6.

There was a time, back in Madison, after the accident, when she thought she was going to get a job, and she decided that she ought to get a picture of the boys to hang in her office.

This wasn't like her. She wasn't sentimental. But now she needed to be reminded of what she had lost and how she had failed. And the people she worked with, at this imaginary job, they would pity and coddle her, and she wanted to show them that she didn't need their pity, that she could take it, having this reminder there in the office with her.

As it happened, she couldn't take it after all. And she wouldn't work again until Reevesport. But she didn't know that yet.

Derek's mother was staying with them—she had come out from North Carolina for the funeral and lingered to help out around the house. As though Elisa, incapacitated by grief, would no longer be able to clean up after herself. This, anyway, was how Elisa chose to see it, Lorraine as an interloper, in collusion with Derek against her. Even from the depths of her misery, she understood that this wasn't the case, that Silas's death had changed her, that order had collapsed in their small house on Gorham Street and Derek feared for their marriage and for their life together: but still, he shouldn't have invited Lorraine to stay. They had lodged her in Derek's study, and she emerged mornings and walked slowly from room to room, coffee mug in hand, alert for signs of disorderliness. She often sat on the sofa with her arm around Sam's shoulders, as though protecting him. At times she gazed into Elisa's eyes and shook her head sadly, demonstrating her sympathy.

Elisa disliked Lorraine. She had always considered this dislike to be a reasonable response to Lorraine's dislike of her, but Derek had long maintained that Lorraine liked her just fine, or as much as it was possible for her to like any lover of Derek's. Derek's father had died young, Lorraine never remarried, and their attachment seemed unhealthy to Elisa. Crypto-sexual. For Derek's part, he shrugged and smiled when Elisa criticized his mother, as though the very thought of the woman charmed him. Of course this was exasperating, but on the other hand, what mother wouldn't welcome this kind of devotion?

Well: Elisa, for one. She had not been a cold mother, or an unaffectionate mother, but she had taken pains to keep a distance, a slight detachment. She had not allowed the boys to climb on her, to sit on her lap, to lie with her when she lounged reading on the sofa or on her bed. She stopped breastfeeding each after one year (Sam, of course, lost out to his brother, who had arrived so soon, so unexpectedly; she might have nursed them both, but somehow this had seemed a kind of taboo, or perhaps a visceral reaction to Silas's fussiness at the breast). What she feared, she would one day realize, was the overwhelming power of love: that if she ever loved her boys with the same level of intensity, the same *fla-vor* of intensity, that had once defined her devotion to Derek, she might never again take pleasure in solitude, in the fact of herself, in her self-containment, the intricacies of her mind. She feared she might give herself over to them, to the boys and men, and exist for them alone.

Lorraine blamed Elisa for Silas's troubles. She was the type of person for whom someone always had to be to blame: there were no innocent mistakes, no accidents. And if Silas was troubled, and Derek infallible, then who else's fault could it possibly be? To her credit, Lorraine never spoke her mind, not to Elisa anyway. But in her posture, her demeanor, the pitying way she looked at the boys, at her own boy: it was clear how she felt. And now that Silas was dead, now that the worst that could happen had happened, Elisa had begun to agree with her. It was her fault. It was. Cutting off the nursing. Pushing him away when she was trying to read. Failing to give the second helping of dessert. Letting him cry it out in the crib. Since the funeral Elisa had become obsessed with the past, with all the wrong turns their lives together had taken. If only she hadn't shouted. If only she hadn't smacked. Wandering through the house, in those days of Lorraine's tenancy, she would slow, then stop, mouth hanging open, staring at a patch of wall, thinking. Seeing herself doing this, understanding how it must look to Lorraine. And Lorraine was pleased to have been right about Elisa; her every gesture seemed to communicate triumph.

Elisa would have liked to discuss this phenomenon with Derek, but he didn't believe it to be real. He believed that his mother meant well and harbored no ill will toward Elisa at all.

In any event, and in spite of everything, she thought she would soon be going back to work, and she thought she would like to have a photo of the boys there. They rarely took photographs, they weren't that kind of family. They owned a small digital camera that now had a year's worth of pictures on it, on the memory card, that they had never transferred to a computer, or gotten printed. The camera was always lying around somewhere, in the basket of pencils in the kitchen drawer, or on the coffee table, or in somebody's bag, and every now and then one of them would pick it up and gaze at the photos on the tiny screen.

Elisa was looking for the camera. She couldn't find it. Sam and Derek didn't know where it was. She searched for twenty minutes before discovering it, at last, in Lorraine's room. Later, when Lorraine came home—she had taken Sam and Derek to the movies—and saw the camera in Elisa's hands, she said, "I see you found the camera."

"What did you do?"

"I'm sorry, dear," Lorraine said, "I don't know what you mean."

Derek was standing beside his mother, keys still in hand. They were in the kitchen, Derek staring at Elisa, who sat, still gripping the camera, at the table. Where she had been waiting for them. Sam had disappeared. Lorraine was looking at something on the floor, or perhaps just at the floor.

"They're gone," Elisa said. "The pictures."

No one spoke for a moment. Then Derek said, "What do you mean?"

"I'm talking to your mother."

Now Lorraine looked up, her face scrubbed of emotion. "I don't think so, dear. I was just looking at them."

"Not all of them," Elisa said. "The pictures of Silas. I took one of the boys together. It's not in here."

"Well, whatever is on there now, that's what was on there when I picked it up." She swept her hand over the countertop, as though wiping away dust, though there was no dust.

Elisa looked at Derek, who was staring at her with curiosity. Elisa held out the camera to him.

He sat at the table and clicked through the photos with his thumb. He said, "I'm not sure anything's missing."

"All the pictures of Silas."

"He hated having his picture taken." His eyes were still on the screen. "I don't think there were any."

"Derek," she said. "You remember the one where they're in the booth at that diner. And at the state park. And the one where he's throwing rocks into the creek."

"Did he come to the state park with us? Didn't he stay with what's-his-name, that fat kid?"

"He came to the park. You took his picture. *I* took his picture."

"Well," he said, and handed the camera back. "Maybe something happened to them. Some digital thing."

This, of course, was asinine. Derek wasn't an idiot. He was a lawyer, an academic. He was the most organized person she had ever met. (Later, it would be his uncharacteristic unconcern that would tell her their marriage was falling apart: his unwillingness to solve their problems, any problems, however insignificant.) He did not believe that "some digital thing" had happened—and even if he did, he would know which digital thing he was referring to. This was an act he was putting on for his mother. To signal his sympathy for her position, her reason for deleting the photos, whatever it might have been.

"Things are always malfunctioning," Lorraine said from across the room. Her back was turned, and she was making tea at the counter.

Now Elisa stared at the floor. The room was silent. She wasn't going to raise her head to look at him, not just yet. There would be an apology in his eyes. *Indulge me.* She didn't want to give him the satisfaction.

But so what? There was nothing here to satisfy anyone, even Lorraine. There were no points for anyone to score. Later that night she would feel this even more powerfully, as she imagined the conditions under which Lorraine would have deleted the photos: alone in the study, knowing her dead grandson was there, on the memory card, a poison pill. Maybe she was drinking. What did Elisa know? Lorraine picked up the camera in a fit of anger and grief, and deleted them. The seeds of misery, obliterated. It wasn't about Elisa at all. It was what Lorraine's body had done to quell the sadness she did not otherwise know how to express.

The photos were still on there, of course. Elisa herself understood how it worked, the subterfuge of digital storage. The data wasn't overwritten, it remained in place, there on the memory card. All that was removed was the camera's willingness to acknowledge it. Where the camera once saw the photos, it now saw holes: neat blank spaces, like graves.

Flawlessly implemented denial: this is what pressing the DELETE key accomplished, on the family camera. There were places in town where Elisa could take the card to have the data recovered, to have the photos exhumed. But, with much the same variety of inertia that would later prevent them from moving Silas's real grave to Reevesport, she held back. Something had been done, and that was that. A part of Elisa had moved on. She did not want to go back. Indeed, she was grateful, in a way, to Lorraine for eliminating the temptation to look, to prolong her agony. Or she would be grateful, lying in bed that night, once she had more time to think it over.

But not yet. Now, in the kitchen, Elisa gave in: she looked up at her husband. But he wasn't looking at her. He was watching his mother with apparent love and concern, and never did turn to face his wife.

7.

The trouble with driving is that there is nothing for the body to do. The mind sees the body moving; the landscape is rushing by outside. It believes that the body must be occupied. But the body is motionless, and the mind does not accept the experience as real.

Several hours of this state lay ahead of her: she should use them to prepare.

But how can you prepare for the unknown? For the impossible? She wants to know what to do, how to behave, but there are no precedents in her life, or any other life she has heard of, to follow. She can only think of movies. A spy picture: the agent going undercover, pretending to be somebody else, ferreting out secrets. Of course there's always a moment when the spy's cover is blown and he blasts his way out of the alternate life. Or he gets the information he needs and his mission ends. He returns home. He resumes his real life.

Elisa is, in fact, returning home right now. Home is the mission. This is real life.

Or it's science fiction. Someone was doing an experiment, and the fabric of space and time was torn. She is the unwitting victim of a top-secret military project, code-named Omega or Vanguard. Somewhere an angry man in a uniform is shouting, demanding to know what went wrong. In her quest to discover the truth, she'll go all the way to the top. And meanwhile the president picks up a red phone and, jaw tight, says *Get . . . me . . . that . . . woman.*

Or it's a psychological thriller. The heroine has amnesia. That's a real phenomenon, not just a movie trope; it happens to regular people. You forget who you are and what you're doing, and your past disappears. The people you love, the house you live in, they're familiar to you. But you're lost in your own life.

Of course, her past has not disappeared. With effort, she could tell you where she was during any week of her adult life. She remembers every moment that led up to this thing, this state of being, whatever it is. But maybe this past life she believes is hers, is part of the amnesia—a kind of dream she was having. *This* is her real life, the one where she was at the conference. And the other one, the one where she was skinny and wearing cutoffs and driving her old Honda, that one was imaginary.

But she knows that isn't true. Or rather, if it is, she has no intention of accepting it, so it might as well not be true.

In spite of the air-conditioning, she's hot, and feels fat. She wants her old body back, the one she woke up in this morning. It's her father's body, lean, stringy, a little stooped. It embarrassed her in high school and college, but even then it felt good to live in, like the sparse apartments she favored, the casual relationships with boys she preferred, until Derek. She was surprised and grateful that this body came back after her boys quit nursing—she looked just like them.

Now she feels like her mother, with boobs and a gut. Small boobs, small gut, but still. She's reached some critical mass—hot enough on the inside to sweat, and the cold air chilling her. Fuck it! She turns off the AC and lowers the driver's side window. The pressure inside the car changes and her ears pop. She has to open the passenger window too, to even it out. The car isn't built to be driven with the windows open. It's supposed to seal its driver off from the world.

She doesn't want to be sealed off. She would never buy a car like this, not in a million years.

In the rearview mirror her eyes are different, softer somehow, the cheeks puffier, but the face tired. Has this body been up late, worrying? Drinking? Working? Having sex? Or did it lie in bed and watch TV, just like she remembers her real body doing?

Driving, she is surprised at how calm she feels. Her hands on the wheel are still and her right foot maintains a constant speed. A moment of unease when a police siren sounds and flashing lights appear, but the cruiser is moving fast and passes before she even has a chance to react. Still, for the next ten minutes her neck and shoulders are tight and she keeps glancing in the rearview, alert for another. A part of her, ridiculously, always believes that she's the one the cops are after; she is forever in a state of readiness for them to arrive on the scene, point, seize and detain her.

Eight years ago, when the police phoned to give her the news, she could feel some primitive device taking control, creaking and groaning in her mind. There was no breakdown, no fit of grief. She just bore the extra weight. She thought she was doing this for Sam and Derek, but Derek spent all of his time smoking in the kitchen or finding reasons to go to campus, and Sam stayed in his room, and Elisa didn't care to see either one of them. Probably they didn't want to see her, either, or each other. Along with everything else they were feeling, they also felt relief, guilt. Guilt at the relief.

They worried about Sam, especially when he retreated to his room or disappeared for hours on long walks by himself. A therapist prescribed drugs he declined to take. Only after weeks had passed did Elisa realize that he had what he wanted now, he had privacy, solitude. He could live for hours, days, without anyone judging him. His life was simpler and quieter without Silas in it. He put on muscle weight and his skin took on a healthier color. He spoke less, and rarely in complaint. He wasn't depressed—he was learning how to be Sam. And Derek changed as well. He became more serious, more dedicated to his habits, if that is even possible. The world returned to him.

But Elisa wasn't sure, still isn't sure, if she ever got the world back. There have been times, over the past ten years, when she has wondered whether some essential part of herself was missing. She seemed to have lost her capacity for delight—what happened to that version of her that was moved by everything? Whose emotions were so overwhelming, debilitating?

There was a morning not so long ago when she woke up in the middle of the night, sat up in bed, and with absolute certainty knew that she was dead. She actually laughed at the force of this epiphany: it was summertime, the window was open, the sounds of insects and traffic carried through the room on the wind, and she understood that she could rise up out of the bed and fly out that window and disappear into the clouds. And then what? Dissolve into nothing: first her physical form, and then her mind, and then her . . . soul? This isn't a thing she believes in, the soul, but she believed in it that night. Oblivion! It was hers if she wanted it; there was no need to haunt this house, this marriage. She tried to remember how she died; all she knew was that she fell from a great height and never hit the ground. She was still falling.

Derek shifted, groaned, pulled his arms out from under his pillow. "You're dreaming, go back to sleep." His voice had the strange quality it had when he talked in his sleep: the crisp consonants, the slurred vowels. "Oh sure," she said, and she lay down and closed her eyes. Two adults, half-married, half-awake, talking to one another from their respective dreams.

Indeed, that's what it feels like to her most of the time. Their marriage is like sleepwalking: each afraid to rouse the other, for fear of what they'll see when they come to. Elisa does know some things about herself, though. She has hardened, sharpened, intensified. But also calmed. She gained a new steadiness, she likes to think, a new strength. She is proud of what she has become.

But now she seems to have become something else.

8.

As she exits the highway onto county route 31, she begins to think that perhaps all is, that all will be, well. That an explanation for what has happened is just ahead. Everything looks the same as when she left. The same dilapidated barns and rusted road signs and the abandoned farm fields overtaken by woody shrubs and goldenrod. Reevesport is a large town on the southern tip of Kineota Lake, home to the college and a hospital and a factory that makes chains. It's unassuming, and it assumes nothing now, as Elisa crosses over the Reeve Avenue bridge and into the city limits.

Here is the farm supply store, the burger joint, the Asian food market that is still open in spite of the always-empty parking lot and a nearly Asian-free local population. Here is the Walmart, the Hiway Motel, the Italian place the senator ate at once during the campaign. They live in a neighborhood overlooking the lake, but from a long way away; if you go out on the roof through the bedroom window and climb up to the top you can see it, hazy in the distance, green and rippling. She signals, turns, climbs the hill that leads her past the college, past the supermarket and horse pasture and onto their winding suburban street. It is all the same. She actually takes a quick look around the car, to make sure that it's all really there, the binder, the blouse, the power windows, to make sure she wasn't deceiving herself, back on the interstate.

The mailbox is the same and the driveway she pulls into is the same. But the house is not.

It is white, for one thing. It's supposed to be a pale yellow-gray. It had been white when they bought it, but they changed it. The rhododendrons are gone, replaced by a row of sculpted yews. Or rather the yews they tore out a few years ago are still there. The grass, to which she had always been indifferent, is healthy and trim, and the pink dogwood, the one that had seemed certain to die but then rallied and came back to life, that dogwood is gone and in its place stands a Japanese maple.

The house could be described as landscaped, well cared for. It is not an aesthetic that she particularly appreciates or feels capable of achieving through her own actions.

Only when she begins to sweat again does she realize she has been sitting in the car, with the engine turned off, for several minutes. It would seem that she has entered into a minor state of shock. It is one thing to be driving an unfamiliar car, but her house? A motion catches her eye— it's Derek, waving from the front window. She raises her hand to him. A moment later the front door opens and he stands in the frame, smiling at her, at the car.

Derek in the doorway, smiling. Elisa closes her eyes, gropes for the calm, the steel. Her mind conjures a memory, not a specific one but a palimpsest of nearly identical experiences: hauling herself up out of the lake she and her parents used to go to in the summer, somewhere in Michigan: an aluminum ladder, bolted to the dock, the rank water sluicing off her body and out of her swimsuit, and Elisa at last standing steady on the bare wood in her bare feet—goggles on her head, the rubber strap tugging at her wet hair—gazing out over the choppy surface roiled by a coming storm. Up and out of the lake, under her own power, looking back at what she has emerged from: that's the image that will give her strength. She draws, lets out, breath, takes up her purse and conference binder and holds them in her lap.

Then, with deep reluctance, she gets out. She makes her way up the walk and Derek comes out to meet her. He's wearing jeans, a clean white tee shirt, bare feet. He seems to be approaching too fast, and she flinches—but he only pauses to kiss her cheek, squeeze her elbow, and then he is past.

She watches him pop open the trunk of the car and pull from it a small suitcase, hers apparently. Which he knew would be there. She turns, climbs the front step, enters the house.

It's tidy. There's a new carpet. For years they talked about tearing up the old carpet, refinishing the pine floor, but here they have gone and gotten new carpet instead. A chair has been reupholstered. There are different things on the walls. She is startled by the sight of a studio portrait of the four of them, from when the boys were five and six, that she took down soon after Silas died. And here Derek has put it back.

"The chicken's almost done," Derek says from the doorway. "You want a glass of wine?"

"Please." And he nods and disappears.

She goes to the bedroom. It's similar, aside from a new comforter and, again, the carpet. She slips her shoes off, then the stockings, then she sits on the bed for several minutes, taking deep breaths. She says "Okay" and goes down to the kitchen. A glass is waiting for her on the table. It's the same table. But the cabinets are new, the linoleum is gone and replaced by synthetic hardwood, the refrigerator and stove are new. The glass is full of white wine. She doesn't drink white wine, but she drinks it now. Derek is busying himself in front of the stove, sawing away at a roasted chicken in a pan. He turns, smiles again, comes to her and takes her face in his hands. They kiss.

"I missed you," says her husband.

9.

She is impressed with herself, at her ability to pretend. She lets him do the talking. He talks about a man in his department; she's supposed to know who this is. He talks about world events. He looks good—if she has let herself go here, Derek has become more disciplined. He's leaner, his skin has some color. She suspects that he has gotten a gym membership—it's something he used to talk about doing but in the old life never did.

"The old life." It's only been a few hours. Look how she's adjusting!

Derek is cheerful, cheerful, cheerful. The food is good, no wonder she's overweight. The same magnets are on the refrigerator and she is wondering how to tell him what has happened to her.

She gets up to load the dishwasher and he laughs at her. Come on, he says, and motions her into the living room, their wine glasses in his hand, bottle in the other. She expects a crisis—something—a confession—a discussion. Instead they sit down and he keeps talking, and she realizes that he wants to fuck her.

So this is something they do, in this life. She remembers it now, this mood, the barely suppressed laughter, the ridiculousness of their desire. Here, in this life, it has returned. It isn't that sex between them has ended in the other life, it's just that it isn't very funny, or very fun. It's more like a reminder to them that they are married. It's pleasurable and necessary and serious.

They're on the sofa and he's flirting with her. He's stroking her shoulder and her arms and she finds herself saying "Well!" She's playing along, but of course it's easy, this is her, this is Derek, even if it isn't her, it isn't Derek. This Derek is certainly attractive to her, she'll give him that. She feels bad about the extra weight. But then doesn't, not really, as he kisses her, unbuttons her blouse, takes her breasts into his hands. All of her feels a little more . . . luxurious. She thinks of Larry, her lover, the man from the frame shop, and she feels guilty—not as if she's betrayed Derek, but as if she's betraying Larry now. She doesn't feel that way when she has sex with Derek in the other life. She wonders if this Elisa is sleeping with the Larry of this life. Everything is becoming confused in her mind, the Elisas and Dereks and Larrys, but this Elisa is turned on by this Derek. His hand is under her skirt. They're undressing. They're making little sounds.

Suddenly Derek stands up, his shirt off, his pants unbuttoned, and holds out his hand. It's time to go to the bedroom. She follows him, letting her skirt fall onto the carpeted floor. It's quiet—the carpet makes everything quiet. Suddenly she likes the idea of carpet very much. She climbs the stairs, passing the photo of the boys as toddlers, then moves down the hallway, watching the muscles in Derek's back.

Something catches her eye then, something she saw without seeing when she came up here to take off her shoes, and her mind tells her, *Don't look, just follow him down the hall.* But she slows, looks, stops. There's another photo of the boys here, with Derek this time, and something is the matter with it. The photo has been taken someplace she doesn't immediately recognize, someplace outdoors. Hills and water in the background. They are all wearing windbreakers. Derek is the only one smiling, but you can tell it isn't genuine, he is under strain, setting a good example. He is looking not at the camera but at the photographer, presumably Elisa but she doesn't, still doesn't, remember this. Sam is pale, drawn; he looks like this is his first time outdoors in a while. His face is riddled with acne and his hair arcs over his head in a cowlick. His most awkward time, when most boys had begun to look like men. Eighteen? He must be eighteen or nineteen. But that doesn't seem right. Why not?

It's Silas, though, whom she is staring at now, Silas who is the problem. He's looking at the camera, directly at the camera, as if he is thinking as he does it that it's the future he's looking at, future versions of his brother, his parents, himself, people he doesn't know yet, people who might not even be born. In his eyes is the expression of calm calculation she remembers, of a sneakiness so subtle that he could not be accused of harboring it, not without the accuser looking like a paranoid, a fool. He's smirking, that at least is how she reads this expression. She can't remember where this was, she can't remember, and it is suddenly very important to her that she remember, and she reaches out a hand to steady herself against the wall as she tells herself to remember, remember, you have to remember.

"Lisa?"

Derek, I want to come down the hall, I want to make love in this strange body, to your strange body, but I have to remember now, I have to remember this impossible thing or I am going to scream, because Silas didn't live to seventeen, or even sixteen, he was dead two months after his fifteenth birthday, and this photograph cannot exist. And so I need to be wrong now, before we go to bed, I need to remember this moment.

But it's hopeless, because the moment never happened, not anywhere in her memory. And so she doesn't go to Derek, doesn't go to the bed-

room, instead she stumbles into the bathroom, collapses onto the toilet
seat, and bunches a bath towel into her hands and covers her face with it
and screams and screams.

⁕ *10.*

When Derek knocks and enters she is still holding the towel in her hands.
It's unclear how long she's been sitting here. She doesn't look up because
she doesn't want to see him.

"Lisa?"

He's kneeling in front of her now, inserting his head into her line of
sight. He says, "Tell me what's wrong."

"I'm confused," she says.

"Okay."

"I think I had a stroke."

His forehead creases and she can tell that he is more doubtful than
concerned. She can't blame him. He opens his mouth but most of a second passes before he says, "Do you want to go to the hospital?"

The hospital, at this moment, sounds wonderful to her. Clean and
sensible. She nods. He nods. He extracts the bunched-up towel, drops
it on the floor, helps her to her feet. A few minutes later she has somehow gotten her clothes back on and so has Derek and they're in his truck,
on their way to the opposite side of town. It's a long drive. This is the
wrong side of town to have had a stroke on, she thinks. Downtown traffic is backed up because of a passing freight train. People are honking for
no reason. Someone up ahead has a stereo cranked and the bass makes
her feel nauseated. She shuts her eyes. The coins in the ashtray buzz: she
thinks of Brownian motion, atoms vibrating too fast to see. Everything
around her is vibrating. Her forehead is pressed against the passenger side
window and Derek is holding her hand.

"Is anything tingling? Is anything numb?"

"I don't think so."

There is irritation in his silence. Surely she should know if she is tingling or numb.

She says, "I'm confused."

"About what?"

"I don't remember things."

"What don't you remember?"

She doesn't answer. She wants to tell him everything. Traffic begins to move again.

They wait in the emergency room while Derek fills out forms. It's strangely silent, among the ferns and rows of airport chairs, though the room is filled with people. There's no music, shouldn't there be music? Elisa uses one hand to massage the other. Her breathing is shallow; her body feels insubstantial. Somehow the act of coming here—the act of *agreeing* to come here—has lightened her. She is no less terrified, but the terror is like the wings of some small bird, beating ineffectually against her. Where is her steely resolve? The image of the lake, of pulling herself up out of the lake, is of no use; she thinks of it and she can feel the dock swaying and lurching under her feet, and the boards are slimed with algae.

They are called in to the examination area and led to one of a dozen rooms surrounding an open central zone of cubicles and workstations. It's more like an office than it should be. She is given a thin gown and asked to undress and sit on a small bed. Then they wait again. Eventually a doctor introduces himself, Dr. Mayles. He's bespectacled, nerdy, and friendly. The word *socialized* springs to mind. It's the learned friendliness of a man who is not naturally friendly. He is around the same age as Elisa and Derek, and she suddenly imagines the three of them in a play group at the age of four—it's as if they all grew up together, making their slow way toward this moment, this little tableau. She almost laughs.

Dr. Mayles asks about her medical history, though Derek has already written it on the clipboard the doctor now holds. He shines a penlight in her eyes, holds her chin gently and studies her face. He takes her pulse and blood pressure, taps her knee with a tiny hammer, all the while talking slowly, quietly, asking her questions. What year is it? What's five times seven? Who's the president?

2012. Thirty-five. Obama.

She tenses. What if the president's somebody else? But it seems to be the right answer.

"You have two sons," the doctor says, reading from the clipboard. "What are their names?"

And as she says the names she realizes that she doesn't want to be here, doesn't want to have had a stroke, has made a terrible mistake. She says, "I'm sorry."

"Why are you sorry?" the doctor asks.

"I'm fine. I think I'm fine actually."

Derek is standing beside the bed, both hands gripping the side rail. He is studying her. "You said you couldn't remember things," he says.

"What can't you remember, Elisa?" says the doctor.

The fluttering wings again. She feels her heartbeat growing faster and weaker. "My . . . job. I was on a trip—I didn't know what it was for. I don't . . . I saw a photo in my house. Of our sons. And I couldn't remember where it was taken. It was unfamiliar."

The doctor seems to have adopted Derek's reckoning gaze. It's contagious. He says, "When was the last time you had a CT scan?"

"Never?" she says.

"Okay. Let's make sure everything looks normal up there." Meaning, presumably, her head. "The nurse will take some blood. And then we'll get you down to radiology." He sounds disappointed. A look passes between him and Derek. But then Derek turns back to her and there's nothing on his face but sympathy and worry. He takes her hand again.

"Your job? What about it don't you remember?"

She squeezes her eyes shut.

As promised, a nurse arrives and draws blood from her arm. She doesn't look. Later she's asked to sit in a wheelchair and is taken to the room where they keep the CT scanner. It looks like a giant toilet seat. Derek is asked to remain outside. She lies down on a table and a nurse, a different one, injects a dye into her arm, not far from where the blood was taken out. *They are replacing my blood with dye,* she thinks. A technician instructs her to remain still, the room clears, and the machine knocks and hums as the table she lies on makes abrupt gradual movements.

This is the most relaxing part of the entire experience. She is alone here with the machine. She isn't thinking of anything at all. The machine is rocking her gently. She falls asleep.

In the end, there's nothing. Her brain looks normal. Her blood is normal—she's maybe a little anemic. The doctor prescribes eating. "And B vitamins. You could maybe pick some of those up at the supermarket." He tells Derek to keep an eye on her.

"Are you beginning to remember?" he asks her, almost as an afterthought. She manages a smile. "It's all coming back to me now."

II.

It went this way:

He wasn't driving. The driver lived but ended up paralyzed and in a coma. The boy in the passenger seat was killed, as was Silas, who was in back with a fourth passenger.

The fourth passenger was a boy named Kevin Framus. His injuries were not serious. He was the one who told the police what happened. There was an alley behind the brick factory, on the southern shore of Lake Monona, with a stone retaining wall that ran along one side and a chain-link fence along the other. The alley was long and lightless, and the driver, a twenty-seven-year-old man named Richard Samuelson, liked to drive down it at high speed with the headlights off.

"Did he ever say why he liked this?" the prosecuting attorney asked Kevin Framus, many months later, during Samuelson's manslaughter trial, which Elisa and Derek watched, over several days, from the hard wooden benches behind the attorney's table, their backs sweating and aching, their minds exhausted, blank.

"He liked getting rushed up."

"And this meant what?"

"That's what he used to say. Like, all excited. For the adrenaline rush. We were going out looking for girls."

This man Samuelson was a high school dropout. He played the drums in local bands. Silas had learned to play bass and was in one of the bands. The other boys in the van were band members. Samuelson, it emerged, hung around with schoolboys in order to attract underage girls. He and his companions would pair up with the girls and have sex with them in the van. The van was full of candles and incense and drugs. Apparently Samuelson liked to watch the younger boys having sex with their girls, while he was having sex with his.

On this night, they never made it to the girls. A police cruiser was patrolling the factory grounds and pulled into the end of the alley.

"And why didn't Mr. Samuelson stop when he saw the police car?"

"Objection," said the defense attorney.

"Did you notice anything about Mr. Samuelson that would indicate why he didn't stop?"

"He had his eyes closed," said Kevin Framus.

"Did he always have his eyes closed when he drove down the alley?"

"Every time I was with him."

"And you never objected?"

"I figured what was the harm. I never saw anybody back there."

"Did you see the police car on the night in question?"

"No, I was in back."

"And so you didn't try to stop Mr. Samuelson."

"No. Silas did. He never came with us before."

"And so he didn't know about Mr. Samuelson's habit of driving behind the brick factory with his eyes closed."

"No. This was the first time he came. Silas wasn't . . . he didn't like this kind of thing. He didn't like to, like, hang out. He liked to do stuff. He was pissed at Ricky that we were just, you know, fucking around." To the judge he said, "Sorry."

"All right," the prosecutor said. "And how did Silas react when he saw the police car?"

"He started shouting at Ricky to stop."

"But Mr. Samuelson didn't stop."

"No. Silas was grabbing for Ricky when we hit. He got up and he was between the seats." He paused. "Silas didn't belong there. He was . . . we were idiots. Silas was all right."

"And when the van struck the police cruiser, he was thrown through the windshield."

"I guess. I didn't open my eyes until after."

"Did Silas say anything about the police cruiser? Did he specifically tell Mr. Samuelson that the cruiser was there?"

"I really don't remember. It was just screaming. I don't remember."

"Do you have any idea why Mr. Samuelson didn't listen? Why he didn't open his eyes and look?"

The defense attorney didn't object. He was staring at Kevin Framus. He seemed to want to know the answer himself.

Framus said, "I don't know. I just . . ." He paused, seemed to consider a moment. "Honestly? I always figured he didn't really have his eyes closed all the way. Otherwise how could he keep it straight? He never scraped the wall or whatnot. It was always straight down the middle."

"So he was just pretending to close his eyes."

"Yeah. He'd make little slits, you know. He didn't really close them."

"So you think he knew the police car was there."

The defense attorney seemed to wake up. He objected, flailing his arms in the air.

This Samuelson was the kind of person nobody knew but would pretend to have done so later, after it was all over. That he was bad news, a notorious town character. In truth he was more or less anonymous, a cipher. The police didn't have him on their radar. It was the trial that taught Madison about him, and a few weeks after it was all over they would forget entirely. The trial revealed his insistence that nothing more than white cotton briefs be worn by band members during rehearsal, the suspicious fire that claimed his childhood home and the lives of his mother and sister, his dishonorable discharge from the Army. They learned about his bust for cocaine possession.

For Elisa and Derek's part, they had met the man once. They hadn't thought well of him but agreed that the band was a good thing for Silas and that they should not interfere with his private life as long as it was legal and safe. It had been neither, but they didn't know, and now he was dead.

A few days after his trial began, Samuelson stopped breathing in the middle of the night, and then he was dead, too. The two police officers who were in the cruiser were treated for their injuries and recovered. Kevin Framus hadn't been injured. He wasn't charged with anything. Six months later his family moved away, and the family of the other dead boy moved away, then Elisa and Derek and Sam moved away, too, and that was the end of that.

It was not the kind of thing that people remembered later. In Reevesport, maybe it would have been, but Madison is a big town, and more important things soon pushed it from memory. Indeed, except for the handful of acquaintances Elisa might run into on her visits, who could be forgiven for regarding her arrival as more of a burden than a pleasure, nobody thought about it much at all. It was just a thing that happened, and it was over now.

12.

But if Silas is alive, then it never did happen.

She is lying on the bed, half-naked. Derek has covered her with a duvet and brought her a cup of tea before retreating back down the stairs. The tea is now cold and her head throbs without actually hurting. It's growing dark outside.

"Tell me when you're ready to talk," he said when he left the tea. She can't imagine that moment arriving.

The darkness deepens. She's cold. She turns a lamp on long enough to confirm that none of her usual clothes are in the closet. Of course not. Some digging does reveal her favorite nightshirt, long and blue and covered with clouds, wadded into a ball in a far corner of the shelf. She undresses, allows herself a glance at her body in the mirror, hauls the musty shirt over it. What on earth could have made her stop liking it? Who is this woman?

She goes to the door, opens it quietly, steps into the hall. She hears Derek shifting downstairs but he doesn't call out. In the bathroom she rubs her face, examines it in the mirror. She is prettier here. This Lisa takes care to pretty herself. She strips off the nightshirt and then showers, careful to wash off all the makeup, not that there was much.

Back in the hallway she pauses beside the incriminating photo. There are things she needs to see and do, to figure out, and she doesn't know how much, if any, to explain to Derek. She recalls his earlier ardent affection and feels a kind of longing. But she doesn't go downstairs.

Instead she makes her way to the door of the room they called the box room. In the old life. When they moved in, they chose their bedrooms, she and Derek and Sam, and there was one left, the one that would have been Silas's. Or, rather, it would have been Sam's, as Silas, though the younger, would have taken the larger one, if he was alive.

Or maybe not—if they gave Sam the choice, Silas could make him feel, somehow, that the larger was inferior. He could find a way to make Sam uncomfortable there, make him wish he had chosen differently. And so perhaps this room, the old life's box room, is now, in fact, Silas's.

Of course the boys are grown now. They don't live here. Or maybe they do and simply aren't home? She is alarmed not to know this. In the old life, Sam has maintained his old room more or less as it was when he was in high school. He has left his posters up, kept his old mix CDs, the model airplanes he was obsessed with, belatedly, during the years he spent puzzling over his sexuality and his uneasy relationship with her and Derek. Even today, with a job and (she suspects) a boyfriend, he still hangs out there, in evident satisfaction, when he comes over; he still smokes cigarettes sitting cross-legged on the bed beside the open window, with earbuds in.

Maybe he's there now, in a world she evidently no longer inhabits. She misses him, that reality, suddenly, painfully. She hasn't seen Sam for days—or, alternately, for a lifetime.

The box room was where they put Silas's things. Derek had packed them, quite neatly, into plain cardboard boxes, and when they arrived here they chose a room for these things, and told the movers that anything unmarked should go in this room. Over time, the boxes were opened, rummaged through, crushed into corners or piled into stacks. Sam took what he wanted, music mostly, a stereo receiver and turntable and speakers, and took them to college and then later brought them back home. Derek removed some impersonal things—a radio, a lamp, a rug—and sold them at a yard sale. But the rest is still there, in the other life, along with other unwanted items, behind the always-closed door. Whenever one of them needs something from the box room, it is like entering a tomb that has been excavated from the floor of a desert. The stillness is so complete it seems to have a physical manifestation, like a liquid form of air.

Hand on the doorknob, Elisa has a sudden memory of Silas at fourteen, in his room in Madison, music emanating from the walls, filling the house: ludicrously repetitive heavy metal songs (*progressive metal,* Silas would correct her), some of them more than ten minutes long, interrupted only by, alternately, the mumbling and shouting of a crazed lead singer. This is the music he did his homework to. It drove her nuts. How could anyone concentrate to that? (Derek: "Let us be glad he is *doing homework.*") He listened at high volume, on vinyl records, sometimes for hours on end, transferred the records to recordable CDs and listened to those in the car or on headphones while he was walking around town or, presumably, the halls of his high school.

Elisa had learned to tune it out, mostly anyway, while she was preparing dinner or trying to read, but one afternoon something about it was bothering her: the song that was playing had been playing too long, the words and chords repeating with uncanny precision. She stepped into the hall and concentrated. There: a hiccup in the progression, a missed beat. The record was skipping. It had been skipping for twenty minutes.

"Silas!" She was banging on the door, but either he couldn't hear or was ignoring her. Two singers, engaged in an incomprehensible conversation: *Ah mutter-mutter-mutter. Ah mutter-mutter-mutter? Ah mutter. Ah mutter. Ah screaaaam! Ah screaaa— Ah mutter-mutter-mutter. Ah mutter-mutter-mutter? Ah mutter. Ah mutter. Ah screaaaam! Ah screaaa—*

"*Silas!!*"

The door was flung open, the music belched out its full spectrum of loud, she could feel her teeth itch. He got right up in her face. "*What!!*"

"*Your! Record! Is skipping!*" Elisa screamed now, to match his screaming, to overwhelm the singer's.

He appeared for a moment as though he might explode in anger at her, for criticizing, for daring to interrupt. But then his face went slack, his head tilted, his eyes unfocused, and he blinked. The record skipped.

Silas almost smiled. It was funny, it really was. But something held him back. The eyes found her face, locked on, and his mouth tightened and he said, "Maybe I like it that way!" before slamming the door and, with a little scrape, lifting the music out of its closed loop.

Something there that she missed. Some opportunity. She doesn't know how she might have played it differently. Surely there was a way: they might have ended laughing.

She opens the door and turns on the light.

It's a home office. There is a computer desk and a laptop and a small radio. Derek's diploma is on the wall. The only boxes are sitting open on the floor, and they're filled with files. A bookcase is lined with law books, Derek's.

In the old life, Derek doesn't work at home. He stays late at work.

Elisa backs out, turns off the light, closes the door. She goes to the other room, Sam's room, and it isn't Sam's room, it's a guest room. It is even tidier here than the rest of the house. There's a brass bed and a caramel-colored bureau and signed prints of sentimental rural clichés: a basket, a barn, an owl. A large vase of dried flowers occupies a corner. The room bears the marks of Lorraine's taste. So—in this life, Elisa has allowed Lorraine to decorate a room in her house. She can't decide what this says about her—that she has no integrity, or that she has so much that she can allow such things without feeling insulted.

Or maybe this Elisa likes Lorraine. Maybe they're friends.

She stands in the hallway for some time, just breathing and feeling her body against the nightshirt. Her feet are cold but the rest of her is warm from the shower and from the agitation of her mind. She has to face Derek, has to explain what just happened—the bathroom, the interruption of their lovemaking, the hospital, the non-stroke—and she is trying to determine how to do it.

Eventually she walks down the stairs. Derek is there, on the sofa, and he smiles at her. He must have sneaked into their bedroom to change while she showered, because he's wearing his pajama pants and bedroom slippers. There's a beer on the table beside him and a law journal is open on his lap.

"Are you all right?"

She can hear, in his voice, the old irritation and doubt. He thinks she is hysterical, that nothing is wrong with her, that they went to the hospital for no reason. All these things may be more or less true.

"I think so."

"Haven't seen that in a while," he says. He means the nightshirt.

She sits down on the other end of the sofa and Derek closes the book and sets it on the table. He folds his hands together and faces her squarely, his eyes locked with hers. This gesture—this readiness to listen—is unfamiliar. And it occurs to her that he has to have learned it somewhere. Therapy? He has had therapy, or they have had it together.

She says, "I need you to tell me our story."

13.

He looks at her. He says, "Something happened at the conference."

"No."

"You're not the same."

"I'll try to explain. Maybe not right away. But first I need to hear everything up until now. From you."

He appears confused. "Everything since you came home?"

"No. No. Everything. Our story. Since we met."

A kind of fear ripples across his face. He sighs, looks out the window, and it appears to be an effort for him to turn his head back to her. "'Need.'"

"What?"

"It's disturbing that you are coming back here and saying you need things from me. That you're just asking for this and expect to get it."

She is eager to respond, to defend the request, but of course she can't. She gazes at her own tightly folded hands in her lap and waits.

"It's your tone, Lisa. Making this demand. This weird demand."

"I'm sorry."

He grunts, shifts his body. He doesn't like the apology, either.

But he says, "Okay. Our story. From when we met, that's what you want?"

She nods, puts her hand on his knee, withdraws it.

He begins talking. Grudgingly at first, and not without sarcasm. But then he warms to it. It's good to hear his voice. It's like it was back when they met, hearing him late at night, talking about his family, trying to tell her everything. To fill her in, so that it would seem they'd always been together. Those first months, they barely slept. Friends mocked their tired eyes, made sexual jokes, but it was mostly talking, talking, talking that kept them awake. He's telling her this now, and of course he is talking now the way he talked then, methodically, linearly, with the kind of confidence that renders editorializing as incontrovertible fact. He's *good.* She doesn't understand why he didn't become a trial lawyer; he could convince anyone of anything. When they were young, this was bracing for her—the antidote to her parents' equivocation and moral relativism. He said things he believed were true, as though they were true, and she accepted them. Then, in bed with him, listening, she laughed, thinking of her mother's recurring admonishment: "Accept what is offered." The trouble with that world was that nothing offered was ever any good: a ratty paperback book, marred by some anonymous fool's notations; a flavorless stew; a heavily qualified compliment ("Good work, but don't get a big head about it"). Well, she accepted what Derek had to offer. Strong opinions, a strong body, a strong will. She opened herself up completely and let him pour in whatever he liked.

He is enjoying himself now. "You were into me," he is saying. "We were into each other." And though he is deep in the past, and is not, she thinks, referring to the way things have changed, she understands that it is no longer so, that they are not into each other now. It isn't merely the inevitable passing of desperate infatuation, the settling and hardening of love, it's that they no longer dominate one another's frame of reference. They are not the most interesting thing in each other's lives.

Derek says, "You were the only woman I'd ever known who actually listened to what I was saying. The way you concentrated. Even if you didn't know what the hell I was talking about—you figured it out. You asked questions. I liked answering your questions."

He pauses, and his face flushes. Maybe because he has realized that's what he's doing now: answering her question. Or maybe because he is contemplating what he says next:

"You fucked me. Not like other girls. You wanted it and you came and got it. You didn't give a shit how that might look to me."

"It looked good to you," she says.

"It looked good to me."

Maybe too good, she thinks. He drew out the narcissist in her. The self she saw reflected in him, she came to mistake for her real self. She forgot how to desire things that weren't him. She would blame him for this, later. Unfairly. Now, recalling that state, listening to his voice, feeling bad that she ever found fault with anything, she takes his hand in both of hers. He lets her do this. He tells her about his proposal ("You will marry me, won't you?"), their wedding (family only, no church, which ought to have pleased everyone but pleased only the two of them), their first rental house, a crumbling bungalow two blocks from the Willy Street Co-op, with crooked floors, squirrels living under the roof, and mushrooms sprouting in between the bathtub and wall. Eventually that house was condemned, then collapsed on itself, folding spontaneously into the ground, a briefly famous neighborhood event.

The time his older brother Nate, drunk, groped her. She did not take it personally—it was something between Derek and him, a rivalry with deep and mysterious roots. Maybe it was about Lorraine, or about their dead father. At any rate Derek simply grabbed his brother by the back of the shirt, dragged him to the door, pushed him outside, and locked it behind him. He left Elisa to drop Nate's duffel bag and car keys out a second-story window. She had known of many such rivalries in her life—there was a time, in college, when she thrived on other people's stories of familial disharmony—but she had never heard of one that ended so suddenly or endured so completely. She has never seen Nate again, rarely even heard his name uttered—even now, retelling the story, Derek refers only to "my brother." *You're dead to me.* Derek would never say anything so dramatic, but he could mean it, live by it. He is a man of regulations, absolutes.

He is telling her, now, about the time he broke up a fight on the street and ended up in the hospital. (She remembers she was angry at him, and proud; frustrated that he should insert himself into someone else's life in this typically masculine fashion. But why is he reminiscing about this, of all things? Why is it important to him, to their life story?) And now he begins to tell her about the boys. (His gaze leaves her face and body and drifts to the window; his voice quiets. He does not want to discuss this. But he will do as she has asked, what he *has agreed to*.) Sam: the pregnancy test in the convenience store bathroom. Her craving for peanut butter cups. Lorraine's absurd objection to certain baby names: "If you call it that, I will never speak to you again." Elisa waking in the night, eight months pregnant, telling him the baby didn't feel right. The drive to the hospital, the midwife's vexation; Sam had shifted; he wasn't where he belonged. The doctor's efforts to shove him into place, the sudden gush of fluid onto the table, the emergency cesarean. And Silas, eleven months and three weeks later: unexpected, uncanny. Her obstetrician had retired in the interim and the new one, a young, nervous man, advised against a natural birth. She insisted. She knew it would be easy. It was easy, waking to labor, arriving at the hospital just after eight, birth by noon.

It is all the same so far, the story is as she remembers. But his voice is growing increasingly strained, as if he has been forced into a lie. Then he stops, and says, as if exasperated, "Does this have something to do with them? With the boys?"

She doesn't respond.

"Is something going on that you haven't told me?"

"No, no. They're—when was the last time you talked to them? The last time we talked to them. Remind me."

His eyes widen, then narrow into a scowl.

"I don't remember," he says. "Why are you asking me this?"

She doesn't know what to say. She folds her legs up under her nightshirt.

"Is it Sam?" he asks. "Have you heard something from Sam?" As if this is a plausible circumstance, as if he's been waiting for it to happen.

"No. I don't know. I don't know, that's why I'm asking."

He stares at her a long time. She says, "Please, just go on with the story."

He closes his eyes, slowly, draws breath. There is a very fine sheen on his forehead. He tells her about their place on Gorham, Elisa's abandonment of her studies. He says this carefully, as though it might hurt her to hear it. The boys' early childhood. The Montessori preschool where they ate brown rice and seaweed for snack and made toys out of sticks and leaves and feathers. Or was it Waldorf? And shouldn't she have cared enough to remember? She hated the place at first, until she met the aide, a kindly old German woman who told the children violent folktales in a barely penetrable accent while waving her fat arms over her head. Sam's fall from his high chair, his stitches, the scar he still has (why does so much of this narrative consist of injuries, accidents, fights?). The time Silas went missing: they spent an hour and a half stalking through the neighborhood, calling his name, searching the park, knocking on doors. Panic, terror.

She remembers a thought that came to her then that she has repeated to herself many times over the years and that she still doesn't fully understand: *I have finally gotten what I deserve.* (In the end Silas had crawled under their bed and fallen asleep.)

And now the stories focus on Silas. He begins to change. His unwillingness to take naps. His boredom. At four, he is no longer content to hear a story or to play with the toys he has. He doesn't listen to what they tell him, or rather he seems not to hear. He is impassive in the face of punishment: where his brother wails with frustration and regret, Silas tends to endure, quietly, with evident puzzlement. If Sam is absorbed in something, Silas will disrupt it. It isn't the behavior that disturbs them, but the evident lack of malice. He isn't being mean. It's as if he is conducting a social experiment. He will tear a magazine out of Elisa's hands and throw it across the room. Or he will spill his dinner on the floor, then quickly turn to Derek to see his reaction.

They learn not to react emotionally. Or to react at all. They leave the spilled dinners where they lie. They finish their own meals deliberately, silently, while Silas pounds the table in a monotonous rhythm and Sam cries and cries.

Derek hesitates now, in the telling. He says, "And of course the time . . ." He pauses, his expression sour, and glares at her.

"Derek, don't, you don't have to," she says, because she knows where this has been going. It all leads to this, for him. She feels, suddenly, as though she has made a major tactical error—that this, on the heels of the fake stroke, the hospital visit, has led her into a cul-de-sac she can't get out of. Surely she seems completely insane to him.

"There's the time I hit him," Derek says.

"Derek, stop, it's okay, I didn't mean—"

She squeezes his hand but he pulls it away. He says, "That night at dinner. He threw the sippy cups on the floor. And then while we were trying to clean them up he grabbed your glass and then mine—"

"Stop, stop. I know this, you don't need to do this."

"—and he smashed them on the table until one broke. And he cut himself, cut his hand," Derek says, gazing levelly at her, "and I hit him, didn't I. Open-handed across the cheek. I knocked him over."

"It's all right," she says, "stop."

"And raised bruises on his face."

"Derek," she says. "Stop, please." He is staring at her, slack-jawed. Elisa feels a deep sympathy for him: he had been looking forward to this day, the dinner, the wine, going to bed. She has fucked everything up for no clear reason. Now he shrugs. He's finished with the story.

Of course she remembers it, too. When Silas smashed the glasses, he flinched—Derek flinched, but he didn't cry out, and he didn't shout. Instead he stood up, leaned over Silas, drew his arm back. Elisa thought, Do it. And he did. A moment later Silas lay on the floor, broken glass around and beneath him, the first expression of genuine surprise they had seen on his face in months. Silas cried this time, for sure. Then Sam, then Elisa. Then Derek.

He says, "Why are you doing this."

"I'm so sorry."

"There had better be a goddamn good reason." He leans back, covers his face with his hands. "A stroke, Lisa? You didn't have a *stroke*."

"I thought . . ."

"Something happened. You met somebody."

"No, no."

"Then what." His voice muffled by his fingers.

She says, "I can't explain, not yet. There's no one else." Though there is, there's Larry.

He's waiting.

"Just tell me about one more thing. One more. From later."

It takes a moment for him to react. To understand, evidently, that she needs him to agree to hear her question. His hands slide off his face and lie limp at his sides. "All right," he says.

She has grown cold now, even in the flannel nightshirt, and she bunches her hands into fists and shoves them together into her lap. "When the boys were fifteen and sixteen," she says.

"Okay."

She hesitates a moment before saying, quietly, "Was there a crash? In a van?"

She expects him to gape, shake his head in disappointment, walk out of the room. Or, *Of course there was, he nearly died, why are you doing this?* But instead he only blinks. He is bewildered.

"A crash?"

"Yes."

"I don't . . . no. No? I don't remember a crash."

"Silas was in a band, a rock band with a guy named Ricky. He was older, he was in his twenties. And that boy Kevin."

"Uh huh," he says, but he doesn't remember. And then he does. "Oh," he says. "They were in a crash. They were playing chicken or something?"

"Yes!"

"And they died, some people died."

"Yes, yes. And Silas?"

"Silas? There was a funeral, we tried to get him to go. He wouldn't go."

She says, "He had nothing to do with the crash? He wasn't in the van?"

He coughs out a little laugh. "No!"

"Nothing happened then. To Silas. Around that time."

"Well," Derek says after a moment, "there was his lost weekend. Was that before or after the van thing?"

She wants to say "Lost weekend?" but bites it back. Derek goes on. "I barely remember the van thing, I can't tell you when that was."

She says, "Tell me about the lost weekend. I want to know how you remember it."

The eyes again narrow. When he speaks, she can tell that he's had nearly enough of this game: he's going to quit soon. He says, "All right, well, he left school that Thursday afternoon and didn't come back. Somebody saw him out in the parking lot, smoking, as though he was waiting for somebody—I remember the school secretary told you that, on the phone. And then we didn't see him again until Monday night." He is staring at her. "Monday night? Is that right?"

"I think so," she says, quietly.

"The police were looking for him, we took turns driving all over town—I think we were out all night two nights running, then we just couldn't stay awake anymore. I canceled my appointments Monday, and we just sat at home, waiting. You said, 'He's never coming back.'"

"I did?"

There is a tightness to his voice when he says, "Yes, you did." He pauses. "I thought so too. As you well know. As we have discussed many times, alone and with Amos."

She does not ask who Amos is, though she wants to. Then she wonders if this is a test, if there is no Amos, and she is supposed to ask who he is. But no, why would he do that? In any event, Derek has moved on.

"He never said where he'd been. But he'd lost weight—he looked terrible and reeked of cigarettes and body odor. He appeared, in every respect, homeless. His school attendance was poor after that. He rarely spoke. Then I got my job offer and we moved here, and entered into the next phase of our strange life together, Lisa."

He's angry. She turns away from him, looks out the window, into the darkness; superimposed over the glass, her face looks heavy and old.

Derek gets up, delivers his empty beer bottle into the kitchen. When he returns he passes by the sofa and climbs the stairs to bed. Halfway up, he turns. "I still think there's somebody else," he says. "I think this was all about the third rule."

She doesn't know what this means.

He waits.

"I'm sorry. The third . . . I'm forgetting . . ."

His mouth turns down in a way that she recognizes from the real Derek, the one she knows. Polite displeasure. He thinks he is being mocked.

"Refusing. You refused."

She says, "Refused . . ."

Angry now: *"Intimacy."*

"I don't—" But now she is just making it worse. His shoulders and jaw are tensed.

"You fell in love with somebody, and you thought you could come home and pretend it never happened, but you couldn't. You panicked." He shakes his head. "A *stroke.*"

"It's not like that. That's not what's happening."

"So *what's happening?*"

Elisa's throat is half-closed, and her voice is strangled when she says, "I don't know!"

He twitches, as if he's about to reply. And then she watches him master himself—the eyes close, the muscles relax. He lets out breath. "I love you," he says, quietly and with resignation, then turns and continues on his way. A few moments later she hears the mattress groan underneath him.

It's an hour before she is able to join him, and another before she sleeps. The first day is over.

14.

She's awake at four thirty. She is lying in the bed beside Derek, not touching him; his chest rises and falls in the gloom but he makes no sound. She permits herself a moment of hoping that yesterday never happened, or was a dream, but this is folly, even lying still she can feel herself occupying the wrong body.

Out of bed, down the stairs. The carpet bothers her now, it's like she's still in bed. The place smells different here—synthetic, unlived-in.

In this life, there's a laptop computer sitting on the kitchen island. Maybe it's just where Derek does his work. But she doesn't think so—he has his study. The computer must be hers. Beside it lies the binder she brought back from the conference that she has no memory of. As the computer boots she opens the binder, stares at the pages, at the printed-out e-mails. Her palms are sweating, her feet are cold, her behind hurts where it meets the hard wooden kitchen stool. She feels hung over.

She has to make a decision.

When the computer is ready, she brings up the SUNY Reevesport website, finds the biology department, reads about it. (They have wireless internet in this life, like a normal professional family.) It's fairly well regarded, particularly for plant biology. She recognizes some of the names of faculty members—people whom she has encountered through her lab in the old life. There's a guy who did some important work on fungi, another who is an expert on fatty acids in seeds, and won an award for it.

There's a list of support staff. And there she is. Graduate studies coordinator. No picture, no job description.

She could call in sick. It would be easy—she's been out of town, she could have picked up a virus. Nobody would find this unusual—it would buy her some time.

But then what? She will have to go to work eventually. She will have to do something.

The way she sees it, there are two choices. Fake it, or not. If she chooses not to fake it, to quit her job, she'll be starting over. She'd have to depend upon Derek's love and patience, which, however devoted (*resigned* might be the better word) he might seem in his present incarnation, she knows have their limits. In this life, she will be the woman who suddenly dropped out, who had a nervous breakdown—though she is not dropping out, is not having a breakdown. Or, at least, she doesn't *feel* as though she's having one. Is a breakdown a thing you feel, or a thing that changes your relationship to other people? In any event, friendships will end—though what does she care? She didn't have many in her real life, and she is not invested in this one.

It occurs to her to wonder what this means. She thinks, I expect that this is temporary, and that I will soon return to my real life. But, if this *is*

my real life, then I am a woman whose only emotional investment is in
an imaginary life. Thus, I am insane. And so I'd better hedge my bets—
I'd better be invested in this life. Just in case.

She realizes now that she will never be able to explain to anyone what
has happened. No one she knows now, at least not in her real life, would
understand. Elisa doesn't understand, for that matter. How could she
explain?

No—she will have to fake it. How hard, really, could this job be? It's
summer—there are no graduate classes in the summer, right? It isn't academic application season, she doesn't think. From Derek, she knows that
summer is the time for overhauls, for long-term projects. There will be
time and space to figure it out. And once she has done so, she can figure
out the rest. Whatever it is that has happened to her.

It's decided, then. She's going to give it a try. She's going to go to work.
Of course the implications of that decision won't begin to reveal themselves for several hours, but there's nothing she can do about it now.

There is something she can do, however, and with Derek still asleep
and the house quiet, this seems the time to do it. She moves the cursor
to the search bar and types Silas's name into it. She reaches for the ENTER
key, lets her finger hover over it a moment. Pulls it away.

It isn't clear when this happened to her; perhaps it happened to everybody at once. But at some point the internet became more real than the
physical world. There was a time when it seemed like a dream—an impossible thing with uncertain implications. And then suddenly it was
everything. There are people, she knows, who don't use it, who have no
presence on it, who can't be searched for, who can only be accessed by
going to their house and knocking on their door. But those people are the
dream now. They're like ghosts.

There was a time, she thinks, as her hand moves back toward the key-
board, when a physical artifact—a letter, a piece of clothing, a room full
of still-unopened boxes in another world—was the conduit to what could
be known about a person. Touch that thing, hold it, smell it. Inhabit it.
Close your eyes and remember.

Now, you search first, remember later. We don't need memory anymore—
the internet has replaced it. And it's a good thing for Elisa, because it is all
she has. She lets her hand fall. She hits ENTER.

There are, it turns out, many Silas Browns. A blind computer scientist, an audio recording engineer. But it doesn't take long to find her Silas, her living son. He is a programmer for a video game company. There he is, photographed in a parking lot in front of a low buff-colored cinderblock building, standing unsmiling in a small crowd of other unsmiling young men. She leans close to the screen. Her throat catches: he's an adult, he's really there. He's wearing sunglasses.

The company is called Infinite Games; they make violent first-person fantasies for game consoles. Titles like Berserker 4 and Ultimate Warlock. She searches a little more. They're popular, these games, but not all that popular. Popular enough, though, so that Silas appears to be quite successful. He is quoted in magazines and on gaming websites. There are a lot of pictures of him, almost always in direct sun. He wears his hair slicked back, gelled, and his arms are crossed. It's tempting to think that this is how she imagined he would be, if he'd lived, but the truth is she'd never imagined such a thing, never allowed herself that indulgence. Here, he looks like a third brother, another person entirely.

California, that's where he is. She feels both relief and longing. He isn't near. And it would seem that he is not in frequent touch.

But he's alive. Something has kept him alive, has given him a viable life. Something that was lacking in the other world. The real world.

Because that's what this is, isn't it? Unreal? Or, an alternate to the real? She has been put here for a reason, surely. To do something. To find out what she did wrong in her real life, to find out how she could have saved her son. This is a dream she'll wake up from, once she learns what she is supposed to learn.

But even as she thinks this, Elisa has her doubts. Because she doesn't believe in God. And what else could have put her here?

15.

A few hours later, she is standing in the driveway, ready for work. Derek will drive her there in his pickup—that seems to be their routine. The notion of Derek driving her anywhere seems absurd. The other car is obviously hers, she could drive herself. But this must be something they decided to do. For their marriage?

Everything so far today has been excruciating. She wanted to make coffee—but does she make coffee? Or does Derek make coffee? Their coffee machine was the same, but the can of ground coffee was not in its familiar cave in the freezer, enfolded in frozen years-old hamburger rolls. Instead there were whole beans, and a grinder. How many to put in? How fine to grind them? She made choices, proceeded. The grinder was startlingly loud. Would it wake Derek up? It didn't; he didn't get out of bed, anyway. The coffee brewed. There was half-and-half in the refrigerator—hers? It didn't matter, she drank it black. She was hungry, ravenously hungry—this body of hers was hungry. She wanted to make the oatmeal she liked to eat in her real life, but there was none in the cupboard. She stood for five minutes in the middle of the kitchen, wondering what in hell this woman ate for breakfast. In the end she settled on a banana.

She didn't know what to do after that, so she took another shower. When she reached the bedroom, Derek had woken up and gone downstairs. The clothes in the closet repelled her, but she put some on. Another skirt and blouse. In the mirror, she looked like a moderately attractive office worker.

Probably she ought to put on makeup, but she didn't.

Derek smiled at her in the kitchen but said nothing. They read the paper. She drank more coffee. She looked at the clock. She said, "I'd better get to work."

He appeared surprised. "Why so early?"

"There's some stuff from the conference I want to get in order."

Derek frowned. "I can go in early." He folded the paper.

"You'll drive me?"

"Of course," he said.

Now he comes out the door, locks it behind him. They get into the pickup. He pulls out and they head toward campus.

He says, "No makeup."

She can only beg, with a look, for his patience.

"You look pretty."

"Thank you."

She puts her hand on his thigh, just for a moment, then removes it.

When he stops the car, she opens the door, takes up her bag and binder. She kisses him—this seems expected.

"I'm sorry," she says. "About yesterday."

He nods, gently unsmiling.

"We'll have to . . . we'll . . ."

But his face tells her he's had enough. She shuts the door and he drives away.

She recognizes the building. It's gray cement with an angled roof and small square windows that don't open. She has come here from time to time, as part of her real job, to meet with researchers or deliver results for outsourced work. The entrance is on the other side, on the science quad, so she walks there. She passes a few graduate students, a man she thinks she recognizes, but nobody says hello. It's already hot and the wind blows her hair into her eyes. She wonders how she usually does her hair—probably not this way.

A directory inside the entrance tells her that administration is on the second floor. She takes the stairs. A moment later, here she is, in the hall outside the main office. Its double doors are propped open. Beyond them a receptionist or administrative assistant sits behind a desk, typing on a computer beside a nameplate reading BECCA SELGIN.

It's unclear what to do next. Is her office in there, part of a complex? Or is it out here, off the hallway, alongside what appear to be professors' offices and seminar rooms? She walks to the end of the hallway and back, then to the other end, looking for her name. She doesn't see it. There is nothing to do but go in.

The woman called Becca looks up. She is in her twenties, pale, over-weight. A dish of candies sits beside the nameplate. She smiles at Elisa but not without some restraint, some reluctance. "Morning! You're in early."

Elisa holds up the binder. "Lots to read."

"Oh yeah, how was it?"

"Very informative." This is going well, she thinks. Then she says, "Any mail for me?"

The girl appears a bit flustered, as if this is not something she is often asked. "Uh . . . maybe? Check your box?" Her eyes dart to the left, as though that's where the mailboxes are.

"Thanks, Becca," and she walks left.

There is a small room off the main one, accessible from the hall, with wooden pigeonholes on either side, and after a moment Elisa finds her name. There is no mail. But she can see now that the administrative offices lie along two short hallways, one on this side of Becca's station, one on the other. She leaves the mailroom and walks down the hallway on this side, looking for her name on a door. The doors are all closed. She's glad she came in early.

"Are you looking for Judith?" It's Becca's voice.

Sweat is breaking out under her arms. Is she looking for Judith? She supposes that's what a person who would be walking this way should be doing. So, after an excruciating pause, she says, "Yes."

"She'll be late. She's got a doctor appointment. Oh geez, maybe people aren't supposed to know."

"It's all right."

This, then, means that her own office is not in this hallway. Correct? Because if you're going down the hall toward your own office, nobody asks you if you are looking for Judith. So she draws a silent breath, turns on her heel, and crosses in front of Becca with what she hopes comes off as a purposeful stride. She is wearing the pumps she wore to the conference. They're the only shoes in her closet that she is sure have been associated with work. Becca says, "You look different."

Elisa doesn't stop, it's a conversation she is not prepared to have. Over her shoulder: "Oh?"

"Oh God, I didn't mean bad. I'll just shut up."

She's down the hallway, peering at nameplates. "Don't worry!"

And here, finally, is her office. A note card, hand-printed with her name, is taped to the wall beside the door. The door is locked. She takes out her keys, finds one she's never seen before, shoves it home. The door opens. She pushes inside, closes it behind her.

16.

She stands with her back against the door, breathing shallowly. Her relief is profound.

The room is perhaps twelve feet square. Several plants, a coat rack, a desk. On the desk is a phone, a printer, a computer. There is a file cabinet, several chairs, bookcases covered with papers and binders. The shades are drawn, as if against afternoon light.

She crosses the room and opens them. Now she sees a photo, on the desk, of Derek and the boys, the same one that shocked her in the hallway last night. She opens a drawer and puts the photo in it.

Hours might pass before anyone knocks. This is what she hopes. She boots up the computer.

The computer desktop is uncluttered, the background image generic. It's like her machine at the lab, which in this life, she supposes, is someone else's lab. There are links to various web pages, which she double-clicks. They lead to university sites, administrative resources, that require a password.

She tries the password she used at the lab, a random series of numbers and letters. It doesn't work.

Though there is nothing in the world she wants less to do than open the door and go to Becca's desk, that's what she does.

"Hey!" says Becca. She's eating a granola bar.

"I am totally discombobulated today," Elisa tells her.

"Tell me about it!"

"And I am spacing on my password."

This gets her a pair of raised, excessively plucked, eyebrows. "Seriously?"

"I know, right? Do you have a list somewhere?"

Becca shakes her head; her voice takes on a more businesslike tone, as if some line has been crossed. "You gotta go to the SRIT web page and enter your e-mail, and it'll ask you the secret question, you know, and then you can change the password. I'll send you the link." She turns to her computer and starts typing. "They tell you not to, but I write mine down. It's on a sticky under the desk."

Elisa goes back to her office. No sticky under the desk. On the computer, there's an icon for an e-mail program, and she opens it. And there's her day's work, laid out before her: thousands of e-mails, doubtless stretching back months, years, that will tell her what she said and whom she said it to, and presumably what on earth it is she is supposed to do here all day. The sight of this list, and the nested series of folders where the e-mail of the past has been archived, paralyzes her. She feels the way she did when, as a little girl, she pressed her nose to the glass of the TV screen to see what static really was: a mesmerizing and random and utterly boring thing that nevertheless compelled and frightened her. Then, as now, she felt fascinated and doomed. She opens the e-mail Becca has sent, and clicks the link. Enters into the browser window the e-mail address she has just learned. Hits "FORGET PASSWORD?"

The security question is "RULE 2."

This was all about the third rule, Derek said.

Shit, fuck, damn. What the hell are these rules?

Elisa is certain that, should all else fail, she could walk over to the IT office and act like a dumb bitch and make them hand over the password. It's a nice morning and already she is longing for a bit of fresh air. But she wants this finished now. She wants to crack this thing without getting up off her chair. She rubs her eyes with the heels of her hands and groans. Okay. Okay.

She picks up the phone and calls Derek's office, and he answers. He says, "Is everything all right?"

"Can you answer a question for me?"

"Sure," he says, after a moment.

"What's rule 2?"

The silence that follows is long.

Elisa says, "I just . . . I don't remember the order. And I forgot my password, and rule 2 is the security question."

"All right."

"I'm sorry."

Another silence. She can hear people talking in the background, perhaps in an adjacent office, and a truck rumbling by outside his window. He says, "Lisa, you understand that I am just . . . this is just completely baffling to me. I am just . . . going along with it now. Because I don't know what else to do."

"I'm sorry, Derek, I . . ."

"I know you're sorry, I can tell, but that's not the point. The point is . . ." There is the creak of his chair, an antique wooden office chair that his mother bought him when he accepted this job. "The point is you're something else too, not just sorry, and I don't know what it is."

She whispers, "Neither do I."

"That's not a comfort to me. Or an explanation."

Perhaps it's best to say nothing. She says nothing.

Derek says, his voice deepened by resignation, "Rule 2 is 'Blame yourself first.'"

She remembers Derek on the stairs, the way he closed his eyes, his anger giving way.

"Oh God, of course."

"Uh huh."

"Thank you, Derek."

Again, silence.

"Nothing yesterday," she says, "was your fault. But I can't explain now."

"I know it's not my fault."

"I'm not having an affair. There isn't anyone else. It's nothing that happened or anything you did, it's just me. Do you believe me?"

He laughs. "Yes. Sure. We'll just . . . sure."

"We'll just what?"

His breath catches; the chair creaks.

"We'll carry on . . . we'll just carry on."

17.

By nine thirty she has more or less worked out what she does for a living. Processes applications, deals with graduate student complaints, updates databases. Reminds professors how to do things: computer things. She has been reading the old e-mails, many hundreds of them, and in a spiral notebook she found in the desk has begun to take notes on each person she seems to have regular contact with. Her fellow office staffers; professors, students, the assistant dean. Every e-mail offers a few more small details, and each detail serves to confuse the overall picture of her job. She can see the parts but doesn't know how they fit together. The job is both wildly intricate and completely boring.

By ten she is wondering if she should take a leave of absence. But after that, then what? The sooner she learns the better.

People have been moving around in the hallway for half an hour now. Female voices. She has never much liked other women. Derek had wanted daughters both times, but she was glad to have boys. Even when things got bad with Silas, when Derek reiterated his wish that they'd had girls (and in a tone that suggested it might be her fault, that her contrary desire had somehow expressed itself through her womb), she remained glad. If Silas had been a girl, it might have been worse.

She has known for an hour now that only women work in this office. And that every last faculty member is male. There are two female graduate students, both with foreign names—she wonders if she knows them, if she likes them. Probably not. Probably she likes the professors. She likes scientists. She *is* one.

And it occurs to her to wonder if the other her, the real one, has continued to live her life, her real life. She feels a moment of panic. *She* is living *my* life! Or perhaps they've changed places, that Elisa and this one, and the poor soft housewife, the woman bound to her husband by rules, is now panicking in that bony body.

Ruining it—ruining her body with excess. And grief. Because that Elisa has just discovered that her son is dead.

Her jaw tenses and her heels drum the linoleum floor. Then there's a knock on the door and a woman's head pokes in and says, "How was it?"

Judith. This must be Judith. She is page one of the spiral notebook—the single most e-mailed person in the sent box. And Elisa recognizes her. Late thirties, bespectacled, curvy and loud, this woman has hovered around the edges of her real, her remembered, professional and personal lives for years. People at the lab know her. She's at the coffee shop or the supermarket, talking on her phone. Men Elisa knows like this woman, want to sleep with her. Larry knows her—she gets dumb art framed, pastel-colored prints of chickens and barns, old magazine covers. His gentle mockery of her that tells Elisa that he wants to sleep with her, too.

Of course Elisa dislikes her. Judith is one of those people you don't know but know you'd hate. Which for Elisa is most people. But now, here, they are friends—the best of friends, to judge from the e-mails. She has read at least thirty e-mails she herself has written to Judith, all of them in a tone—one of sly, wisecracking cheerfulness—that seems utterly alien to her own sensibility. Somehow this woman has awakened some undignified part of herself: gossipy. Sassy.

"Boring," Elisa says, and tries rolling her eyes.

Judith slips in, shuts the door behind her, flops down into the only other chair in the room. "Any hot guys?"

"Maybe a few."

"And didya fuck 'em?"

"Ah . . . not all at once."

Is this working? Elisa feels close to hyperventilating. She has the fingers of one hand looped through a drawer handle on her desk, and she is hanging on for dear life. Judith gives her a slow smile. "Does Derek miss it when you're gone?"

What does this mean? Sex? "Oh, God," she says, "I barely have time to put my bags down."

Judith laughs. She appears relaxed, as though this has been a normal exchange. Her hair is short and dark and frames a pretty but undistinctive face. What is it that men like? What is it that *she* is supposed to like?

But then Elisa gets an inkling of what this is—what it's like having a friend. This is something women, some women, need. This woman must know her secrets. This woman was her friend when whatever happened with Derek happened. Maybe she knows about the rules. Maybe she can tell her something about Silas.

Only an instant has passed, in which Elisa considers telling her everything. Listen to me, hear me out. Between friends. I'm not crazy. I'm someone else.

But when Judith says "What?" she changes her mind.

"What 'What'?"

"You got a look."

"Passing thought. I'm tired. I have a lot to do."

Sage nodding. "We must change our wasteful ways."

She is referring to the university-wide budget crisis. This is why she was sent to the conference, Elisa has discovered. She has been asked to cut corners. This means staff—consolidating jobs, firing people. It might have to be Becca—Becca would go, and someone from the back office would do her job at the front counter from now on. Callers would get a voicemail menu. In the long run, it won't make much difference. But nobody wants to give up her private office and sit out in front.

"Yep," she says. She ought to produce some witty banter, she knows, but the strain is too great. It's been less than twenty-four hours, and every moment has been an effort. To pretend. Her throat tightens and she gulps air.

Judith seems to get the message. She gets up, smacking the arms of the chair. "Back to the grindstone! Lunch later?"

"Sure."

Judith turns on the way out. Says, "Lisa."

"Mmm?"

"When you're ready. You can just go ahead and tell me whatever it is. Okay?"

She can only nod in response. When Judith is gone, she crosses her arms on the desk and lowers her head onto them.

18.

They eat at a campus café run by art students; Judith leads her there without asking where she wants to go. They must eat here every day. Judith talks about her latest conquest, a man who works in development and is "sort of married." Elisa knows about him already, from the e-mails. She has been worrying all morning about this lunch but it's easy—Judith will happily do all the talking, if she is allowed. Another good reason to like the woman.

Back at the office she selectively writes to certain people, complaining of an imaginary computer crash and asking for updates on various projects and situations. She clicks all the links on her desktop, figures out how to use things. It isn't difficult. Indeed, it's like her other job, except with less direct responsibility, thus easier to fake. By four o'clock she is feeling more confident that she'll be able to do exactly that. She has learned the names of the other women in the office—Linda, Tessa, Jane—and what they do. She has seen a few professors she recognizes, passing through on their way to the lab, and she says hello. It is good to have something dull and necessary to think of.

Because her real preoccupation is not, shouldn't be, this job. It's Silas. That he is in this world, alive. She can't shake the feeling that he has somehow engineered this: that he has brought her here, to show her something. To prove something. The internet has told her that he makes worlds. That's how he puts it. "I make worlds." At Infinite Games, he is known as a rebel. This is how he presents himself. She has found an interview with him, in an online trade publication, in which he flogs a new game he designed, called Mindcrime: Destiny's Mirror, and criticizes his rivals. The gaming industry, he says, is made up of emotionally stunted engineers with no imagination. Only he, Silas Brown, is doing anything of lasting value.

INTERVIEWER: But your projects don't sell. At least they don't sell compared to Berserker and the other big titles at Infinite.

SB: Sales aren't the point. Vision is the point. I'm trying to invent a new paradigm. Designers are stuck on the notion of story. As if it's the story that makes a game worth playing. But nobody gives a fuck about story. Nobody cares what happened in some guy's past, like if bandits raped his mom or kidnapped his sister or gunned down his buddies or whatever. That shit is stupid. It gets in the way. Games aren't stories, they're games. They have to invent themselves. Like life.

INTERVIEWER: But isn't life made up of stories?

SB: No. Stories exist to make sense of life. But they're a pointless exercise. Life is inherently nonsensical. Drawing strands of meaning together is for idiots. All there is, is right now, this moment. Noticing things and doing things. Making things happen. Building a tower of blocks, kicking them, making them scatter. Do it again and again, the pattern of blocks is different every time. You can't replicate it. That's what I want to evoke in a game. The first-person shooter, in its current conception, is moribund. Nobody gives a fuck about missions, about assuming some dumbass motivation some other guy thought up for you, like having to assassinate an arms trafficker or getting revenge on some guy or whatever. It's a fake moral justification for what the gamer really wants, which is to make shit happen. To manipulate the controls and watch things die and be born. To make worlds with your hands.

INTERVIEWER: But obviously people do want missions. Those games sell better than your games.

SB: People don't know what they want. I do.

If there was any doubt in her mind that this world was real, that this Silas was real, that interview has put it to rest. Silas is alive. That's him. She remembers a discussion she had with him one night, while he lay in his bed, a handheld video game on pause in his lap, an impatient expression on his face. He was thirteen. She was asking him, begging him really, to change his behavior at school. Because, when he got into trouble, it made trouble for his brother. Because the people who cared about him got upset. Because he had a future, and everything he did now had an effect on that future. Didn't he understand? He did not live in a vacuum. *Everything he did had an effect.*

By this time, Silas had begun to assume the imperious air that he would carry with him for the rest of his short life. He betrayed little emotion aside from stoic endurance. He looked at her and said, "That's not my problem."

Weakly, with profound exasperation: "How can you *say* that?"

And Silas said, "If I have an effect, then so do other people. So they can have their own effect to push against *my* effect. Can't they?" And he looked at her with real curiosity, as though truly interested in the answer.

"Some people can't."

"Then that makes it their problem."

"But Silas—it's not all about you. It's about other people, too. Who are close to you. Don't you want to help them with their problems?"

He frowned, turning back to his game. "When have they ever helped me with mine?"

As was often the case when she dealt with him, the rage came fast and hot, and she clenched both fists and pressed them into her thighs to suppress it. She said, "We *try,* and you don't *accept* it."

Bleeping, digital music, the sounds of explosions. "Well then that makes it *your* problem."

Video game design. Why didn't they think of that? They might have gotten him on that track early, won his respect by giving him the opportunity. Of course they never considered that such a thing existed. Games were distractions, unconnected to real life. They did not think of them as made things, as designed things. Another blind spot. They might have saved him.

But here, in this world. Did they save him? What was different? What *had been* different? Was there a split, a single place where the universes diverged? Did they—did she—make a different choice here, a choice that kept him from climbing into that van? What small thing, what word or deed, would have been enough to change this?

Or perhaps there was no single place where the worlds diverged. Maybe many things separated the two. Maybe it isn't a matter of cause and effect, but of random variation. Brother universes, forever at odds.

19.

She is staring at the ceiling, thinking, when she hears her name being called, a pounding on the outer door. She jumps up, hurries into the hallway. Everyone else has gone home. It's Derek.

"I've been waiting for twenty minutes."

"I'm sorry! You should have called."

"I shouldn't have to," he says. He is following her back down the hall, to her office. He stands, peering around, while she gathers her things. She notices him looking at the empty space on the desk where the family photo should be.

"You're right."

"We're going to be late," he says.

And without thinking, she replies, *"For what?"*

He stares at her. "Our session."

"Oh God," she says. "I'm sorry."

She follows him out and pulls the doors shut behind her. On the stairs, after a moment's thought, she says, "The conference—I thought today was Monday."

"It's all right," he says without turning around. It is obviously not all right.

Derek drives ten minutes in silence until they reach the city limits, and then says, "It has not escaped my attention that you are only forgetting the most important things."

She sits with her hands folded in her lap. She wishes she were back in her office.

"The things," he continues, "most germane to the survival of this marriage."

"I don't—" she says and then stops.

"It feels like sabotage. I am not saying that it is. I do not know your motivations. But it feels to me like you are trying to sabotage us. For some unseen purpose."

"I'm not."

"I don't think I believe you."

Eventually they arrive at a renovated farmhouse on a lonely stretch of road between villages. The driveway leads to a barn in back that has been fitted with sliding glass doors and a discreet wooden sign that reads AMOS FINLEY, MFT. Derek slides open the door and steps in, and Elisa follows.

They are in a bright carpeted room with wood paneling and an unmanned reception desk. From behind a green-painted door come plaintive voices. A clock reads 4:56. They are not late.

After a moment the door opens and a young man and woman walk out, the woman leading, red-faced, the man trailing behind with his hands in the pockets of his jeans. They pass by Elisa and Derek without a glance. A small bearded man emerges now; he is thin and long-faced, about fifty, dressed in tan pants and a big floppy cotton sweater. Elisa has never seen him before. He says, "Derek, Lisa. Welcome."

They follow him through the door. The room is capacious, but comfortable. Wide windows look out onto a meadow. Rag rugs lie on a polished wide-plank floor. The man sits on a small sofa, tucking one shoeless foot under the opposite knee. Derek sits in an upholstered chair half-covered by a blanket, and Elisa takes a seat beside him, in a similar chair.

"How are you this week?" the man asks them.

Derek looks at her, and the man follows suit.

"Fine," she says.

From Derek, a quiet exhalation.

The man gazes at him, then at Elisa. He says, "Lisa?"

"I forgot about our session today. I thought it was Monday."

"She was on a trip," Derek offers. "Over the weekend. So she missed work yesterday."

The man waits, expectant. Derek doesn't speak. Elisa is developing a headache.

"Is one of you forgetting the second rule?"

The man, the therapist, is almost smiling. He is filled with life—this conflict seems to delight him.

"Elisa," he says, "perhaps you'd like to remind us of the second rule." At least, a question she knows the answer to. But she remains silent.

"Derek?"

"'Blame yourself first, circumstance second, your partner last.'"

The man turns back to Elisa. "Elisa, Derek seems to think there is a problem this week. Do you want to claim it?"

The headache comes into focus just over and behind her left ear. She tips her head back. A crack seems to run diagonally across the skylight, then disappears. A twig, perhaps, blown by the wind.

Elisa could panic, if she wanted to give herself over to it. She hoped to be heading home around now—at least there she has already had a few small successes. She has made coffee, she has found her favorite nightgown.

But what is happening now seems impossible to navigate; it makes no sense. Of course they have been in therapy before, separately and apart. But that was about the boys. And it wasn't with this man, this strange, almost jolly creature. She is inclined to think of him as sinister, the instrument of her impending downfall. But there is a part of her that likes him, liked him immediately upon seeing him. He feels to her like the closest thing to an ally she has in this room, maybe in this life, at least so far.

She'll take the path of least resistance. To the ceiling, she says, "I broke a rule. A different one."

"And which did you break?"

"I . . . refused intimacy."

"You can refuse intimacy."

Elisa tips her head forward and looks at the therapist.

"But," he goes on, "you have to offer something in its place. Did you forget to do so?"

"Yes."

"Perhaps Derek would like to suggest a substitute for intimacy?"

Derek shakes his head. He is clearly annoyed by this avenue of discussion. "She is leaving things out."

Amos Finley has continued to gaze at Elisa. "You have the floor now, Lisa, do you want to explain?"

She does. She wants to tell him everything. Instead she says, "Last night.

I . . . panicked. I don't know why. I thought something was wrong with me. That I was sick. So we went to the hospital. But it was nothing."

Derek is agitated. It's clear that he would like to leap to his feet, pace in front of the judge's bench, take her story apart. But he resists.

The therapist stands up, smoothes his pants and sweater. He gazes over their heads, out the window. He sits down on the sofa again, this time with his legs crossed, Indian-style. He says, "Something has changed this week. Let's get to the bottom of it. Lisa, you went to a conference?"

"Yes."

"Did something happen there? Something that has caused your behavior to change?"

"No."

Derek breaks in. "There has to be. You're different."

This is true. She can't speak. She reaches down and rummages in her bag for her aspirin, but for some insane reason there isn't any there. When she looks up, the therapist is holding out two tablets for her. She takes them. "Water?" she asks, and he stares at her a moment before pointing to a second green door in the corner. It's a small restroom with a sink and toilet. In the mirror above the sink, she looks red and disheveled. She swallows the aspirin and comes back into the room.

"Thank you, Doctor," she says.

The man laughs.

Derek rubs his forehead. "Are you mocking me?"

She has not sat down. She stands in the middle of the room and feels sweat blooming under her arms.

"No!"

"She said she had a stroke," Derek says, gesticulating at the therapist. "She didn't have a stroke! We went to the hospital, and we came back, and she made me tell the whole story of how we met. Of our entire marriage, the trouble with Silas, everything. She is forgetting, or pretending to forget, everything. She forgot the rules. She forgot about this appointment."

The therapist is not looking at Derek, but at her, gazing at her with a strange intensity, as though for the first time, as though she's naked. She is still standing.

"Lisa," he says quietly. "Have you forgotten these things? Or are you trying to . . . make things difficult for Derek?"

"I'm not trying to be difficult."

"Why did you call me Doctor?"

"It was a reflex, I'm sorry."

Derek says, "She is doing everything differently. She sat at a different place at the table. She wore an old nightshirt." He seems embarrassed at the last, as if suddenly aware of some deep pettiness once hidden from himself.

"May I sit down?" Elisa says, then takes her place without waiting for permission.

The exchange has changed the mood of the session. The fight has gone out of Derek. The therapist steers the conversation around to other things, he is talking more generally now, about trust in the marriage, restoring and maintaining trust. It sounds like a canned speech, some shtick from a book he wrote. Elisa ought to be paying attention, there is likely plenty to learn here, but her attention drifts to the window, to a cluster of white-tail deer browsing at the edge of the woods, and to the motion of the wild-flowers and grasses in the breeze. The sky has clouded over, everything appears warm and lush. She longs powerfully for her real life.

The session is ending. Derek and the therapist are standing up and so Elisa does too. The therapist asks Derek to go out to the car so that he can speak with her alone for a moment.

Derek's compliance is instantaneous and disconcerting. He turns and walks out the door and is gone. The room is very quiet now. The deer are gone from the meadow. There is a movement to her right and when she turns the therapist is standing there, holding his eyeglasses in his hand.

"Lisa," he says.

She remembers, just in time, not to say *Doctor*. But when she utters his name, quietly, it comes out wrong, blunted and slurred. *Amos*. They face each other, breathing in and out.

"There's nothing you need to tell me?"

"No."

His eyes are large and tired and faintly wet. They blink. "But there is something you want to tell."

She doesn't answer.

"I think we should meet one on one."

She is heavily conscious of her body in the room and, though she is dressed, she wishes she had something—a bathrobe, a blanket—to cover herself with. There is an intimacy between them—between the therapist and his idea of her—that makes her feel disturbed and excited and envious. Because it's *her* intimacy, the other Elisa's. She pictures that woman in her own real body, trapped in it, in her thin body and vacant marriage, driving out here, pulling over at the side of the road, gazing at the therapist's house and office with loneliness and longing.

And like that, she has an epiphany. In her real life, she is *lonely.*

"We've come a long way together," says Amos Finley. "You know you can tell me anything. Don't you?"

"Yes."

"When you're ready."

She is moved, suddenly. She sort of wants to hug him. He seems to notice and draws back, almost imperceptibly.

"All right," she says.

He smiles, slides his glasses back onto his face. His eyes recede and focus and he holds his palm out, inches from her shoulder, and says, "Go to your husband."

PART TWO

20.

She tells Derek she'll be going in to work early every day, in order to re-organize things. He agrees to drive her, though she wishes she could just drive herself—but never mind. This still buys her an extra hour and a half alone, at the office, studying . . . this job, ostensibly, but actually, this life.

She has found several very old e-mails to Sam in her sentbox, overly cheerful exhortations to take care of himself and not drink excessively and not be hurt by the things his brother says and does. The tone embarrasses her—it's artificial, desperate. These chipper notes stopped more than a year ago, and don't appear ever to have been answered. He is living in Santa Monica, apparently the same place Silas lives. Why?

She needs to call him.

It is Wednesday morning. She is sitting in her office. Her inbox is filled with responses to her queries: people have sent her project updates and status reports, as she requested. She reads them, and begins work on a slate of recommendations for the reorganization of the office. It isn't hard. They won't have to fire Becca. She will have Judith read it at the end of the week.

Elisa is disturbed, a little bit, at the ease with which she is occupy-ing this position, one she had no inkling even existed just two days ago. Does this say something about her? Are her talents so generic as to be adaptable to any job? Or is this job so generic that anyone could do it?

More vexing still is the way the job foregrounds, in her mind, the rea-sons she left science in the first place. She was convinced, remains con-vinced, that if the world of biology had consisted solely of herself, a lab, and an unlimited budget, she would still be doing it. Indeed, she would be very, very good at it. As an undergraduate, she had been part of a genomics project right on the forefront of the field; she was the only undergraduate on the team, and the only woman. At first she thought she'd arrived—that to have crossed those lines was to have been accepted.

But of course it didn't work that way. To the other students, even to her professor, her inclusion gave them license to let their guard down, to indulge their pettiest selves. She was mocked the day she wore a skirt, then mocked the rest of the time for wearing jeans. She was told, many times, that her safety goggles flattered her, or didn't flatter her. A tittering tour group, passing through the building, was presented with "the girl scientist." Then she made the mistake of dating a grad student for a couple of months, a man of lesser intelligence to whom she was supposed to defer; and when they broke up, his friends on the team ignored her questions, sabotaged her work, talked about her in stage whispers when she was in the room. "Hey!" she called out one night in the crowded lab, "Will somebody please look at me and answer my fucking question?" It was her ex who answered, to the amusement of his friends, "I thought you didn't like people looking at you. We're just trying not to be *sexist.*"

Her professor, who before had treated her with a certain amount of respect, now came on to her. "You look pretty today," he said, and when she replied "Please don't talk to me that way" a heavy curtain came down between them and he never asked her to do anything again.

The project was tainted. She tried to get on another, to no avail. People told her she was crazy to want to quit. Her adviser, the only woman in the department, told her this. "That project is going somewhere," she said. To Elisa's complaints of sexism, of bullying, of disrespect, the woman turned steely. "I'd like to send you back in time twenty years and see how you like it."

She hated the bureaucracy. She hated the corporate money, the suggestion that certain outcomes were acceptable to the administration and certain outcomes weren't. She hated the fact that all the people working in the department office were women and all but one of the professors were men.

Now, here, she has become one of the women in the all-woman office, in a department where all the professors are men. They are decent people, the professors who are here this summer, but she is not real to them: they don't acknowledge her as anything more than an office worker. Even at her lab job, in the real life, even when she is doing the same kind of organizational work she does here, she is regarded as a person who *does science.* But this job seems to have been perfectly okay with the Elisa Brown who accepted it.

Then again, why should anyone treat her differently? And maybe part of being a good scientist is knowing how to parry insults, how to navigate bureaucracies. How to seize authority and respect, rather than waiting for them to be conferred. Indeed, maybe these are the defining traits of a good scientist—maybe the things that made her think she was a good scientist thwarted, were actually clues that she was not a good scientist at all. And maybe this Elisa has, for better or worse, accepted that.

She considers, briefly, that perhaps the same could be said about being good at marriage. Or parenthood.

It makes sense, she supposes, that in this world where Silas is alive, she isn't in touch with him. But Sam? It's hard to imagine the offense that would drive him away—that would compel him to move to California, to live near his brother, and never answer her e-mails. Maybe they write letters—there could be letters somewhere, tucked into a drawer or cubbyhole somewhere at the house. She'll look later, when she gets home, but somehow she doubts it.

When things were at their worst—with Silas, and with Derek, too— she could always talk to Sam. Even when he was small, when he could barely speak, he was interesting to talk to—habitually quiet, he became voluble when they were alone, asking questions, remarking on the scenery, trying to figure things out. *He* would be the scientist, she thought. He wanted to know how things worked. He had ideas about how they might—compelling ones. By the time he was five or six his questions fell outside her ability to answer, what-ifs about the nature of time, existence, the limits of the universe. He did excel at science in school, for a while, but his grades suffered as Silas intruded more and more upon their lives, and they never really recovered, even after the accident. By then Sam had come to think of himself as an indifferent student, and so he was.

But he was still smart. She would like to tell him what had happened to her, to ask his opinion. He would certainly have one. He'd dismiss immediately the notion that she had lost her mind, go right for the science. "Where did Han Solo go?" she asked him once when he was six, having watched him, in play, tuck his action figure behind a sofa pillow. "Sucked into a hole in the space-time continuum!" was his reply.

Twenty minutes seem to have passed, here in her office. The document file open in front of her makes no sense. She closes the word processor, opens a web browser, and clicks in the search box.

She is thinking of Sam when she types the words "parallel worlds," then adds "physics" and "study" and "university." This is the kind of thing they talk about these days, in her real life, summer nights out on the porch when he has come over for dinner and Derek has gone to bed, Sam smoking with his chair tipped back and his feet up on the railing. Sam would take the idea seriously, at least for an hour. But what the internet gives her is a lot of science fiction. Television shows and novels. There are scientists who have theorized the existence of parallel universes, but nobody who is actually trying to figure out what is in them. This is the purview of cranks, dreamers, and Hollywood screenwriters.

She wants to look harder, to find somebody who is actually looking into this idea, who thinks of it as palpably real. Instead she finds herself googling Silas again, digging more deeply into the search results. There is a reference to "Silas Brown of Infinite Games, minefield on gamedev.org." She searches for minefield, gamedev, and ends up on an internet forum for hardcore gamers, video game testers, and game developers. And there is indeed a member named minefield.

Minefield appears to be belligerent, impulsive. He has been banned multiple times. In the hierarchy of the game development world, he appears to be among the most successful professionals who still post on internet forums. There are celebrities in this world, and he is not among them, but he has some small fame here, in this community of hobbyists, wannabes, and up-and-coming professionals.

He is clearly among the most knowledgeable members of the forum, and Elisa can tell, after half an hour of reading the threads he visits, that questions are often asked with the sole purpose of luring him into the open. At times he is very generous with what must be basic advice. He answers a question about coding convex rotating polygons. He advises somebody on creating realistic intelligent motion in virtual crowds. (None of this makes any sense to Elisa; it's like a map of a foreign country. She has never played video games, beyond Pac-Man once or twice, at the pizza shop, with a boyfriend, in 1984.)

But every now and then minefield will respond to a question with withering personal criticism. *You're fucking pathetic. You come here expecting something for nothing. That is the stupidest fucking question I've read on here in six months.* He tells people they'll never amount to anything. He mocks their ideas, their spelling mistakes, their screen names, their graphic avatars. His victims fight back, weakly, trying to justify themselves. The forum breaks into camps, attacking or defending minefield. Members say they've had enough, threaten to quit the board. Moderators are summoned and issue warnings. Minefield mocks the moderators. The thread is locked. Minefield is banned. Minefield comes back, feigning contrition, and it all begins again.

It has to be Silas. He is everything she remembers. He is as charming as he is vitriolic; you feel proud when he accepts you, and when he turns on you, you blame yourself.

Elisa remembers something now, something from the months leading up to the crash. Silas brought a girl home after school one day. She might not ever have known it had the girl not sneaked out of his room to use the bathroom: Elisa saw her at the end of the hallway, darting across from one door to the other. They must have come in while she was out, or entered quietly through the back. Whatever the case, they were here, together: Silas and a girl, in the house.

She heard the girl return to Silas's room. She waited a few minutes, then sneaked down the hall.

They were very quiet. Elisa could hear them kissing, hear them shifting on the bed. Then the girl said, "I really need to do this, Silas."

"Shh." Silas groaned quietly, then spoke to her in a tone she hadn't heard before: commanding, certainly, perhaps condescending, but gentle. He said, in a near-whisper, "All right, let's see it."

The bedsprings creaked; Elisa heard a zipper. Not her clothes, her backpack. Then a grunt of effort as something was hauled out of it. The pages of a book, being turned. "What don't you get?" was Silas's question, weary, skeptical.

"The whole thing," she said.

"Dude," he said, "this is easy."

"Dude," the girl said, not without sarcasm, "for you. Not for me."

Their conversation continued, with Silas dominating, talking about straight and curved lines, the slope of a line. F of X, F-prime of X. Derivatives. He was explaining calculus to her—helping her with homework.

Elisa withdrew. She had never seen or heard him with a girl. He never brought one to the house. This one must have insisted. She withdrew to the kitchen, where she could still hear the doors open and close, and idled until the girl seemed to be leaving. Then she headed down the back stairs and busied herself in the storeroom, pretending to look for a particular can of paint, so that she could catch a glimpse as the girl headed out the back.

It worked. She was alone, a small thing with a giant backpack. She started when she saw Elisa there, gasped.

"Oops, sorry," Elisa said.

"Yeah, sorry, hi," the girl said, hiding her face behind her hair and scuttling away, through the door, across the patio, and into a gap in the hedge. Elisa was surprised again—she wasn't pretty. Plain, in fact, the face flat and broad, lank hair, thick glasses. She was done up like a punk, with pierced nose and lip and a black leather jacket. Her jeans were tight on her heavy hips; her exposed hairy ankles must have been cold, as it was a dry clear winter afternoon, near dark.

Were they having sex? Something she would wonder, later, after he was dead: had he ever slept with a girl, or with girls; this one or others? She wouldn't find condoms or any other evidence among his possessions, afterward; but then again she would never look very hard. Some of his things are still there, in boxes, in the other life. They might contain anything at all, or nothing.

A week later Elisa was at the supermarket and saw the girl there, buying a can of Coke and a chocolate bar. She was with a friend, a skinny blond-haired thing in a ratty knitted hat. "Oh, hey," the girl said, hiding her face behind a curtain of hair, and Elisa said, "How are you?"

"I'm good," Silas's girl said. She appeared eager to leave; Elisa was on her way in, these two on their way out.

And then Elisa said, quietly, conspiratorially, "I hope he's treating you well," and the girl's face froze, and her friend's mouth made an *O* of delighted shocked surprise.

"Uh huh" was the reply, and they were gone. Elisa imagined them gasping and cackling in the parking lot, and felt as embarrassed as she had ever felt in her life. She was worse than her mother, worse than Derek's even. She had visited humiliation upon this poor child, and brought it down on herself as well. But she had wanted to warn the girl. Silas was trouble, after all.

After he was dead, she came to believe it was only Sam they failed—they allowed his brother to dominate him, to wear him down. Maybe if Silas had been the older one, they would have pushed back harder. Maybe there was some part of them that believed Sam ought to be able to fend for himself, being bigger and (so they thought, at first, and maybe they were right) smarter. Maybe they knew all along he was gay, maybe on some level it made them uncomfortable. *C'mon, don't be a pussy, fight back.* Later, when Sam came out to them, the first Christmas of his college career, she wondered if Silas had ever abused him, had subjected him to incest, if Silas had somehow made him gay. Nothing in her memory would suggest that Sam had ever been anything but what he was, yet she thought it nevertheless. Derek too. Sam's sexuality a problem, Silas its cause.

But that's what Silas was like. Even in death, he dominated their thoughts, their way of seeing. The likelihood of Silas's influence simply seemed greater than the likelihood of random chance; Silas was easy to blame things on, when so much was his fault.

Wasn't it?

Elisa's palms are starting to itch. Minefield is mesmerizing, mercurial; to read his helpful posts is harrowing. *Does this make sense to you? I'm not sure that's the best example. If that doesn't work, let me know, I've got another idea, too.* It's too perfect, too reassuring, too accommodating; reading it, you wait, hushed, for the explosion, you sense everyone on the forum waiting with you. And then someone, some hapless newb, betrays his ignorance—*wait uh I dont get it what?*—and Silas pounces.

She wonders now what she did then—is it all theater? Is the charmer merely a stalking horse for the bully? Or is the charmer for real, a genuine part of Silas that he simply can't sustain? If it's real, what does it feel like

for him, proffering this part of himself, then having to snatch it back? Is
he ashamed? Does he feel remorse?

They should have asked themselves that more often, she thinks. When
he was bad, they punished him, or tried to. But maybe it hurt him to be
bad. Maybe he wasn't so hard, in the end—maybe it was all armor, a way
of defending his most sentimental, most vulnerable self.

But she doesn't like to think about that. If that's true, then they did it
wrong. If that's true, then Silas is more like her than she wants to admit.

21.

Elisa tells Becca she's having a business lunch with somebody from Killian
Tech, and will be back at two. Becca doesn't seem surprised or concerned,
and Elisa walks out into the July sun.

Killian Tech is her lab—the one that, in her memory, she was managing just a few days ago. It's a dozen blocks from the Levinson Center,
closer to the lake, and she walks briskly, suffering in the heat.

The people, the houses all look familiar. She is alert for differences in
this world that do not involve her husband and sons. But none are evident. That's not to say they don't exist, only that she has never been as ob-
servant as she might have liked to think. How could she be? Her thoughts
have always been more interesting to her than the world itself. She remembers what she liked best about her lab work: data. Having data to
pore over, on the filthy computer in the corner by the window, while
the other students fussed at their experiments behind her. She loved that
world, the world of abstract representation. She loved making numbers
make sense. That's what she did here, at her old lab.

The Killian Tech building is a flat, one-story structure with windows
on all sides. It used to be dental offices and is wedged incongruously into
a residential neighborhood. Its owner, her employer, lives in fear of zon-
ing complaints from neighbors. But so far there haven't been any. They're
quiet and unobtrusive.

Elisa's office is on the northeast corner of the building, facing a bus stop
and a NO PARKING sign. From the sidewalk, through the windows, it looks
more or less the same: a desk and computer, some plants. She made few
changes to it when she took the job, and whoever is working there now

clearly took the same approach. Where Elisa had hung a black-and-white photograph of a cobblestone street, this person has hung a diploma. The filing cabinet is larger—Elisa had always meant to do that. There's a photo of a blond-haired woman on the desk, and a little wooden box containing some sand, some stones, and a tiny rake.

She pretends to wait for the bus but continues to watch the workings of the office. The techs aren't visible from here—most of the lab facilities are behind an interior wall, where the light can be controlled. But she doesn't recognize the people coming and going through the lab door. Of course she hired many of the techs herself and wasn't here to do so, in this world.

Eventually a thin man walks into the office, smiles at her through the window, and sits down. He begins to read his e-mail. She remembers doing the same thing: meeting the gaze of bus passengers, turning to her work.

Something occurs to her that surely she has thought of before: the world doesn't need her. The highest compliment you can be paid at work is that you are indispensable. *We couldn't do it without you.* But of course they can always do it without you. Killian Tech is doing it without her. Her sons are doing it without her. In her world, the real world, when Silas died, the world knitted itself back together behind him, and all that was left were a few scars, nearly all of them in their house. Maybe his girlfriends were sad for a little while. Then they moved on.

Perhaps the reason she is afraid of Derek here, in this world, is that she knows he doesn't need her. She's seen it. He can find other people to talk to, to have sex with. So can she. His attachment to her here is superfluous: there is a part of her that wants to just get it over with, to betray him or be betrayed, to leave him or be abandoned. Because it can happen, and the fact that it hasn't is a hanging thread, an unresolved note.

The man in her office looks up again and she realizes she has been staring at him. He is not her, looks nothing like her, but in this world, to those people, he *is* her. His brow is creased; he is gazing at her frankly, and with puzzlement. Elisa feels self-conscious now, and turns to go. At this moment a bus arrives, and she impulsively steps onto it.

There is a moment of frustration and embarrassment, as the bus pulls away, that she cannot find her bus pass. Indeed, it would appear that, in this life, she doesn't have one. She smoothes out a crumpled dollar and feeds it into the cash box, then takes her seat.

This is the number 20. It goes down to the park by the lake and then out to the western edge of downtown before circling back. The air-conditioning is on high and a soft-rock radio station is playing a song by Journey. She shivers. No, she didn't board the bus on impulse: she intended this all along.

She gets off at the main depot by the library and walks east. After three blocks, she turns south. The frame shop is the fourth building on the right, a small converted cottage, again on a residential street. From the outside it appears identical to the one she knows—cedar shakes stained a slightly artificial brown, louvered windows with gold text: AURORA FRAMING.

He's there, standing at the main counter, a broad work table arrayed with mat board samples. Behind him, the walls are covered with frame corners. He is typing on a small laptop computer.

He looks up at her with a completely generic smile and says, "May I help you?"

Larry. He's trim, early fifties, and an inch shorter than Elisa. Clean-shaven, with hair cropped close. He looks subtly different to her—perhaps it is his failure to recognize her. She hasn't seen this expression on his face, one of expectant politeness, directed at her since the day they met.

Of course, here, this *is* the day they met.

"It's silly, really," she says, and hates the sound of her voice. "Maybe not worth your time." She draws from her purse the family photo that used to stand on her desk. "I'd like this put into a decent frame."

He takes the picture, turns it over in his hands. "Do you intend to hang it? Or stand it on a surface?"

"Hang it," she says.

He turns it over again, as she knew he would. He is deliberate, thought-ful. This is the sort of movement that, in the old life, would quicken her breath, make her tongue find her lips to moisten them. But her body doesn't want to catch up with her memories, not yet.

"Are you after a contemporary or more traditional look?"

"Traditional. But not gaudy."

This makes him glance up. Or maybe he just wanted a second look at her. Another small smile, then he turns around and reaches for one, then another, frame sample. His shoulders are broad, for a small man's, and his jeans hug his hips. He pushes some papers out of the way, removes the photo from the frame and places it on the countertop, facing Elisa. He selects a sample piece of cream-colored mat board, lays it down over the corner of the photo. Arranges a frame sample at its edge.

"This will give it a warmer look than what you had it in," he says. "Now this . . ." He swaps out the mat board for a different piece, this one a pale gray. "This will complement the colors of the stones here, behind the figures."

"Ah," she says.

"Your family?"

"Yes."

He looks up at her. "Handsome boys."

"Thanks."

"Do we know each other?"

"I've seen you around town." There is a quaver in her voice. She extends her hand. "I'm Lisa."

"Larry."

Their palms touch, his dry, hers clammy. He holds on exactly as long as is appropriate. She says, "I like the cooler one. And the plainer frame."

"Good choice, I think. We can have that for you in a few days."

He opens a drawer, pulls out a form, takes pen in hand. She is reminded of the way, after sex, he picks up his glasses and puts them back on. She is trying to remember, with unexpected difficulty, what he is like in bed, what his body feels like close to hers. He writes "Lisa" on the form.

But Elisa has already backed up. She is nearly at the door. She says, "No need for that. I'll be back."

Larry looks up, apparently surprised. Doubtless there is a deposit policy. But in the end he says only, "All right then."

Back on the street, she admits to herself how much of this encounter she planned out ahead of time, how many hours some small ashamed part of her mind spent blocking out the movements, working on the script. Perhaps this is why she expected something more—a feeling of something gathering momentum. Instead it feels like the first steps up a steep hill.

Was it really that different, in the old life? Did she want him right away, or did it take time? Maybe she is misremembering the sudden, inalienable erotic pull, the feeling of inevitability.

Or maybe this is the real life, and that one was fantasy. Erotic fantasy.

No. It is just that lust is physical. Maybe it bypasses the mind, like the impulse that pulls the hand away from a hot stove. Lust is in the body, she thinks, boarding the number 20, shoving her dollar bill into the slot, and this is not my body.

22.

It's a few nights later. She's home alone, Derek is out buying a six-pack of beer from the supermarket, and the phone rings. The caller ID tells her it's Lorraine. She decides to let the machine get it.

But then she picks it up. She can't stop herself: she's curious. "Hello, Lorraine."

"Hello there, dear, how are you?"

"I'm good, I'm good . . ." Already it's different: Lorraine never calls her dear, doesn't ask her how she's doing.

"I expected to hear from you—how did the conference go?"

"Fine, it was fine." She is analyzing every word for hidden content: the "I expected" is typical Lorraine, but not in this context. Lorraine expecting to hear from her? The question does not sound sarcastic. The intent does not seem to be to mock and humiliate.

They make small talk. Or Lorraine does, and Elisa tries to. Elisa doesn't know how to do small talk. This is why they never have anyone over. Or perhaps in this world they do—maybe they have parties, lavish boring parties. Lorraine is telling her about her book group, a novel they read, the comments some of the other women made. She describes a television show she watched the night before, and offers some details about the child of some neighbors who has just graduated from Harvard.

Elisa feels as though she's supposed to offer something in return. Some little morsel. She mentions getting the photo reframed.

Silence. Then, "Maybe you should just take it down, dear."

"Maybe," Elisa says. Another silence follows, so she continues: "Do they . . . do you ever speak with them?"

"You know that I don't." This quietly, uncertainly.

It feels like an opportunity to Elisa, but she isn't certain what kind. She says, very quietly, "Lorraine. It's all right if you do."

She thinks she must have made a mistake—Lorraine says nothing, then draws a deep, ragged breath.

"Thank you," she says, and nothing more.

A moment later she hears Derek coming through the door. Does Lorraine want to talk with him? No, she doesn't. "I just wanted to catch up with you, dear," she says, with audible relief.

"Well, thank you."

Some pleasantries, which Derek listens to as he arranges beer bottles in the fridge. "My mother?" he says, when Elisa hangs up.

"Yes."

He shakes his head. "All she ever wanted was a daughter. Sometimes I think she likes you better than me."

23.

She starts bringing work home. The binder. Budget materials. It's all begun to make sense, but she wants it to be intuitive. Natural. Out of all the things that are alien to her, she thinks, if I can master this, then I can master it all. Evenings, Derek cooks, she clears the table and puts the dishes in the machine and wipes the table down. Soon she has her glass of wine and is working under the bright kitchen lights. Surely this is not quite right—there are things she's missing, things Derek expects her to do. But he says nothing. Sometimes he looks at her too long: this is when he's waiting for her to discharge some obligation. Nights he appears anxious, frightened even. He says good night, then waits. She might get up and go with him, and in bed he will reach out and touch her shoulder, then withdraw. She might remain seated in the kitchen. They haven't had sex yet.

Friday night, she stays up after he goes to bed. She has been in this world for five days. Laptop open in the kitchen, she searches the internet for references to Silas. Then she composes an e-mail to Sam. It reads, *We want to see you.* She doesn't know if this is even possible—if they or he have the money to travel. Surely they do—they did in the real life. The e-mail sits on the desktop, unsent.

She wonders what the other Elisa is doing. If she is adapting, or if she is floundering. The latter, Elisa tells herself—this Lisa, the one she is impersonating, is soft, pliable, defanged. Or perhaps she is merely flattering her real self. In any event, if that Lisa has adopted her old life, Silas is being mourned again.

The memory of Silas's death—his funeral, his burial, and her subsequent months, years of grief—no longer compels strong emotion in Elisa. The way a factory worker, forced to listen to the same clang of metal against metal for years and years, will lose that frequency for good: that part of her is worn away. But the thought of that woman, her doppelgänger, experiencing this for the first time, stops her breath. A little hiccup of misery convulses her body; the stool barks on the linoleum. The poor thing.

But then again, maybe the Lisa who once inhabited this body, who endured the challenges of a living Silas, has had to evolve a more agile mind. Maybe I'm the weak one, Elisa thinks—the woman who couldn't hold her marriage together, who cheated and lied, who couldn't get along with her mother-in-law. And now the smarter Lisa, the stronger Lisa, is making better use of her freedom than the real one ever could. Maybe the fake Lisa mastered Killian Tech even more quickly than the real one mastered the Levinson Center. She has seduced Derek and resisted the advances of the creepy frame shop guy, who keeps calling her, though they've never met. She is working harder, thinking more clearly, feeling more deeply. What does Silas's death mean to her? In this world, the wrong one, he might as well be dead. He isn't in her life anymore.

She still hasn't sent the e-mail. After a moment's thought, she signs it *Love, Mom* and hits SEND.

As if in reaction, she reaches out and snaps the computer shut. A wave of terror rises up in her and then subsides. On the chair beside her lies her purse. She has carried it with her everywhere all week and has barely looked into it, except to remove and replace her wallet. Now. This is a good time for it.

She pushes the computer out of the way and hauls the bag onto the table. She begins to remove its contents, item by item.

First, makeup. A compact, a lot of lipstick. Eyeliner and rouge. Lipstick she has worn before, but eyeliner? What on earth is this woman supposed to look like? There are Tic Tacs, orange and mint, and two half-empty packets of tissues. There is a pocket calendar. It gives her a moment of panic, until she realizes that it's from 2007 and is completely empty after the month of May. Lots of receipts, some itemized and listing items that are also in the purse. An eyeglass case containing her same old glasses, which she has kept ever since switching to contact lenses years before. Contact lens case and fluids. Wallet. Keys. Phone.

There are pockets on either side of the main compartment, fastened with a snap. One is filled with pens, as it was in the other life, where the second compartment was empty.

Here, though, the second compartment contains a piece of graph paper folded twice over on itself, rounded and furred at the corners. She removes it, pushes the bag out of the way, and unfolds it on the table in front of her.

It's in her own handwriting, and it reads:

1. Pay compliments and express gratitude.
2. Blame yourself first, circumstance second, your partner last of all.
3. If you must refuse intimacy, offer something in return.
4. Account for your time.
5. Do not use the children to attack your partner.

24.

Elisa lies awake beside Derek wondering what else might be different. She remembers the moment of the switch—has been trying to remember it more precisely—and is certain that there were more or fewer clouds, or that the clouds changed position. And if the weather was different, then a lot of other things must be different. Right?

But then wouldn't Silas himself, Silas's existence, be the thing that changed the weather, changed everything that is different now? No. There was something before the van crash that kept him from going along for the ride, and something before that, and something before that. And so the world was already altered, and Silas's death or survival trivial. The world must be indifferent to Silas, to her affairs and her appearance and her personal demeanor. She is a casualty of circumstance, not the center of the universe. And so this change, this transference, cannot be meaning-ful. It's something that happened by accident: a glitch.

For this universe not to be about her, not to be made with her in mind, then, there would have to be more than just the one where Silas survived. There would have to be one where Silas was maimed, and one where Silas was never born, and one where he was a delightful and well-adjusted child, and one where he was a houseplant.

How many would there have to be? All of them.

Of course it's easier just to say she's nuts. She's the glitch. At least that way, she can imagine how she might ever return, if that's what she wants to do. The mind is more malleable than the universe, as far as she knows. You don't need to be a genius or a video game character or from the future to manipulate the mind. The mind is made to be fucked with.

This, then, is the most likely, the most sensible, explanation—the world is the same, and Elisa Brown is the thing that is different. There's a phenomenon she has read about, not déjà vu, but *déjà vécu,* false mem-ory. You think you remember something, but it's your unconscious mind that has created it, for purposes the conscious mind can't fathom. The thing you remember seems real. But in fact only the thing before you is real. This room. This bed. This man.

She wonders what time it is. The clock is on Derek's side of the bed, turned away because its glow is too bright. Has she slept yet tonight? She feels that she hasn't, but there's light outside, almost. Or maybe that is the moon. At this hour, whatever hour it might be, anything and everything seems possible, anything at all could be true. What has happened seems real. The possibility of return seems real.

If she isn't insane, and if she could return, what would that mean? That is, if her consciousness leaped from one body to the next, then who is to say the body it left is still alive? Maybe the other Lisa isn't in it, mourning now for Silas; maybe that body is dead. Maybe it ran off the road and through the guardrail and there is a funeral in that world, for her, going on today. Maybe Derek is waking up alone today to bury her.

Or who is to say that this consciousness wasn't just copied, that the other Lisa is the same as ever, working at the lab and carrying on with her lover? Even if she could go back, maybe there is no place for her to go. Her body there is already occupied by the original.

And if this is so, then what happened to the woman who occupied this body? If Elisa leaves it now, perhaps it will drop dead, too.

Of course all of these thoughts are predicated on the idea that the consciousness in question is, in fact, a thing. A thing that has to be somewhere. And this is not a notion Elisa Brown has ever believed in. The soul. The God who tends it. All of it, nonsense. The soul is chemistry, it dies with the body. Consciousness is an illusion, a piece of software. When the machine shuts down, the program isn't merely resting. It doesn't exist.

What has happened to her does not fit into this worldview. Yet there is none she knows of that will accommodate it.

Derek stirs beside her. She doesn't want to wake him. She slides out of bed, pads to the toilet, and then down the stairs to the kitchen and her computer. She is hoping that when she powers it on she will find an e-mail from Sam. But what she finds instead is one from Amos Finley. It reads, *Lisa. Have you thought about seeing me one on one as we discussed?*

The e-mail has been cc'ed to Derek.

Her reply goes to the therapist only. *No, I don't think so.*

She is startled, first at this apparent breach of privacy, and then even more startled that the therapist is awake and sending e-mail at 5:00 a.m. on a Saturday.

Elisa sits and considers. There is some code here, some message that she does not understand. What is the value of betraying her to Derek in this small way? It is an effort to force her to reform. They are ganging up on her, the men.

As if the e-mails have summoned him, Derek appears, wrapped in his thin cotton robe.

"Who are you e-mailing?"

His back is to her. He has opened the coffeemaker and is dumping the grounds in the trash under the sink. He does this with the brusque, exaggerated movements that suggest displeasure at her not already having done it.

She says, "The therapist is suggesting a private session. With me. He cc'ed you."

"What therapist?" he asks, filling the coffee urn with water.

She says, "Our therapist."

"Why are you calling him 'the therapist'?"

"Sorry," she says, after a moment. "Amos."

He doesn't respond. Something in the curve of his back indicates that he believes he's being fucked with. *Please, Derek,* she wants to say, *it's me!* But she says nothing.

He asks her, "So when are you going?"

"I'm not."

"Why not?" Derek turns, straddles the stool across the table from her. Behind him the coffeemaker begins to pant and moan.

Instead of answering, she says, "It's strange that he's e-mailing at this hour."

"It's strange that *you* are."

Their eyes meet. His hand reaches for a mug of coffee that isn't there yet. Fluidly he transforms this motion into a gentle stroking of the table's surface.

And just like that she would like to have sex with him. She is startled by the thought, and he seems to notice, and to notice what it is that caught her attention. He moves, just barely—the head cocked a fraction of an inch, the single eyebrow twitching over one eye. She closes the laptop, slides down off the stool, and walks out of the kitchen without a glance behind her. She takes off her nightgown on the way up the stairs. By the time she's standing naked by the bed he has crossed the threshold of the bedroom, his robe billowing around him.

It's quick and intense. His body is better here. Stronger. He doesn't seem younger—indeed, he looks and feels his age. But this is better than the concealing softness of the other Derek. Her own, heavier body feels more erotic. She makes no sound other than a single deep involuntary groan.

For those moments there is nothing to apologize for and everything makes sense.

They lie beside each other, touching at the hip. Down in the kitchen, the coffeemaker beeps five times.

"You're different," he says, this time without hostility or accusation.

"Yes."

"Do you know why?"

"Not entirely."

For a moment she thinks he's going to let it go. Then, "Do you want to tell me what part you know?"

"Not yet," she says.

"Will you tell Amos?"

"No."

Immediately she feels this is the wrong answer. Does it violate a rule? But he slides his hand up onto her hip and across her belly. Perhaps this is something they haven't had together for some time: a small secret.

25.

Two hours later they have eaten breakfast and drunk their coffee in comfortable silence. It's almost possible to consider the situation normal. There's a newspaper to read, so she stares at the words for a while, turns the pages. She tries and fails to empty her mind.

In the afternoon Derek goes out on errands. She opens her laptop and finds an email from Sam:

> Mom
>
> Nice hearing from you
>
> No time/money to travel
>
> Sorry
>
> Sam

She reads the message several times. It feels heavy with meaning. After a few minutes' thought, she writes back: *I want to come see you.* She sends it before she can change her mind.

A few minutes' idle clicking later, she shuts the laptop, paces around the kitchen. They keep a phone list magneted to the fridge in the old life, but here there's nothing. She opens and closes several drawers, then finds an address book—neatly maintained, implausibly, in her own hand—in the drawer under the phone. She looks under *Brown* and then *Sam,* and finds an address, two phone numbers.

She picks up the phone, stares at the keypad. Puts it down, goes to the front window. No Derek. Goes back to the phone and calls the first number.

There's a click, and then she can hear a city street. For a moment, no one speaks.

Elisa says, "Hello?"

Sam says "Hi," elongating it into a question.

"Are you all right?"

Another pause, and then, "Sure. Are you?"

"Yes. Yes, I'm fine." Elisa lets out breath and experiences a moment of lightness, dizziness. Relief. She hasn't understood until now just how anxious she has been, how terrified of this moment. And for what? That he wouldn't be real. But here he is. She hears a car horn, voices speaking Spanish. "I'm sorry I've been . . . out of touch," she says.

"Uh huh . . ."

"This must seem . . . it must be strange to hear from me."

"Yeah . . . yeah . . ."

"Thanks for your e-mail. Did you get mine? I guess you didn't, I just sent it."

"Oh really?"

"I want to come to see you." She hesitates. "You and your brother."

He doesn't respond to that. He seems to be speaking to someone else—buying something at a store, perhaps. Somebody thanks him in a foreign accent. After a moment, she goes on.

"I hope that he hasn't . . . I hope Silas isn't . . . hurting you, Sam. Or making things . . . harder for you."

There's a long pause. Elisa feels the need to fill it.

"I realize that things haven't been good between us. For a while now. I . . . want to rectify that. Start to rectify that. If you'll let me. Some things have happened to me—" And here, she is suddenly and unexpectedly moved, and her throat closes. She has to pause. She takes a breath, says, "Some things have happened to, to change the way I see my life. And I need to try to make things right. With you and Silas."

He laughs, but it's fake—forced.

"Sam?"

"*That* guy." The voice has changed now.

Elisa says, "I don't—"

"*Silas.*"

Here in the kitchen, she becomes aware of the ticking of the wall clock, and it seems very loud. Her voice is very loud, even though she is nearly whispering. "Is there a problem with—"

"That guy is *such a dick*. Seriously. He's *so* mean to me."

A chill goes through her. The receiver creaks in her hand: she is holding it tight enough to break it.

The voice that comes out of it says, "He's so *mean!* I hate him. I wish he would just leave me alone."

She says nothing.

"Boo hoo hoo," says the voice.

"Silas," Elisa says.

"I do hope you'll visit, Mom. Maybe you can tell him to stop bothering me? He never listens to me. Whoops," he says, "gotta run. It was great talking to you!" And the conversation is ended with a click.

She has just spoken to her dead son on the phone.

Forty-five minutes later, the sound of Derek's truck rouses her from sleep. She is on the sofa, her head tipped back on the cushions at a strange angle. Her neck hurts. Derek walks in and his body language communicates disapproval. He dislikes napping in general. In the other life, he overcame this prejudice, with effort. She sits up. "Hi."

"You're not getting enough sleep."

"No, I guess not. Where were you?"

"Home Depot," he says. He's wearing a very clean pair of jeans and an old tee shirt and standing on the living room carpet with a plastic sack dangling from his hand. It is about to start to seem strange, his standing there, when he lets out a small grunt and sits down. He drops the bag on the floor and takes her numb hands into his. "This morning," he says, "was nice."

"Yes."

"I want you to go see Amos. Please."

She makes herself sit up, cranes her neck, trying to get the kink out. Derek releases her hands and begins to rub her shoulders.

"Thank you."

"Will you go?"

She wants to answer him, but it's as though the whole charade has hit a wall. She exhales, feeling his hands on her. Her throat tightens and her breath catches and she tells herself that she isn't going to cry.

"I'm sorry," he says. "This is . . . everything has gone insane this week. I don't understand what's happening."

"We have to put this behind us," she says, finally. A shot in the dark. "Amos. Everything."

Her eyes are closed, she can't see his reaction. But there is despair in his voice as he says, "I don't understand how you can say that."

"We can do it. We *have* done it."

"I haven't. I haven't, not yet."

But she meant in the other life. For a moment she wants, very badly, to tell him. To come clean. She remembers how it felt last night, the secret between them, the information she planned to conceal from Amos. A path to a new life, a third one, that begins right now.

Isn't this something she has wanted, every now and then? Hasn't everyone wanted this? To just throw it all overboard, the bad decisions of the past, and start over? Her life, at this moment, is a nightmare: she is tired of pretending, she is tired of trying to figure things out. Let it go. Derek would do it with her, he would let it all go. Wouldn't he?

A new life. Starting now.

The phone rings once. Neither of them moves. It doesn't ring a second time. She feels it, that ring, as if it's a nail the universe has created, that has pierced her and fixed her to the sofa. She doesn't move or speak, other than to squeeze Derek's hand, a gesture that could mean anything. *Sorry. Please. Love. Help. Get closer. Go away.* In the end, he goes away. He kisses her sweating forehead and disappears with his plastic bag. A few minutes later she hears, from a distant part of the house, the sound of an electric drill.

That night an e-mail arrives from Sam: *I don't get it. What are you doing?* When Derek goes to sleep, she books a plane ticket for California.

26.

By the end of the following week she has mastered her job. It hasn't been hard. To other people, she has just appeared forgetful. She's made up for it with excessive cheerfulness. Half her day she spends online, following Silas on messageboards. She thinks she has found iterations of him in other places—other gaming forums, a forum about motorcycles, another one about serial killers. The latter, she discovers, is famous for rumors that some members of it are actually murderers—twice in the past, apparently, new members who joined discussions of killings turned out to be the killers. Silas is very interested in this phenomenon—he is always accusing people of being killers, and then, as on his game developers' forum, ends up temporarily banned. Finding him has been easy—though he uses different names on every forum, he always has the same signature line on his posts, an unattributed quotation: *He saw himself in a strange city with his friend, except that the face of his friend was different.*

The first part of the week went this way: after work on Tuesday, she appeared at the usual time to be picked up by Derek. But instead of getting into the car, she leaned in the window and told him she wasn't going to therapy. If he was going home, she would ride with him. But if he was going to see Amos, she would walk.

He appeared stricken. He gazed through the windshield and gripped the steering wheel with both hands and said, "I'm going to go."

"I'll walk home."

"In those shoes?"

"I brought sneakers."

They looked at each other. She should have kissed him. Instead she took a step back. He said, "Lisa. Are you going to leave me?"

For too long, she said nothing. Because that's another thing she could do with this third life. She could start over on her own. But she did eventually say, "No."

"Do you love me?"

"I love you."

She sounded certain of it, to her own ears, but she didn't know if she meant it or if her conviction came from her need to say it. Derek accepted it, accepted her love. He drove away. And she changed into her sneakers there on the curb and walked home. And in fact she has continued to walk home every day, even in the rain.

Now it's Friday, not quite noon. She could leave if she wanted to, but this office has slowly turned into a sanctuary. She likes it here: it's the place where she knows what's going on. She has a set of papers in her hand—printouts of some budget material for an interdepartmental committee, on which handwritten notes have been made. It needs to go to physics. She reaches for a campus mail envelope, then stops herself. It's a nice day.

Physics is on the other side of the science quad. She walks in a perfectly straight line, ignoring the cement paths, cutting through the grass, diverging only to avoid hitting trees. A young Asian man holds the heavy wooden door open for her; she nods her thanks.

The office is hot. They don't have air-conditioning, for some reason—just fans. There is a sense here of confusion and dishevelment—she likes it. She finds the department's equivalent of herself and hands her the papers. But of course that's not really why she came, is it. She doesn't admit it to herself until she is standing at the front desk, where the assistant, a woman around her own age, is chatting with a second woman, this one younger. They are talking about a movie they have both seen.

"Sorry to bother you," Elisa says to the assistant. "But I have kind of a strange question."

Both women look at her.

"Is anyone in this department—any of the scientists—studying the concept of . . . other . . . that is, parallel, or multiple, universes?"

The assistant says, "Like science fiction?"

"Well—not really. Or I guess maybe, but I mean in reality." She feels like a fool.

"Oh, geez, I really don't know," the assistant says.

Elisa claps her hands together, steps back from the desk. "Thanks. Sorry to bother you." Only once she's nearly to the stairs does she let out breath—she doesn't know what made her think that was a good idea.

But a voice stops her—"Hey! Uh, hello?" It's the young woman. She is half-jogging down the hall, in the manner of someone who rarely moves faster than walking speed.

"Hi."

"Hey!" The girl is out of breath. She arrives where Elisa is standing, gets a panicked look in her eye, takes half a step back. "I'm a postdoc here?"

"Ah." She is small and cute—cat-eye glasses, blue hair. A physics woman.

"I'm Betsy. I'm . . . yeah. So the multiverse?"

"Oh! I'm Elisa. Is that your field? Parallel . . . whatever?" She's embarrassed now—embarrassed to utter these words in this building, embarrassed to say "whatever" to a woman half her age.

"No, no. I'm doing experimental stuff—radiation patterns from quarks."

"I see."

Betsy takes a wallet out of the pocket of her jeans—a man's wallet—and slides a business card out from behind her driver's license. Her hands are trembling slightly. Elisa is impressed, for some reason, that she has business cards. It reads BETSY OROSCO, PHYSICS. And a web address. "That's my site," she says. "It's kind of a . . . physics blog?"

"Cool," Elisa says, and feels herself blush.

But the girl is encouraged. "Yeah, and, ah . . . I'm kind of interested in this stuff. The multiverse stuff. I mean, I post about it sometimes. It's a hobby."

"Physicists have hobbies?"

"Yeah, more physics!"

Betsy invites her into her office, and Elisa follows her to the end of the hallway, up a flight of stairs, and around a corner. They have to duck as they pass beneath an inexplicably low section of ceiling, and then they're in a little cul-de-sac with three doors. Betsy opens the one on the left and leads Elisa inside.

The office is intimate, cramped even, but higher than it is broad, with bookshelves on three walls covered with textbooks, papers, and unusual objects: toys, oddly shaped bits of wood, machine parts, circuit boards. The fourth wall is empty save for a tall narrow window. In front of the window there is a green aluminum desk and, on a filthy Oriental rug, two stained aluminum-frame upholstered chairs. Betsy climbs behind the desk. It bears two laptop computers, a cell phone, and many stacks of books and papers. Elisa sits in one of the chairs, which is familiarly uncomfortable. She says, "How long have you been working here?"

"A year."

"You've really made yourself at home."

Betsy's face reddens. "I like to make a nest." And then, surprisingly, she says, "I'm thirty-two, you know."

"Oh?"

"Did you think I was younger?"

"I admit I did."

"My mother says I'll look like I'm twenty until I'm forty, and then I'll suddenly look sixty."

Elisa says, "Thanks, Mom."

Betsy settles in her chair until its back rests against the windowsill.

The motion upsets a small cactus there, and its pot clanks faintly against another one sitting beside it. The younger woman doesn't seem to notice. "I know, right?" she says, laughing. "But she thinks I'm a lesbian and that science is a phase I'm going through. So yeah but . . ." She leans forward. "Do you know you could make a universe? Like, in a lab?"

Elisa doesn't say anything.

"Or your house even."

"Really."

"In theory! I mean, I can't. You can't. Well, maybe you can, what do I know."

Betsy is excited. She seems to enjoy having Elisa here. Out the window behind her a corner of the building is visible, this very building, and beyond it the science quad. They are in some kind of wing or extension. Yet this seems miraculous somehow, an optical anomaly. A building that is visible from inside itself.

"How?" Elisa asks her.

"I was just reading about this. You'd need a seed. A little tiny thing. Ten pounds of matter, packed into a really tiny space. And if it's all packed in there enough—so that it's basically a black hole—then the repulsive component of gravity, which yes there is such a thing, should be enough, once you trigger it, to expand that matter into a whole other universe."

Elisa says, "A little tiny one."

But Betsy is shaking her head before Elisa has even finished speaking. "No, regular size. Like with stars and galaxies and everything. Like this one."

At the words *like this one,* Elisa experiences a chill. For a moment, she can't believe it—she is actually talking about this.

She says, "Wouldn't it . . . blow everything up?"

"Nope. It would occupy its own space. Another space."

"And you could make this. A person could make this."

"Yeah. Well—in theory. You would need to smash the right particles together. To make the seed. And then, to trigger the expansion—it's tricky. I mean, nobody has done it. As far as we know."

Elisa leans forward. A cloud has covered the sun, the quad is in shadow, but light is still striking the corner of the building that is visible from the office window. "But maybe somebody has."

"Maybe this is it! The universe somebody made."

After a moment, Elisa says, quietly, "A person could go there?"

"In theory."

"But in reality?" Elisa asks. "Is that possible? Can you go there? To the other universe?"

"Well . . ." Betsy says, and there must have been something in Elisa's tone, some excess of hope, that is causing her to pull back from her initial enthusiasm. "You'd have to go through the black hole somehow. Which of course there's all kinds of complications there. Like it would compress you into a stream of atoms, which is to say you're dead. And then, you know, it's a black hole. So."

"So?"

She shrugs. "Even if by some miracle you survived the trip. You could never come back."

27.

"But listen to me," Betsy is saying, "blathering like an idiot."

Elisa shakes her head. "No, this is exactly what I wanted."

"I am kind of giddy, having a nonstudent visit my office. So, wait, you're . . . what's your deal then? Do you work on campus?"

"I'm an administrator," she says carefully, "in the biology department." After a moment, she says, "I used to be a scientist, too."

This seems to please Betsy. "So okay, wow. Physics? Not physics."

"Plant biology. Genetics."

"So how did you get interested in this? This stuff?"

Up until now, the meeting has seemed like a lovely bit of serendipity—the realization of a fantasy she didn't realize she'd harbored. Betsy Orosco is perfect: a probing intelligence wrapped in a sheath of innocence, good humor, and charming clutter. Indeed, Elisa could not have invented a better person to explain these things to her. It's almost as if she has *created* this strange little room, up in this obscure dusty corner of campus.

Elisa's palms are sweating. She grips the greasy burlap armrests of the chair. If this universe, if any universe, could have been created by someone, then who? Could she have created it herself? By accident? Is there a universe where she stuck with science? Moved from biology to physics?

Worked on a particle accelerator? Smashed the right things together? Created new iterations of herself, her husband, her sons? Could this be only one of many? Could this be only one of an infinity? Did she mean to do it, or was it a mistake? Does she even know she did it? Maybe she didn't even notice that it happened. Maybe she thinks the experiment was a failure.

She is vaguely aware that an awkward silence has sprung into being. She looks up to find Betsy looking at her, biting her lip.

Elisa says, "I'm . . . trying to understand something. That happened to me. That is happening."

Betsy's response is quiet and tentative: "What happened to you?"

"I'm not sure I want to say."

The two of them gaze frankly at one another for a moment, and then Betsy turns away, leans back in her chair. The cactus pots clank.

Here it is again, the moment to tell or not tell. She thinks of the billions of women throughout history who have silently endured this same moment of indecision, the little fermata before confession. A last breath before the uncomfortable intimacy is forced onto the friend, or the lover, or the mother, or the sister. *I was raped. I'm married. I'm in love with you. I'm gay.* She's lying to Betsy: she is quite sure that she does want to say. What she isn't sure about is whether she wants to be heard. Because there are only a few possible good outcomes, and an infinitude of bad ones. *Sorry, I have to go. No, that's crazy. Why are you telling me this? You need help.* It's narcissistic, isn't it, this need to tell—to hear oneself give voice to one's feelings, to watch them register on another person, to watch the person shoulder the burden. There's no rational reason for it, just the relief from solitude. Betsy says, "Then maybe you shouldn't."

Her face is alert, the eyes wide, the lips pulled back revealing straight white clenched teeth. She appears alarmed—whether at the possibility of further, perhaps unwanted, intimacy, or at the sound of her own words, Elisa can't tell. Both, probably. The words are not unfriendly; Elisa senses, strongly, that Betsy likes her, likes that they are both women, both scientists. There is a great deal, it seems, that they might understand in one another, that they wouldn't have to explain, should they become closer. Elisa would like coming here, to the physics building, to meet her friend for coffee. She would like to hear more about Betsy's work, about her strange ideas, her speculations.

Too close, too soon: that would ruin it. Elisa is disappointed and relieved. She nods, grips the armrests of the chair, readies herself to get up and leave.

"No, wait," says Betsy, "I'm sorry."

"I should be sorry," Elisa says. "I'm taking up too much of your time."

Betsy's half out of her chair, her hand extended over the desk, the fingers splayed. "No, no, no. Please."

They are frozen like that for a moment. Okay, then, Elisa thinks, we're going for it. She relaxes back into her seat, and Betsy returns to her chair.

"You were going to say something that's important to you. I shouldn't have interrupted."

"You don't know me," Elisa says.

"Maybe that's good." They both sit in silence for a minute. Somewhere a door slams. "So."

"It'll sound crazy."

She's hoping for a *No, no, it won't,* but instead Betsy shrugs. Her face is expectant, but what is she expecting? To feel interested, compassionate? Or for a good story to tell her boyfriend, about the crazy lady who came to her office?

Well. No matter. Elisa sits up straight and looks out the window where the corner of the building is visible and says, "I was on a road trip. A few weeks ago. And everything changed. Everything around me. And me. My job, my body. My car. Things in my family are different."

She ventures a glance at Betsy, who is scowling in concentration.

"I mean, everything changed at once. It was all different. Instantly. The whole world. Or that's how it seemed to me."

They are both quiet as Elisa gathers her thoughts. The room is very hot. Now somebody walks past in the hallway outside. By the sound of it, this person is dragging a large cardboard box along the floor. Eventually there is silence.

"It *still* seems that way. It's still happening. It's like amnesia. Things have happened that I don't remember. Except I remember a whole other life in its place. My real life." She gazes directly at Betsy. "It feels like I switched from one life to another. And I'm not crazy, I don't think. Do I seem crazy to you?"

"No," Betsy says, but she is still scowling, still thinking, thinking, and it's not clear if she means it.

"I started doing research. Into different explanations. I'm . . . I thought maybe this . . . this theory could explain it."

Betsy's expression hasn't changed. She's sitting very upright in her chair, with one leg tucked underneath her, like a child. One hand hangs out of sight by her side and the other rests flat on the desktop. If she lifts it up, there will be a print there, outlined in condensation. Elisa closes her eyes and waits, and eventually Betsy says, "You mean you think you're in a parallel world?"

"I didn't say that."

"You think . . . you think that *could* be a *possible* explanation for your situation."

"I'm saying that's what it *feels* like. I am trying not to draw any conclusions."

Elisa opens her eyes again: it's time to look. The younger woman wears a curious expression, head tipped back, eyes unfocused, her lips slightly parted. Both hands lie flat on the desk now, and she is biting her lip. She says, "It's hard to see how it's possible."

"I'm just saying how it feels."

"No, no, I know, I get it." Betsy appears to lose herself in thought for a long minute. When she turns back to Elisa, she says, "You know this whole multiverse idea, you know where it came from? Who thought it up?"

Elisa shakes her head.

"William James. The psychologist. He wasn't talking about physics—he was talking about morals. Like, he was rebelling against the idea of pre-destination, of a universe that was a finished creation. A *finished* world. Where you have a role to play. And a God that cares about that role." Betsy is sitting up straighter now and gazing directly at Elisa. "For him, in a moral multiverse, your choices matter. You have free will. And what you do means something. It makes something happen."

The physics Lisa, she thinks, smashing the right things together. "Are you saying I made this happen?"

"I'm saying . . . that something made *something* happen."

"You think it's all in my head. Not out in the world."

Betsy is shaking her head, but there doesn't seem to be a lot of conviction in it. "I don't know what it is or where it is. Maybe your head and the world are the same thing."

Elisa is exhausted. Her hands are shaking and she is slumped in the chair. She is given to think of Silas, the interview she found. Games, he said, have to invent themselves. Rain, briefly, spatters the window, then abruptly stops. Did she do that? Did she make the rain? She is suddenly very confused; it's as if she is drunk, or high. "I don't think I know what you mean."

"Me neither," Betsy admits. She seems resigned to something, it is not clear what. "But let me have your e-mail. I know a guy. He would probably find you . . . interesting to talk to."

28.

Since Monday she and Derek have kept their distance from one another. When they have spoken, it has been politely. There has been no more sex. They're too nervous. He appeared thoughtful when he returned from the therapy session she didn't attend, but he has said nothing about it. So far she has resisted asking, but now, Friday night, over dinner, she looks up at him with the intention of doing so.

He's looking at her. They both turn away, then turn back. She smiles. He doesn't.

She used to talk a great deal, she remembers. Before Silas. When she drank, she would talk even more. She loved it—it felt . . . *low class.* They would go out with friends, or with another couple, and Elisa would find somebody to talk to, to talk at, and she would just go for it. Sometimes she would be off-putting to this person, and the person would notice, and would shift her attention to the group, or to someone else. Sometimes her interlocutor would be patient, would endure her. Sometimes something would click and this person would respond with equal enthusiasm. If the person was a man, the encounter would sometimes feel sexual. Derek both liked and didn't like this. He liked that she relieved him of the need to make conversation, he liked her energy. He didn't like it when she became too intimate, too quickly, with strangers. His heavy hand would grip her leg under the table, midway between the knee and the waist. This was a warning but it, too, was sexual. His fingers would land close to her crotch and they would stay there for a while. Sometimes she dialed it back a bit; sometimes she kept going, just to bother him. At these times his grip would tighten. They would argue on the way home, then go to bed.

She is wondering where this person went. This talkative, combative Elisa. She wonders if this Elisa has come back, in this world—if Amos Finley has brought her back, and now here the "real" Elisa is inhabiting the poor woman's body, dragging her back into reticence, into the realm of mystery. She wants to think of something to say to Derek that will evoke the old days, her wilder self, but she's at a loss. He lowers his gaze, sets down his fork, draws breath.

She says, "Have you ever played one of Silas's games?"

He's surprised. "Silas's *games?*"

"Have you?"

"You would know if I had."

She says, "Where can you get them? Do they have them at the mall? Are they for regular computers, or do you need a thing for your TV, or what?"

Derek shrugs, eyes wide.

"I want to try one."

He doesn't say anything, though it appears that he is trying to.

"Come to the mall with me," she goes on. "There's a game store."

He stares at her. Then, as though after long calculation, he nods.

He drives them to the mall in his truck. (In this world, they don't seem to like her car. She's glad; she doesn't like it either. The truck feels good—there is only enough room for the two of them in the cab. For their marriage. It's their marriage truck!) Elisa is surprised how many people are at the mall on a summer Friday night. She would expect they'd be out having a good time instead. Or perhaps that's what this is. She and Derek make their way past clothing and gift shops. Elisa, suddenly ebullient, takes Derek's hand.

He gives her a strange look but doesn't let go.

The video game store is adjacent to the food court. They walk in and are instantly confused. The walls are lined with little boxes depicting heavily armed and graphically stylized men and women. The games are made for different systems, but they all look the same. Everyone else in the store is under the age of twenty. To Elisa's surprise, there's a pretty girl behind the counter. She's wearing a nose ring and asks if she can help them.

"We're looking for something by the company Infinite Games."

The girl nods. She wants to know which game.

"Uh . . . Mindcrime's Mirror or something, is that one of them?"

"Mindcrime: Destiny's Mirror. Yup. It's pretty okay." Then she recommends a different game and gives them an appraising look. "The other one's kind of confusing. If you're newbs. Are you?"

"Definitely," Derek says, and Elisa is mildly surprised he even knows the term.

"I think we really want that Mindcrime, though," she says. She can feel Derek's eyes on her.

"Okay . . ."

"Does it run on a regular computer?"

"It's a console game," the girl says, more kindly now that she understands how clueless they are. "Do you have an Xbox?"

"No," Derek says quietly.

"Do you sell them here?" Elisa asks.

"Oh yeah, sure." The girl shows them a display of boxes. The consoles are expensive but not as expensive as Elisa assumed they would be. She says she'll take one, and a copy of the game. The girl suggests an extra controller and Elisa says fine. Derek is staring at her.

"You're serious?"

"It's one of Silas's," she says. "The game."

He nods as if any of this makes sense. He appears so confused here, among these strange young people, and all the light and color. He belongs in a library, surrounded by brown things. She touches his shoulder, kisses him.

The girl looks on in apparent amusement. "Don't get discouraged," she says, as she packs the boxes into a large shopping bag. "This is like the worst first game you could ever play. Do all the training. You need to figure out how to work the controls. After that, it's about a twenty-hour game."

"I'm sorry," Derek says. "What does that mean?"

"That's how long it takes. To finish."

He appears flabbergasted. "You're kidding."

"For you, though," she says with a smile, "longer."

Now they are driving home. It's hot and the sun is in their eyes. Derek drives with the stiff, silent precision that indicates there are questions in his mind. Elisa takes the opportunity to gaze at his face. She has not looked at him directly for more than a few seconds at a time since whatever is happening to her happened.

He is harder here, to be sure—cleaner, more controlled. This was always a part of his personality, of his physical self. This advanced containment. She met him, or rather saw him for the first time, at a party a boy had taken her to. The boy was a law student, an undergraduate. The party was mostly grad students. Her date was proud to be invited—he went around introducing her to people he barely knew and tried to burrow into conversations that were over his head. She didn't find this appealing. One of the conversations was with Derek and two other men, and while the other two men bantered with and gently mocked Elisa's date, Derek merely stood still, sipping his drink, his face hard. Not angrily so. Impassively. He struck her as a passionate man who had mastered his passions. She couldn't keep her eyes off him and didn't learn his name.

The boy took her home and she went to bed with him but never returned his phone calls after that. She started studying at the law library, a place she had never previously so much as entered. At first it was in the hope of seeing the man from the party. But eventually she came to like the anonymity of the place, the inscrutability of the information it housed. All of the facts were there, but none could be seen, not immediately. Not without searching for them, without knowing where to look. This was not like science. Scientists had to generate the data with experiments. The law, its precedents and interpretations, were written down. The law was here—all of it, right here, all around her.

Scientists, of course, didn't hang out in this library. She was the only one. One afternoon she was sitting at a table in the third-floor reading room and looked up to see Derek coming toward her from the stacks. Deliberately, almost defiantly. When he arrived he crouched beside her, crossed his arms on the tabletop. The hairs of his forearm were touching her notebook. He said, "You were at a party last semester." Elisa nodded. "Come get a drink."

(Later, months later, he would tell her, "I was terrified." This was the first time he ever disappointed her, not because he had been terrified, but because he hadn't been, but found it necessary, or perhaps just advantageous, to lie that he was. He wanted to appear more susceptible to strong emotion, and more experienced at managing it.)

This Derek, the one now driving home from the mall, is more like that Derek than any Derek she has seen in years. In the other life, raising the boys broke down his defenses, made him transparent, but threw his flaws into sharper relief. His willingness to blame others, Elisa in particular, for shared problems. His incapacity to accept a problem as chronic and unsolvable, and to readjust his expectations accordingly. By the time of Silas's death, he was worn out. The world had disappointed him. If you asked he would have said he was happy, and he wouldn't have been wrong. But it was the kind of qualified happiness that he never expected he would have to accept.

Here, though, in this world, the fortress of Derek has been partially rebuilt. It must have cost him real effort. And he doesn't want it to crumble again—surely, if it did, he would lack the will, the energy, for another recovery.

She loves and pities him. He is ill equipped for this life, for the other life, for any life. Though she supposes you could say that about anybody.

29.

It takes Derek about ten minutes to hook the video game console up to their television set. It's black, and the controllers are black—to Elisa they look like amoebas, with the various buttons and sticks as organelles. The game comes in a DVD case, with a picture on the cover of a man, a young man in tee shirt and jeans, seen from behind, peering into a distant yellow light. The box is hard to open, so Derek goes to the kitchen for a knife.

"This is stupid," he says, but he's laughing at himself.

"This is what people do on Friday nights now," she tells him, though what does she know about what people do on Friday nights?

Inside the box is the game disc, with the title printed on a black background. In a slot on the inside cover is a glossy black paper that reads "INSTRUCTIONS: FIND YOURSELF."

Derek turns the paper over, looks again at the box. "That's it? That's the manual?"

"I guess the game tells you how to play it."

"Ay caramba."

They sit cross-legged on the carpet in front of the TV, power up the console, and slide in the disc. It whirs. They expect some kind of credits, some title sequence, but instead they hear a click and a whine, and a yellow dot appears in the center of the screen. It expands, rapidly, like the picture on an old television, into the image from the cover. This version of the image is subtly in motion—the man is panting, his shoulders heaving, the muscles of his back trembling slightly. He is scratched and bleeding; his clothes are dirty. A bass chord sounds, and then a male voice, echoing as though in a cave: "Who am I?" Then the chord evolves into a slow orchestral dirge, and options appear on the screen. GAME. EXPLORE. CONTROLS. OPTIONS. EXTRAS.

"Explore?" Elisa asks.

"Nah," says Derek, and expertly manipulates the joystick until PLAY is underlined. He presses a button and the menu screen disappears.

"How did you know how to do that?" she asks him.

Derek shrugs. He seems mildly embarrassed and pleased. It's the sort of thing he can do—pick up a tool, or a gadget, or a computer program, and just use it. It is, she must admit, a bit of a turn-on, as is his pleasure at his own facility. A few notches more self-satisfaction, though, and it would be insufferable. This is a key to his appeal: confidence bordering on, but not crossing over to, arrogance.

Their Man is standing in a forest, alert and subtly breathing. A message appears on the screen: PREPARE TO FIND YOUR DESTINY. This is the training the girl told them about—they have to teach themselves to run, climb, throw, hit. On-screen icons indicate which controls to use. The screen shows their character, the Man, in various environments—a forest, an empty house, a road, a ship—where some obvious task, like scaling a wall or opening a safe, has to be accomplished. He is always shown from behind, his muscles working, his thin hair flopping on his head. Elisa is amazed at the photographic quality of the graphics—it looks like a movie. The training is fascinating and vexing, and the game proper doesn't seem to have really started yet. Derek says, "Jesus. Are they all this complicated?"

"The girl said no."

"Jesus."

When they decide that they've mastered the controls, or come close enough, Derek gets up and comes back with a bottle of bourbon and two glasses. They haven't drunk the stuff together in years, at least not in the world she knows. The ceremony in his bearing suggests they haven't in this one, either. He pours the drinks over ice and they clink them together.

"To an unusual evening," Derek says.

"To Silas."

The warmth drains from his face and he turns away from her, to the screen. "So are we playing this thing or not?" He drinks.

"Let's."

As it happens, they can't both play at once—it's single-player only. They take turns manipulating the controls and exploring the world of the game.

It is, of course, a mystery. The player is a nameless Man who wakes up bruised, beaten, and starving somewhere in a forest. He has nothing in his possession save for a compass—which doesn't appear to work here in the woods—and a creased and torn photograph. The photograph is familiar to them both: it is clearly based on the family picture from the lake, the one that Elisa remembers she has left at the frame shop with Larry. Though she hears Derek draw in breath, neither of them remarks on the resemblance. The faces are different, but the poses are the same.

During the first fifteen minutes, they die repeatedly by falling into holes or out of trees. Only when morning breaks in the game are they able to make their way out of the forest; they do so by following the sound of passing traffic. When at last the Man climbs onto a road, Derek says, "So, how long are we going to be doing this?"

They are both on the second bourbon. Elisa is shocked. It's only ten. She has no intention of stopping. "Oh, I don't know," she says. "Another hour?"

Derek shrugs. She can see that the game has caught his interest, but he doesn't want to stick with it. It's bothering him. She gets up and refills her glass. She is beginning to get drunk.

They flag down a pickup truck driven by a grizzled old man. *Where to?* he wants to know, and they hear the Man say *wherever.* Eventually the driver buys him breakfast at a diner. Then a waitress comes on shift, tying her apron around her waist, sees the Man, and screams.

Derek actually cries out and drops his controller. "It can't be!" the woman is saying. She backs into the kitchen, weeping.

"Rosie, you got a problem with this guy?" says a voice, and the Man turns to find a burly biker type standing behind him, cracking his knuckles. There is something sickening about this sound: it is wet and deep, like the popping of greenwood in a fire.

"Fight him! Fight him!" Elisa shouts, and when Derek makes no move to pick up his controller, she punches him on the arm. He flinches. "Derek. Derek! We have to fight this guy!"

"Let's pause," he says. "Can you pause?" They both try various buttons until they hit upon the right one, and a menu pops up: EXIT. OPTIONS. Derek exhales, seeming to shrink to half his size. He says, "I think I've had enough for tonight."

"You're kidding!" Yes, she is a little drunk.

He pats her shoulder. "I'm beat, Lisa. I wrote lectures all day."

"Oh."

"You kind of hurt my arm."

"Sorry," she says. She glances at the screen, then back at him. "Mind if I stay up?"

"Go ahead." He stretches. "Don't forget to save the game. In case you die."

"Thank you," she says. And then, "Derek. I'm going out to see them."

"See who?"

"I bought a plane ticket."

He's silent. He is staring not at her but at the biker on the screen. She says, "In three weeks. I'm taking the Friday off."

His response is very quiet. "Why?"

"Do you want to come? You aren't teaching. You can come."

"I don't know."

"When was the last time you flew out to see them?"

He gets that look—the fear that he doesn't know what's going on. "You know."

"When?" She feels reckless. "Just say it!"

He doesn't reply, just stares at the screen. After a moment he rubs his face. Says, "He could be funny sometimes. Silas."

Derek has half gotten up to go to bed and then sunk down again, so that his legs are folded under him, as though he's getting ready to pray.

"Just cuttingly, shockingly funny," he goes on. "The way he would impersonate people. Walking by. Do you remember that?"

She nods.

"Even when he was, Jesus, eight or nine. He would do those conversations between people. At restaurants? Do you remember the old man with the cowboy hat and the girl with him? In, what the hell was it, the place that used to be where Subway is now?"

"The Arbor? No, the Terrace."

"Yeah, with the plastic ivy. He did the Texas accent, 'Weaaauuul now, darlin', y'all lemme know if ya find a tooth in them french fries.' Remember that?"

"Of course."

"And then the girl, 'Oh, Pappy! Oh, Pappy!'"

It's true, sometimes they laughed at Silas until they cried. He knew exactly what to mock. God forgive them, they even laughed when he made fun of Sam. At the dinner table, faced with a food he didn't like, Sam's chin would drop and tremble, his cheeks collapse, his eyes narrow and moisten. Silas had it down. Sometimes he would even beat his brother to it—as soon as the plate of beets hit the placemat, before his brother had a chance to react, Silas would pull The Face, and Elisa and Derek would convulse with laughter.

Oh, God, it was wrong. It was so wrong to encourage, but it was so funny. She thinks of minefield, Silas's online alter ego, and she wonders where that part of her son went. By the time he died, it was gone. His mockery wasn't funny anymore. And here, this game. There's no humor in it. Yet it compels her all the same.

Derek has stood up to leave. He says, "Maybe you could turn the sound down a little."

"Sure."

He drops to his knee, kisses her on the head. "Good night," he says, and he grips her shoulder as though to fix the moment, as though she might run away. "I still don't understand what you're trying to do and

I'm afraid you're going to ruin everything. But I love you." And then he goes to bed.

30.

She only means to play for another hour, then join him. But she ends up playing all night.

She doesn't fight the biker, in the end—instead she backs off, leaves the diner, and while she's in the parking lot the waitress comes out to find her. "Is it really you?" she says. She's young and pretty, and Elisa can't help but see her through Silas's eyes. Is this a girl Silas made? A girl he wishes were real? There is a tenderness here in the way the girl's features are rendered: her red-brown hair, tied back loosely, a nose slightly too large for her face. The way the clean apron nevertheless bears faded stains that can never be washed out, and the way it creases when she gestures, the fibers frayed and weak with age. How is it even possible to evoke these details in a video game? It is impossible, immersing herself in this world, not to feel that she has missed something about Silas.

Of course every aesthetic decision here cannot have been Silas's. There is probably a team of programmers, graphic designers, and the like. And yet she feels, powerfully, that this character, this girl, is the product of her son's mind. This world, the world of the game, is Silas's, as well—it is as though she has been allowed to enter into his consciousness, to see the way he sees. It is something he made to satisfy himself. And it feels realer, fuller, than any version of him she was ever permitted to see in life.

But then again, how hard had she looked? It's true that, up until his adolescence, his emotions appeared to live on the surface—his problem, as they saw it, was impulse control, an incapacity to keep himself in check. His actions, as they saw them, were the unfiltered product of his subconscious. They lived in the world he made, by necessity, and he refused to enter the world they wanted him to live in.

But he did change, around the time he turned twelve. He fell quiet and began to brood. And though this made their days more orderly— fewer messes, less violence, fewer shouting fights—it also threw Elisa and Derek into a state of paranoia. What was he thinking? What was he going to do next? His quiet hostility became more disturbing than the acting out once had been, and Sam, who had endured their shared childhood with his wits largely intact, began to show the signs of deep anxiety and, eventually, depression: sallow complexion, sunken eyes, bitten fingernails. Sam hid in his bedroom much of the time, while Silas haunted the halls with a kind of regal insolence. He frightened them.

But perhaps there was nothing to fear. Maybe it wasn't merely his demeanor that had changed, but his desires, his emotional aims. Maybe he was waiting for Derek and Elisa to discover them.

Instead they nurtured their paranoia, let it grow and spread. Each accused the other of trying to sabotage the family, of giving up on Silas, of giving up on Sam. Each accused the other of infidelity before either was actually guilty of it, and each used the accusation as justification for the act. There was a strong sense, in that household, of impending dissolution. Both of them were tired. They indulged the part of themselves that just wanted to get it over with.

But what if, behind Silas's seemingly impenetrable affect, lay a nascent empathy? What if he was trying to find a path out of the wilderness of his childhood, through the games he played, the books he read? What if the Silas who made this game was, in fact, that Silas—the one they chose never to get to know?

She has stopped drinking, but the night has the quality of a bender, with periods of sudden strong emotion, and of blankness, and of pointless hilarity. The girl, it turns out, knew the Man from a period, some months before, when she was under the control of some thugs who lived in her trailer park. Then, the Man had gone by the name Jack, and though he was only passing through, he managed to chase the men out of town and help the girl, Rose, pay her mother's medical bills. Jack, she explains now, wouldn't say where the money came from, and indicated that Jack was not his real name. He said goodbye and good luck, and disappeared.

But now he's back. What happened to him? The Man shakes his head—he doesn't know. Rose gives him the only thing he left behind—a torn sheet of notebook paper with a six-digit number written on it in an unfamiliar hand.

"I have to get back to work," she says. "Don't mind Rocky—he's just trying to help me and Mama." If the Man is looking for information about himself, Rose tells him, he should try the motel in the center of town—that's where he stayed. And when he finally figures it out, "come back for me" she says and runs away, into the diner.

The motel gives way to a bus bound for the city, which, as the hours of night pass by, leads Elisa down a spiral of increasing ridiculousness: the criminal underground, domestic spying, terrorists, government conspiracies. The number on the paper is a combination—there's a safe, a post office box key, an encrypted document.

It is all, of course, adolescent in conception, but beautiful in execution: lavishly detailed, astonishingly full. Maybe all games are like this now, what does she know. But every time she tries to enter a building, there is something there for her to see. Every time she approaches a character, that character has something to say. Silas, whose motivations, whose desires, were always so inscrutable, has created a world and left it open to whoever might wish to enter.

When the sky framed by the living room window begins to lighten, she glances at the clock and sees that it is nearly five in the morning. She climbs the stairs to bed, sleeps until noon, eats a sandwich and drinks a glass of orange juice, then returns to the game.

She sees Derek a few times as the hours pile up; sometimes she can hear him in the kitchen, preparing food; at one point he walks past with a hammer, and several minutes later she hears pounding somewhere in the house. He pauses behind her a few times to observe her progress through the game—a visit to a mental hospital, then a run-in with the FBI, digging in the woods for a buried time capsule and riding the bus to a distant prison for a visit with an inmate—and she tries to fill him in, glancing occasionally over her shoulder to make sure he's paying attention. But mostly he seems to be waiting, waiting for her to finish.

It is late on Sunday morning when she finally comes to the end. A slow trudge up the driveway of a white-clapboard house in an affluent subdivision. A knock on the door. There they are, the family in the photo, the people who rejected him, who sent him away because of his choice to become a government spy, a killer. But there was no choice—he'd been framed and it was the only way out. It doesn't matter, he is told by the family patriarch, who refuses to let him over the threshold, behind which his mother and sister cower in fear. They want nothing to do with him. Go away, they tell him. We don't want you here.

Elisa can retaliate, if she wishes. She has learned how to do things. She can beat these people to death with her fists, burn their house to the ground. She understands enough now about the way the game thinks to know that this is a possible ending, an acceptable ending. Instead, she turns and walks away. Returns to the diner to collect Rose and take her and her mother away from their terrible little town. At the end, they are standing out in the road, hand in hand, facing the sunset, but not yet moving toward it. The Man, exhausted by his efforts, is panting, just as he did at the beginning; the women's hair is lifted by a breeze.

And then, a closing sequence. The camera, though of course there is no camera, lifts up as though on a crane, and a distant landscape is gradually revealed: not mountains, not the sea, but a trailer park, lavish in its dilapidation, pickup trucks and dirt bikes moving through its ragged streets; a commercial strip, populated by crumbling big-box retail spaces and empty cracked parking lots; a landfill, dump trucks and bulldozers swarming over it like ants, and tiny gulls swooping overhead; a cemetery, weedy and overgrown.

That's what lies ahead for the Man and Rose and her mother: suburban decay and ennui, pollution and filth, death and obscurity. Game over.

Elisa wonders what sequence she would have been shown had she chosen to set fire to the family home.

She turns off the television and the game console and lies on her back on the living room carpet. She ought to be tired, but she isn't. Instead, her mind is clear. She closes her eyes and thinks. When she hears Derek enter the room, she says, "You're right."

"About what?"

"I'm going to go talk to Amos."

There's no response. She opens her eyes, tips her head back. There he is, upside down. He's staring at her.

When she calls the therapist, he tells her to come right over.

31.

She gets lost. All she remembers is the name of the road—Orton Road—and that it's on the west side of the lake. Eventually she finds it, goes the wrong way on it, drives for miles in confusion. Then she backtracks and everything begins to look familiar.

Clouds have moved in and the temperature has dropped. There will be a thunderstorm. The meadow behind the therapist's office is empty of deer and the grasses are bent by the wind. When she knocks on the office door, nobody answers. She hears her name being called: he's behind her, on the back stoop of the main house. He turns and goes inside and she follows him.

The house is low and close and smells like frying meat. It has the air of being lived in alone—somehow clean and squalid at once. Books are everywhere and the old windows distort the outdoors. He leads her into a living room, dark and comfortable, with a sofa and coffee table and desk and easy chair. This is where he spends all his time, clearly. He stands in the middle of the room and gestures at the sofa.

Elisa sits down and waits for the therapist to do the same. Instead, he paces for a moment, as though measuring his thoughts. He seems smaller today, more intense and professorial. The kind of professor who doesn't get tenure. His demeanor, his house suggest a man who has withdrawn from active life, declared himself an observer.

At last he lowers himself into the easy chair. He knits his hands together. There is a wobble in his voice, the slightest sign of nervousness, as he says, "You were to have been open with me."

"I have been."

"Something is different."

She has dressed in business clothes, a skirt and blouse. She catches herself tugging the skirt down over her knees.

He says, "Do you want to tell me what it is?"

"I'm not sure I know."

He is agitated. His hands separate and rejoin. She is reminded of cell mitosis, the first time she saw it: a black-and-white film, in high school, that somehow seemed more real for its flickering jerkiness. The jittering little lives, straining to separate. The nucleus, exploding into two, pushing at the edges of its tiny world, stretching the cell walls until they broke. And then each half, identical now save for experience, drifting apart. As if they were never one.

Amos Finley twitches. Flinches, maybe. "The way you are—it reminds

me of the way you were when you and Derek first came to me. You're
being cagey—secretive. But nothing is supposed to be secret here. Didn't
you promise that?"

"Did you make that promise, too?"

He tries on an expression of hardness. But what she sees in his eyes,
his slump, is a kind of panic.

She says, "I can't remember. The promise, I mean."

In response he closes his eyes for several seconds. Sits up. His back
creaks, or maybe it's the chair. When he opens his eyes again it occurs to
her that he might be in love with her. The thought makes her sad, though
not with pity. Rather with a sense of the impossibility of everything. The
number of emotions in the world that can't find purchase anywhere and
are wasted. The therapist, she can see, is at a loss. There is some authority
he had over her that is clearly no longer accessible to him.

"Listen, Amos," she says. In her tone she is aiming for tenderness. "I'm
not trying to be difficult. I honestly don't remember."

He is gripping his knees now, working at the fabric of his slacks.
"What . . . precisely . . . have you forgotten?"

"Everything," she says. "Everything up until a few weeks ago."

He is gazing at her, frowning.

She goes on: "I don't remember coming to you, or any of the promises
we made. When we were here a couple of weeks ago, it was like the first
time I'd ever seen you. I don't recognize my life. My job. Derek—he's—
he's not the same. Do you understand?"

He sits back, sighs. "You come back from a trip you took alone. To
a business conference. And you begin to act nervous and confused, as
though you're trying to conceal something. Then you cease therapy entirely. And now you want to tell me you have . . . amnesia?"

"It's more complicated than that."

She sits back, stares up at a corner of the room. She has a sudden desire to clean this house—to haul these old chairs and lamps out to the
curb, rip up the carpet, scrub every inch of the place. She would like to
reform this man, reform his life. She says, "Amos, were you ever married?
Do you have children?"

The question seems to surprise him.

"Humor me," Elisa says. "Pretend I don't know anything about you."

"Twice divorced," he replies, quietly. "An adult daughter. From whom I am estranged."

"Have we slept together? You and me?"

The question startles him. "No."

"Okay. Good." There's an energy in the room now that she likes—she feels as though progress could be made. She feels like the woman who just finished that video game—a person who can find a path and walk down it. "Good. Maybe you can help me."

"That's what I am trying to do," he says.

"We need to make a new agreement. A new promise. Because the woman who promised things to you and Derek—that was somebody else. That wasn't me. We're going to make a new deal, just between us."

He shifts in his chair. It is clear that he doesn't like it. But he's curious enough to play along. He says, "Go on."

"When I'm here with Derek, I will try to be that woman, but you need to understand, I don't remember. You need to help me out."

"I am here to help you."

"Here's the thing, Amos. It's not that I forgot. It's like I never knew. I remember everything, but I have different memories. I remember my son, Silas, dying, nearly a decade ago. And Derek and me drifting apart. And I'm having an affair with a man named Larry who now, here, doesn't seem to even know me. And I have a different job, and I wear different clothes, and my house is messier."

He is scowling, concentrating.

She says, "A couple of weeks ago I was driving in my car, and it all changed, the car and everything, my clothes, my body, and I became this person. Who is in therapy with you. And is not having an affair, and has a marriage with these rules in it that I don't know where they came from.

"This is *not my life*," she says to him, leaning forward. She is excited, astonished, that she is managing to say exactly what she means to say. "This belongs to somebody else. Some version of me that you know and I don't. And I am pretending to be that woman."

She slumps back in her chair, lets out breath. "That's why I'm different," she says. "Because I'm somebody else."

There.

For a while, Amos Finley simply stares at her, and Elisa stares back. He closes his eyes, rubs his beard. He drums his fingers on the armrest of his chair, opens his eyes again, gives her a long appraising look. Then he gets up and leaves the room.

She hears him in the kitchen. Bottles rattle as the refrigerator door is opened. She hears ice cracking and clinking. A few minutes later he comes back into the room holding two ice waters in pint glasses and hands one to Elisa. She thanks him. He sits down.

He says, "You need to tell me what you want."

The question takes her by surprise. "I came here because you told me to."

But he dismisses this with a shake of his head. "You came so that you could say this to me." He is back in charge now. His voice is clear and directed. He says, "Do you want to be cured of this apparent delusion, this dream of a previous, or alternate, life? That is, do you want to live fully in the life you are now occupying? And that I have helped you create? Or do you want to hold on to what you believe is real, and alter this life to suit?"

Until now, this question might have been easy to answer, had anyone asked. She wanted to hold on to what she believed was real. But now she isn't sure. She admits this to him—she says, "I don't know."

"All right," he says, "then that's something we'll have to figure out. I want to make sure I understand: you believe that Silas is dead, and has been for some time."

"In the world I know, he is dead."

"In the world you know, yes. In your memory, you haven't seen him for years. You know nothing of him, this young man who is now an adult."

She says, "I've been following him online. I know what his job is. I know Derek and I rarely speak to him."

"Do you want to see him?"

"I'm going to," she says. "I've been in touch with Sam. I bought a plane ticket."

He appears surprised. He says, "You understand, much of the work I have done with you and your husband has involved helping you to detach yourselves from your children. Silas in particular. You have chosen your marriage over your children."

"No" is all she can say.

He nods. "That's what you've done. That's what this reality is all about. From my perspective—and I am just telling you what I believe based upon what I'm seeing—from my perspective, you are having a psychotic break. Some part of you is rebelling against the choices you've made. Your guilt has gotten the better of you and you are denying the reality of your children's estrangement from you."

She is beginning to feel uneasy now. "I did not choose my marriage over my children."

He is nodding, nodding, nodding. "The woman I know did exactly that. Sam allied himself with his brother, moved away with him. You tried to separate them, to persuade Sam to come home. You became depressed. You were hospitalized, more than once. This is not your first break. Your marriage nearly fell apart. Finally you gave up on your sons."

"I love my sons. I love Sam."

"That is not in question, Lisa, but you and Derek put them behind you."

It is like the moment on the road just after it happened, the semi blowing past, her head on the wheel, the undented soda can crushing itself in her mind. Panic is blooming in her. She opens her mouth to deny for the third time that she chose her marriage over her sons.

But the truth is that she believes it. That it is possible. The psychosis, the hospitalization. Making the choice. She is, was, capable of this. More so, certainly, than the universe is, of moving her from one reality to another?

This is not your first break.

She has rarely bothered to remember—allowed herself to remember—the year leading up to Silas's death. The van crash was like an exclamation point at the end of a cruel running joke—when they buried him, she took that whole year, rolled it up, and dumped it into the grave with him. They were of a piece.

But in truth, the crash was a fluke—an interruption of that time, not a completion of it. And she can remember feeling close to giving up. Lying in bed awake, making deals with herself. What would she sacrifice for it all to go away? To return to what she used to have with Derek, the kind of love that once defined her life, that was the point of her life, that moved her to give up the life she thought she wanted?

Elisa supposes that, in her world, in the world she knows, she suffered a first break after all. The year of blankness, of losing weight and embroidering until her fingers bled. But what was her first break here? What pushed her to it? What did it take her away from?

She looks up so suddenly from her thoughts that Amos gives a start. She says, "What was it? What broke me the first time?"

The question makes him uncomfortable. He fidgets. "You were addicted to the internet. Groups, forums. Many of them about children with mental illness. And politics, you became obsessed with politics, and you were angry all the time. You stayed up all night on your computer, posting on various forums under various names, and, according to Derek, you would only talk about those things, your children and politics. Sarah Palin, you became obsessed with Sarah Palin. You lost interest in sex. Derek nearly moved in with another woman."

Elisa says, "Sarah Palin? Seriously?" She barks out a little laugh.

Amos doesn't, or won't, smile. His hands are folded in his lap and he is watching her intently. "You became dangerously thin, and chain-smoked."

"I hate politics! I don't smoke."

"You chain-smoked. Your sons moved out west, and you engaged in loud and sometimes inebriated conversations with them on the phone, at strange hours. And you ended up in the hospital, after Derek found you knocked out cold on the kitchen floor. You hit your head on the corner of the counter and the coffee urn was shattered on the floor and you had been burned by hot coffee. You were treated for malnutrition as well as for your injuries, and when you got out and stabilized, that's when Derek threatened to leave. Instead, the two of you agreed to come see me. And we worked out the terms. That you would leave the boys alone, and quit the internet and smoking, and eat regular meals with him. And he would give up contact with the woman."

"Debra."

"Debra." He untangled his hands, wiped them on his knees. "Who, in any event, now lives elsewhere and is married, if I remember correctly."

"Forever?" she says.

"Sorry?"

"The boys, forever? We are never to have contact with them again?"

He groans, and his tone, when he speaks, is exasperated. "*You* were

not to have contact with them. Derek could, if he liked, though he has
not seemed inclined to do so. I don't know. *You* were to cut off contact,
and it could be restored only through mutual agreement. Between you and
Derek."

"I've broken the agreement."

He nods. "Yes, you have. Derek is afraid for you, Lisa. He isn't angry.
Or rather, he has managed to control his anger. He's worried. He is afraid
you're breaking down again."

There is a long pause as she tries to get it all straight in her mind. It
makes a horrible kind of sense. All those aspects of her personality that
she fears, over which she feels she has only the most tenuous control,
those are the ones Amos has informed her led to her breakdown. It is how
things might have gone.

"Lisa?" Amos says, sounding somewhat alarmed, and she is surprised to
find herself standing up. "Where are you going?"

"I'm going home," she tells him over her shoulder, and then she's out
the door and heading for the car. She expects him to be right behind her
when she turns, but he's not: he's standing behind the screen door, looking out at her with his hands at his sides. She waves at him through the
windshield, to reassure him, and he raises a hand.

He looks sad, as though he's failed.

32.

Instead of going home she drives up the lake to the state park. There is almost nobody there, because of the impending rain. A pickup truck is parked
in the lot and a man is asleep on the rocky beach. A fat woman is listlessly
fishing off the end of the jetty.

Elisa stands on the shore beside the stone benches and gazes at the
power plant on the other side of the water. This is where the photo would
have been taken. She tries to imagine what circumstances would have
brought them here together—her and Derek and both boys. In her memory, it was hard getting the boys to do anything, let alone with the two of
them together, by the time they were thirteen and fourteen.

Until now, Elisa used to think of those years, when she thought of
them at all, as a time when Silas had to be endured. And indeed, he was

unpleasant to be around—imperious, disdainful, he rarely opened his mouth except to mock or criticize.

But his mind was elsewhere—he was thinking about his life outside the house. By this time he had friends, sycophants, female followers; he had come into his bad-boy good looks, the James Dean cheekbones Lorraine was pleased to note had come from her; the thick black hair the wind always seemed to blow into an arrangement of perfect, studied nonchalance. He used the phone a lot, went out on his bike without asking, following just enough of the house rules to avoid open conflict. He showed every sign of not caring what they thought.

But Sam simply grew sullen, wouldn't come out of his room. Moved slowly. The collars of his shirts were always frayed and wet from nervous chewing. He licked his lips incessantly, leaving the skin around his mouth livid and peeling. There were bags under his eyes. The older of the boys, he nevertheless seemed like the baby of the family, fleshy and uncertain. Silas, of course, was uncommunicative: he was rarely there, or distant if he was; he answered their questions with the bare minimum of effort before ducking away, back into his private world. But Sam's unresponsiveness was more vexing. He didn't try to escape. He just sat there in the kitchen, or lay on the bed, eyes open and blinking, thin hair stuck to his moist forehead.

"Are you all right?"

"I guess."

"It's late, you should go to sleep."

A shrug.

"Do you want to talk?"

"No."

"Did you get enough to eat tonight?"

Another shrug.

The shrug had become a signature gesture. The shrug, the slump. Sometimes a limp. "Are you hurt?" "No." Elisa began to get the idea that Sam was feigning injury, not for their sake but for his own, for the small pleasure of privately comforting himself. She shared this theory with Derek. He seemed faintly repulsed by the idea.

Lorraine said, "It's genes. Nothing to be done. Luckily," she added, patting Derek's hand, "our family has never been moody."

Moody. Elisa's father used to call it "blue." "Your mother's a bit blue today." "Poor Lisa," he said during meals, when Elisa let her teenage hair fall into her face, and ground her teeth, and gripped the seat of her chair with both hands as though, if she concentrated hard enough, she might be able to fly away on it. "Poor Lisa is feeling blue."

Sam was not blue. He wasn't moody. He was depressed.

Elisa is exhausted from her weekend of gaming and the session with Amos. She finds a picnic table and sits down at it. It's astonishing that it hasn't rained yet; the clouds are heavy and black and the lake surface is lashed by the wind. She will sit here until the first drops fall. She imagines herself making a run for it, hands over her head. It seems important not to take cover now—she wants to be pushed to shelter.

Poor Lisa is feeling blue. Though when she reflects upon the way she actually feels today, it comes to her as no visible color, nothing as natural as sky. She feels like something blinding and artificial and impossible to look at directly. Ultrasomething. Infrasomething. She closes her eyes hard and hears the muscles tightening in her head. Betsy the physicist seems less real to her today, the possibility of madness more palpable.

When she thinks about that last year, before the accident, what she remembers is the desperate, guilty feeling of her love for Sam beginning to fray around the edges. The component of her love that was pity, curdling and turning into a kind of disdain. Resentment at his weakness. At the ways he was like her—or, rather, the ways he was like the parts of herself she disliked. His willingness to give himself over to other people's ideas of him, his willingness to give up.

She stayed up late with him while he lay sweating, and smelling of despair—she sat hunched over with her elbows on her knees, trying to find the right combination of words that would make him talk to her. What is it? Did Silas say something to you? Sam would talk—he wanted to talk—but he wouldn't talk about his brother. Instead he spoke in abstractions, in philosophical conundrums. And not very interesting ones. Why, he wanted to know, should he get up in the morning and go to school when nobody cared whether he showed up or not? (But your father and I care, Lisa told him, over and over. As if that would matter.) What was the point of it all? (She could not pretend to have an answer. The only one she knew was: the pursuit and expression of love. And she couldn't say this to her son, who loved no one and, to hear him tell it, was loved by no one but her and Derek.) Why did people like Silas when Silas was a dick who mocked and belittled them? Why did those same people turn around and mock and belittle him, Sam? And why didn't Silas tell them to stop?

She doesn't remember what she said. But the answer, of course, was that power attracted and weakness repelled. At times, that power could manifest itself as charm, as intelligence: as the positive attributes that people pretended to seek in one another. But it wasn't the manifestations that mattered, it was the power.

(Elisa remembers better what she wanted to say than what she actually did say: *Goddammit, Sam, you're older and bigger than he is. Don't be a fucking pussy.*)

Silas was powerful. And Elisa respected him for it. His evident indifference to, even disgust for, his own mother: she respected it. She respected it because she felt it herself, about her own mother, who liked to preempt criticism of her weakness by calling attention to it, with feigned pride. "Lisa's toes have been poking out of her shoes for three months and I didn't even notice!" "I forgot, completely forgot, to make Lisa lunch!" "I was so thoroughly drunk that night I had to send Lisa to the corner for cigarettes, if you can believe that."

It was true that at the time Elisa liked it. She liked the squirrelly little threesome she made with her parents—the shield of nondescript scruffiness and cultural superiority they suspended between themselves and the world. She felt proud to be her parents' daughter: she thought there was something real, some empirically verifiable quality, that justified their stance of amused condescension against other people. Now she knows it was fear.

It wasn't until she was in college, when she began to meet confident people, powerful people, that she understood. It was Derek's confidence, his ability to approach others to ask for what he wanted, to put the past behind him with finality, that crystallized her desire: he was the antithesis of her parents.

Of course Sam was not Elisa's mother. Elisa herself wasn't even like her, not really, and there was as much Derek in Sam as there was Elisa. But it was impossible not to see him as a manifestation of Gemma Macalaster, casually exerting her influence from afar. Or, rather: exuding, seeping. She was like a fog, like the mildly acrid cloud of cigarette smoke that had always surrounded her, that followed you out of the apartment in your clothes and hair and was with you wherever you went. She could still smell it sometimes, or believed she could, when she was drifting, finally, off to sleep: she could smell her mother's cigarettes in the pillowcase, in her nightgown, as if the old woman had visited just long enough to lie here and imprint her particular brand of passivity on the bedclothes.

She didn't want to think of her mother when Sam slouched off to bed, uncomforted, unconvinced. But she did, she did. And Silas, though he was, she understood, a deeply flawed young man, reminded her of nothing so much as the boys she loved, the bad boys her mother loathed, and the hard and obsessive parts of herself that she most valued.

She is pulled out of her thoughts by a change in the light. Behind her, from the west: sunshine. The wind is steady and slow now, and the clouds have moved on. The sleeping man on the beach is gone and families are arriving, laying blankets on the grass, unpacking baskets. It didn't rain after all. It isn't going to rain.

33.

Derek begins to seem slightly afraid of her. He has stopped asking questions and doesn't attempt to initiate sex. Elisa doesn't either. She feels as though her existence is a cup filled to the brim; she is trying to stand very still until her trip. For this reason she doesn't accompany him when he goes to see Amos on Monday.

When he gets home he looks at her with confusion and distaste. "You're thinner."

"Yes."

"I thought you looked good. Before."

She shrugs. Did Amos tell him what they talked about? Does she care if he did? She knows she should tell him herself. But she is afraid to.

Derek says, "And you're not wearing makeup anymore."

"No," she says. "You're just noticing now?" He doesn't respond, and after a moment he goes upstairs to change his clothes.

There is a part of Elisa, an increasingly prominent part, that wants to follow him, to undress him, to make him love the woman she is turning into, which is to say the real her, the her of the other life. And there is a part of her that wants to push him away for good. The strange thing is, if she could have the Derek of the other life right now, the one from whom she is estranged, the hard one, the one whose love for her is rote at best, vestigial, she would love him, she would take him back and love him. But she does not want to let herself love this Derek, the one who has chosen her over their children.

She resists the temptation. She doesn't follow.

Instead she e-mails Sam to tell him when she'll be arriving—the trip is in a couple of weeks. He writes back within the hour: *I don't think you should come.*

Why not? she replies. But he doesn't answer.

Wednesday morning, still half asleep, she reaches out and wakes Derek by stroking his arm. It's five thirty. He gasps, leaps out of bed, then stands facing the window in a kind of ready crouch.

She sits up. "What is it?"

He turns and says, "I was dreaming." But he doesn't get back into bed, he stands there staring at her, blinking, still in a state of near-violent attention. In the gloom, backlit by dim gray sky, he looks like some kind of animal, or worse, something half human. For a moment she actually hates him.

That day she takes a long lunch and uses her new bus pass to go downtown. She walks the few blocks to the frame shop. Larry isn't behind the counter. But on the low shelf beneath the frame samples lies a small flat package, wrapped in brown paper, with a yellow sticky note attached, and she knows it's her picture. She asks the girl who's there, "Is Larry in today?"

"He's on lunch break."

"I'll come back," Elisa says, and walks back toward the bus station.

But it's lunchtime, after all. She goes into a Korean café. Was this place here in the other life? She doesn't remember it. The worlds are blurring— she is slowly merging with the woman she was before, and she can't remember all the differences. The thought fills her with desperation. Soon they will be so intertwined she'll never get them apart. She sits down by the window. A crack runs through the glass. She stares through it at the people passing, the buses collecting and releasing passengers.

A man is crossing the street toward her, carrying a plastic drugstore bag. It's Larry.

"Can I help you?" says a voice.

There's a woman standing beside her, holding a notepad. Elisa stammers out an order. Larry walks in the door of the café and sits down at a table across the room.

"Anything to drink?"

"Just water."

She has to crane her neck to see him. The café is almost empty—a silent couple in the corner, a man text-messaging over the remains of his meal. She shifts herself to the other chair at her table, in order to face Larry. He is reading the menu, though not for long. He speaks to the waitress for just a moment. A regular. Then he takes a magazine out of his drugstore bag and begins to read it.

He won't look up. She's sure of that. His ability to concentrate is tremendous. It's irritating to go for a walk with him, because he doesn't want to stop and look at anything, he just wants to walk. But when that concentration is trained on her, he sees nothing else. The intensity of his attention, in fact, can be overwhelming. Which is why he's good to have as a lover. But not necessarily to be married to.

The magazine is about music—a jazz magazine. Does she already know this—that this is an interest of his? Perhaps this is one of the things that's different.

She could go over there. If she waits until the food comes, it will be awkward. She could sit down and ask to join him. If he's the Larry she knows, he will be disoriented, will appear annoyed. Then he'll capitulate, adjust, accept. Enjoy.

Yet she must force herself to gather her satchel and glass of water and cross the room. She tries to convince herself that her reluctance emanates from anxiety. That she wants him so much, it is making her lose her nerve. Larry looks up.

"Mind if I join you?"

He is definitely surprised. "I—do we know each other?" But before he has even finished saying it, he recognizes her. His expression is one of puzzlement and slight relief.

"Elisa Brown. From the shop."

"Sure. You didn't give us your contact information."

"I just stopped at the shop, just now."

"Good. So you like it?"

"Ah—no, I didn't—I didn't pick it up. You weren't there—I didn't want to explain myself."

He takes a quick look at the door, then back at Elisa.

"I was already here," she explains. "Sitting by the window. And recognized you."

She thinks, Why are you making this so goddamn difficult? She wants, very badly, her real life right now. Where all this has already been accomplished, and sex is already being had. He says, "Of course. I'm sorry—please sit down."

She sits. He closes his magazine with some displeasure and tucks it back into his bag. Then he faces her squarely and folds his hands in front of him.

Even sitting still, he appears agile, efficient. His features are fine, the eyes alert. He isn't her type, isn't what she once thought was her type, which is men like Derek—larger, broader, more solid, as though they're made of the same thing all the way through. Their strength obvious in their posture, their movements. Larry is more like a machine, a collection of moving parts. You can see every muscle in his face. He could be an adventurer, a traveler. Not that he actually is. In fact he's a homebody. He lives in a tiny spartan house wedged between the lake and the train tracks, west of the park. Or at least he did, he's supposed to.

She isn't sure what she wants to say to him.

"I hope I'm not interrupting."

"Not at all. I can read anytime."

"You like jazz?"

He raises an eyebrow and it seems to pull up the opposite corner of his mouth. "I didn't always. About six months ago I started thinking I needed a new interest. So I began to study jazz. I bought a turntable and amplifier—for some reason I thought I should learn via records, rather than CDs."

The waitress comes out with Elisa's food, looks temporarily puzzled, finds her, brings the meal to their table. Elisa thanks her.

"You were saying."

"Yes—I've become preoccupied with jazz recordings. On records, I mean." This is characteristic—interrupted and asked to continue, he will do so without the slightest hesitation. As though to be offended is beneath him. "There's something about the physicality of it, I think. The needle dragging in the groove."

She had used to find this kind of conversation pretentious; Larry taught her to enjoy it. She's missed it these past few weeks. But now it is irritating her all over again. She sits on her hands and draws a breath.

"You should go ahead and eat," he says.

"What did you get?"

He smiles. "The same."

34.

They walk to the frame shop together and Elisa pays for her frame. She doesn't open it, and he doesn't ask her to. Unspoken between them is almost everything. He's single. He saw her wedding ring.

"We should do that again," he says, as she leaves.

She hesitates before saying, "We should." The hesitation is almost, not quite, enough to be embarrassed by. She is bewildered by the effort it is requiring to achieve the proper mindset for infidelity. It seems important to want him. *We should.* A necessary obligation.

She returns late to the office and nobody cares. At her desk, she unwraps the photo. It's a nice frame. Silas leers out of it—it's as if he's in a rock band, posing for an album cover. The cocky self-satisfaction. The pleasure of knowing that the family has shaped itself around him. (Stop that: He's just a teenager. Of course he's cocky. So were you.) She puts the picture back into the drawer it came from.

That last year, the year before he died, Elisa and Derek considered separation, seriously enough to make plans, to announce them even. They would separate the children, as well—in fact that was the entire point, or so they told themselves. Derek actually volunteered to take Silas. It was like him to do this. He was better at managing his aversion to Silas

than he was his pity for Sam. Silas had begun to display the crowing satisfaction of the winner of a card game. He tidied his messy room, packed
up some old things, had a friend drive him to Goodwill to drop it all off.
(Maybe it was Ricky Samuelson, his killer. Maybe in the van he died in.)
He was preparing for the next phase of his life, one he had created for
himself, that he appeared enthusiastic about and eager to get under way.
And Sam resigned himself to Elisa with depressing immediacy, looking
up from the book he was reading, nodding once at her tear-stained face
before returning to the book.

They had said too much, she and Derek. They had pointed out each
other's shortcomings, using the children as illustrations. They indicated
what qualities of each parent had been brought to bear upon the suffering of each son, which problems might have been avoided but for which
habit of being, which blind spot. And each had accused the other of the
very thing they feared the most about themselves: that they regarded their
own child as frightening and repulsive.

Rule 5. *Do not use the children to attack your partner.*

They changed their minds, of course. Self-disgust was punishment
enough. Silas made his disappointment known, and so, cruelly, did Sam,
though it barely had a chance to register before Silas's death rendered it
all meaningless. Did it happen in this life, too—the decision to separate,
the announcement, the retraction? It is too exhausting even to speculate.

She peers at the clock in the corner of her computer screen. Two forty.
She's glad it's still early. She doesn't want to go home. She stalks Silas online for a little while, does a web search for his sig line, trying to find another online iteration of him.

It would be a relief to be mad, wouldn't it? To accept Amos's diagno-
sis and embrace this notion, that the events she remembers with such intensity and conviction are the products of an imagination broken by guilt
and grief. She could submit to more therapy, to medication. She would
be given paid time off from her job. She could wave goodbye as Derek
went to work in the morning, spend the day catching up on her reading, allow herself to be treated gently and a little fearfully, as any sick person would be. She could put that weight back on and give herself over to
Derek's carnal needs. And her own, for that matter.

What does a crazy person look and sound like? Certainly not like this—showing up on time at the office every morning, staying until five, sending and receiving e-mail, taking meetings in clean and tidy clothes. No—she wants to be, she feels like, a person to whom something inexplicable has happened. If there is madness, it belongs to the universe, not Elisa Brown. The mind is not enough to explain it.

This reminds her of something. She does a search for "William James multiverse."

Betsy was right, James coined the term. There are many hits. One of them is a forum, MetaphysicsNet. She reads it for a while. Past lives, alien intelligence, magnetic energy, parallel worlds. The parallel worlds subforum is crowded and extremely active. It's a hot topic, thanks to recent movies and television shows. There are a lot of threads discussing its plausibility, based on scientific and psychological research.

She bookmarks the site, turns off the browser, does a bit of work. Judith comes in, closes the door behind her, whispers "I fucked him," in reference to whom Elisa can't remember, then describes the encounter in detail. Elisa has come to like Judith, she has to admit. Judith is full of life. Judith is abidingly real. In this world, Elisa clearly has come to appreciate things that are alive and present. This Elisa is more accepting. Talking with Judith, she thinks she ought to adopt this way of being, then bristles at the notion that, in yet another way, the worlds are bleeding together.

When Judith is gone, Elisa tips her head back, gazes at the sprinkler and water pipes overhead, falls asleep. She dreams that she is performing oral sex on Larry, that he fills her up like a water balloon, and she begins emitting heat and light like a sun. She wakes up gagging and gasping for breath. Her neck hurts.

The working day is over. Derek picks her up. They go home, eat, drink, end up making love, though without particular intensity, and for no apparent reason other than that it has been a while. They go to sleep. Drifting off she thinks, All of this is impossible, we're doing impossible things. People do impossible things, all day long.

35.

A few days later she is reading an e-mail she has received from a man named Hugo Bonaventure. It's full of exclamation points. He'll be on campus all day Tuesday and Wednesday! He would love to talk about the multiverse! There's a cell number.

Clearly this is Betsy's friend. When she gets to work, she calls him.

"Yes, yes!"

"Mr. Bonaventure?"

"Yes, yes!"

They agree to meet the next day. His office is in the Keller Center, about as far from the biology department as it's possible to get and still be on campus. When it's time to go, she wishes she'd brought shorts and a floppy hat, as the air is very hot under a cloudless sky. She is glad, however, that she has abandoned the pretense of bringing formal shoes to work, and now wears sneakers all day.

She remembers the last long walk she took in Wisconsin, before the switch—around the cemetery and the park down the road. She stood over Silas's grave and for the first time didn't cry. She felt sadness, but also acceptance and relief. The memories this act stirred up were mostly memories of other visits to this cemetery, when her feelings had been more profound. (This is what happens, she supposes, to dramatic events: they create feelings that create other feelings, memories that give way to memories of having them. The older you get, the more life seems like a tightening spiral of nostalgia and narcissism, and the actual palpable world recedes into insignificance, replaced by a copy of a copy of a copy of a copy. The sunshine today agrees: it has rendered the town in high relief, grainy and posterized, the colors too bright. So fake it's a new kind of real.)

But the main thing that day was the trip itself, the way it fit into what her life had become. A ritual for her to wrap her guilt and grief in, so that she could separate it from the rest of her days. And then, eventually, this package, this bundle, began to feel familiar. Comfortable to carry, easy to set aside.

This was the year she realized she had moved on. As much as that was possible. She realized that she had moved on, that her life had been restored to her. And then the thing that happened happened.

She wishes she'd brought a bottle of water, though the walk is less than a mile. By the time she's nearly there she's sweaty and her bra and sneakers are chafing. She needs new clothes. She needs some air-conditioning.

The Keller Center for Theory and Practice is a kind of science-meets-humanities think tank, housed in a nineteenth-century brick mansion. Professors inside and outside of the college apply for fellowships there; they are supposed to get new ideas about their work by talking to one another. They hold monthly lectures and receptions, which she has never attended. Or maybe this version of her has—she doubts it, though. She arrives ten minutes early and stumbles in through the heavy oaken front door, expecting to find a receptionist, some cubicles—an office. Instead the place has the look and feel of somebody's house—someone unusually tidy but blind to the ravages of time. The front room, a parlor really, contains too many sofas, all of them worn and lopsided and from the seventies. She flops down on one and spread-eagles herself, her burning limbs.

The building is silent, save for a slow pulsing drone that must be an air conditioner: it is very cool here. A broad low table before her is covered with academic journals and, oddly, back issues of a glossy men's magazine. Light is blasting through the leaded windows but the room still seems gloomy. She likes it—she wants to move in.

The next thing she knows somebody is poking her in the shoulder and she is reflexively wiping drool from her face.

"'Ello? 'Ello? Is Missus Brown?"

"Oh my God. I'm so sorry."

She gathers in her arms and legs, blinks, tries to look over her shoulder. But he isn't there.

He's in front of her now, on the sofa across from her, a tall gangly man in shorts and button-down shirt. She can barely make out his face, as he is backlit by the blazing afternoon sun. But his hair, his massive ball of curly reddish-blond hair, glows so brightly she can see the shape of his skull beneath it.

"Is very comfortable here, no?"

"I guess the heat did me in."

"So you are tired, yes, I see. We will talk right here then, okay?"

"Where is . . . are you the only one here?"

"Yes! They have all gone away in summer!" He flutters his hands.

"Of course."

"So! So! I am speaking to Betsy Orosco! You want to talk about the multiverse! This is good, people like it, it's in the TV shows and movies a lot, you know?"

"Yes."

He's so tall, and the sofa he sits on so old and sunken, that his knees come up to the middle of his chest. He keeps them spread far apart and his legs are very hairy and she can see right up the leg of his shorts to the outline of his balls underneath a pair of white briefs. Somehow this seems cosmic, profound. Why does a man need two? Why not just one, a big one, dangling beneath the penis like a veined and whiskered egg? No, it has to be twins. She thinks of the poor redundant sperm, born daily and reabsorbed, unused, by the body: a cycle, the two balls in tandem, equal partners, competitors perhaps, in this Sisyphean undertaking. She laughs, but it comes out as something more like a sob.

"So . . ." says Hugo Bonaventure. "Something unusual, correct, you are saying is happening to you, yes?"

"Something unusual, uh huh." She sits up straighter now, rubbing her face. She still can't quite make out Bonaventure's features.

"You are professor of what?"

"It's not . . . I'm not a professor. I work here. At the college."

"Okay, okay . . ."

"I am just a regular person," she says, and marvels that those words would ever come out of her mouth. "I just want to know."

"Okay, okay . . ."

He nods, nods, is waiting for her to speak. And it occurs to her that she has no idea what she wants to say. There is a long silence.

"How much did Betsy tell you? About my . . . situation?"

"Just, how do you say," he replies, making curves in the air with his hands, as though illustrating a voluptuous woman, "you give me the, not the silhouette?"

She doesn't understand, and then she does. "Outline."

"Yes, the outline, thank you, yes. I make the recording?"

He taps his shirt pocket, where there is a bulge the size of a pack of cigarettes. She understands that he has a tape recorder in there and is requesting her approval. Without thinking she tells him sure.

She collects herself and goes through it all for him. Her life before it happened, the trip to Wisconsin, the drive, the moment of change. The differences. She tells him about telling Amos Finley, "my psychiatrist," she calls him. Toward the end of this monologue Hugo Bonaventure appears to grow agitated, impatient. She has discovered that if she closes her eyes for a moment, then opens them while they are trained on his face, she can catch a glimpse of it before her pupils contract from the light. His nose and chin are long, his eyes deep. He appears handsome and a little bit frightening, an exemplar of that extreme kind of effete masculinity accessible only to men without the slightest awareness of its existence. "Okay, okay," he says. "Okay, okay."

"Yes?"

There is a pause, punctuated by nodding, as though he is charging himself up. He says, "Okay, you say this moment, there is a change, can you give the description again? Of what it is like?"

"All right." She tells it again, more slowly this time, trying to add detail. The positions of the clouds. The rivets on the guardrail. The shape of the crack in the windshield. She nearly chokes up describing the crack, realizing that she might never see it again. The chip, like a leaning triangle, where a rock struck it, and the strange way the crack rises from it, ruler-straight, for six inches before it veers off to the left, then right, and heads for the upper corner of the glass. Hugo Bonaventure nods, taps his bare knees with his long fingers.

"Yes, yes, I ask you questions now, okay?"

"Sure."

"When this happens, yes?, there is a sound?"

"What kind of sound?"

"I don't know this," he says, "only you know this, the kind of sound. Maybe there is a ring, a vibration, something—" He claps his hands together and the claps echo off the high ceiling. "—something like a pop, a bang?"

She had not considered this possibility. A pop? A bang? She says, "The window was open, and then it was closed. So the wind noise was gone— the wind shut off."

"Yes?"

"But it was smooth. The change. The old car, it was noisier, and the new one is quiet. More solid. Everything went quiet."

"So a lack of sound. But no pop, bang, ring."

"No," she says. "Nothing like that."

"Okay, tell me, okay, do you smell something different? Or in the air, yes, there is some kind of crackle? Current?" He raises his hands and wiggles his fingers. She can hear them whispering against one another. "You feel anything on your skin? Something electrical? Or maybe some flash, there is light, not outside light but inside, on your retinas, you see?, the pop of light, the impulse, pop!, you see?"

"Yes, I see. Let me think," she says. She is trying to remember. The smell. Yes, it changed. There was the smell of the road and of the dusty interior of the Honda and then the stale recirculated air and plasticky odor of the new car. And the temperature changed, and there was the movement of air, of the hairs on her arm. But there was no pop, no flash. There was no smell that didn't seem to come from what was around her.

She tells him this. She says it was smooth, the transition: sudden, but clean. "There were no . . . artifacts. From the change itself. It didn't feel like something was happening. It was just, there was one thing, and then there was another."

If he is disappointed in this, he doesn't let on. He says, "Okay, very good, now I tell you straight from the bat, yes, maybe I think you are delusional? But perhaps not?"

"Uh . . . all right."

"But this is a thing we, that is, science, this notion, this idea, it is something real? We think, there are many ways for an event to transpire, the laws of physics allow this, there are probabilities, and all these probabilities are perhaps real, they have the same chance of being real, you see? A thing happens, any thing at all, it creates the universe of happening and the universe of not-happening. Do you understand? Always there is the branching, and every branch is a universe, and they are all real."

Her skin is puckering as the sweat evaporates from it and she shivers. She stops trying to make out Hugo Bonaventure's face. He's just a blank surrounded by light. That's enough. She says, "So this is real? The worlds are real?"

"Well, okay, sure. This idea of real, maybe this is not so important for the physics, do the math, maybe it's a little fanciful, one can make it with the math, sure, but to test it, how do you do this, okay?, how do you make the experiment?"

Her shivering has intensified. She feels very strange—as though her body is making energy. As though she is not quite in control of it. She clenches herself, clamps down on herself from the inside, in an effort not to melt here, to lose herself. The sofa is very soft and she feels very far down in it.

Hugo Bonaventure says, "This group, my colleagues, they do an experiment, okay? They take the tiny metal, like a tongue, a tiny thing, you barely see it with your eye, yes?, and they make it very cold, it is called the ground state, the lowest possible energy, yes? And here, at this place, the metal, because it is small and cold, here you don't have the disruption to the quantum state, correct? So they can make the measurements. And they pluck this metal—" He reaches out and flicks a finger. "—they pluck it, and they see that it is vibrating, yes? But it is also not vibrating."

He pauses, as if to let this sink in. She is nodding now, nodding the way he is nodding: they are nodding at one another.

"This is, then, okay, the universe where the object is plucked and the universe where the object is not plucked. My friends, they test it, they see both states."

"Both universes?" she asks him. "At once?"

"That is correct, yes, yes."

"You're saying they have seen this? Another universe?"

"They do, they see this."

She says, "Could they see me? The other me?"

He gets up. He paces for a moment in front of the coffee table. She is still fixated on the spot he has left: the image of his head, the void his head has imprinted on her vision, is left behind.

"Not quite, no, this is not possible. You are far too large." He lets out a kind of cackle. "Ha ha!, no, I cannot say that to a woman, but yes, you are too large for the physics to see. The outside forces, they push against you, yes?, they disrupt the quantum state. But maybe they can test!"

"Test me?"

He suddenly lopes around to her side of the coffee table and sits down beside her. She can see him clearly now: here he is. In profile, he is a study in extremes: his nose and chin appear even longer now, and bent, his brow a shelflike protrusion. His body gives off a moist nervous heat, and she realizes that the air-conditioning has made her really, really cold. The long pants that tortured her on the way over are now woefully inadequate.

He points to her bag, which she has brought with her and which is sitting on the floor between her sneakered feet. He is snapping the fingers of both hands. "You can give me, what do you say, two possessions?"

"I . . . possessions?"

"Two things you own, okay? One thing you have in both universes, the other one you have only here. Ha!, we would like the thing only from the other universe, but you can't give this!"

Elisa picks up the bag, holds it on her lap like an animal. "You want to take my things and . . . test them?"

"Not me to test them, my friends in California! No lab for this here, ha ha, sorry New York State, it's not so good. But my friends, they are doing this research, they can test maybe, okay? You give me two things, I send them, maybe we find something out, you never know." And he puts out a palm and beckons with his long fingers.

She gets it. One thing from here, one thing from there. She opens up her bag, roots around. The first thing she sees is a tube of lipstick she bought for an academic dinner years ago, some gala thing involving a guest of Derek's department, to which she had been persuaded to go. She used it that one time but didn't like the color, and doesn't like lipstick, and she never used it again. But here it is. She removes it and hands it over to Hugo Bonaventure.

"This was in the other place," she says.

"Okay, okay, very nice," he replies, and wedges it into the breast pocket of his shirt, beside the tape recorder. She's a little disconcerted— shouldn't he place it in some kind of specimen bag, affix a little label to it, something? But he's the scientist here, not her, not anymore.

She peers into her bag again. The light is dim; it's hard to see. There's her driver's license, which is different from her old one, but she needs that. She opens one side pocket, then the other. Shoves her hand into each. Comes out with a piece of paper.

It's the list, the five rules. The paper is creased and furred, the words, in her own hand, blurry and fading. She reads,

4. Account for your time.

Her fingers fold the paper, pointlessly, in half, concealing the list, and she hands it to Hugo Bonaventure.

"And this is from only here?" he asks.

"Yes."

"It is, how to say it, it is not from recent, but it is before you see the change?"

She nods. "That's right. It's old. It was in my bag when I got here."

His acceptance of this strange frame of reference appears total. He tucks the paper, insouciantly, into the pocket with the lipstick.

And then, abruptly, he stands up and sticks out his hand. "Well! Okay! I send these things away!"

"I . . . well, all right then."

She takes the hand, thinking he means to shake, but in fact he pulls and she rises, involuntarily, to her feet. For a moment she thinks she might topple over, but she manages to right herself, with the help of his free hand on her shoulder.

"Ha ha!" he says. "It is like we do the dance."

Her limbs ache—the air-conditioning has frozen her muscles solid. She feels dizzy and tiny lights zoom across her field of vision. Hugo Bonaventure is saying something. Then he is withdrawing, crossing the room, climbing the stairs. He waves from the landing, and Elisa waves back.

She goes out into the insane light and begins the trek back to the sanctum of her office.

36.

Next Friday morning. It's August now. She rises early, showers, takes her already-packed bag out to the pickup. Derek would ordinarily be the first one in the driveway, standing next to the open driver's side door, his arm on the roof, or leaning against the hood and scrolling through his phone. But today he's trailing behind. There has been an air of desperation in the house, as though time is running out; his eyes have lingered on her too long, too many times. He's been waiting for her to do something, say something. She knows what it is, and hasn't. This is part of what makes him a good lawyer—his ability to draw out a rival with silence. But it isn't working with her, because she doesn't know what to say.

On the way to the airport, Derek says, "Look, Lisa . . ."

She waits. He waits.

He sighs and again falls silent.

For a moment, she considers telling him everything. What happened to her, what she remembers, Betsy, her session with Amos, even Hugo Bonaventure. Watching him drive, she remembers how much she used to enjoy being a passenger beside him. His calm at the wheel, his deliberateness. Economy of movement. Driving her places, he made her feel safe—or rather, made her feel comfortable indulging her desire to be protected.

But today these same qualities seem to her evidence of a deep conservatism, a fear of inadvertent revelation. She can imagine very clearly what his reaction would be if she tried to explain herself now—silence, a frown, careful consideration. *I believe you,* he would say. *I believe that you think this happened.* He would apply logic, lay out possible remedies, mostly involving the solicitation of outside professional help, the application of psychoactive drugs.

Elisa doesn't want to have that conversation. She doesn't want to embrace his frame of reference. Now, she just wants to live in this new world, delusional or not, and see it to its end.

They are almost there. His hands are wringing the wheel as he says, in a voice edged with desperation, "Will I ever know?"

She can't remember when she's heard him sound this way. Or known him to be in such a position. She is tempted to pity him. "Know what?" she says.

His eyes are filmed over, his voice strangled. He stares resolutely through the windshield, exits the highway. "What this *is.* Why you're *doing* this."

"I'm just going to see our sons. I have to see them."

He sighs. "That's not an answer," he says, nearly in a whisper. They arrive at the airport. She expects him to park in short-term and wait with her. But he pulls up in the white zone. He doesn't even put the car in park. He seems to have gathered himself; she can tell by the set of his face that he is shifting his anger and frustration away from her and onto himself. A dangerous state—it usually leads to a fight. Not now, though— she's leaving. He says, harder now, "You are coming back, right?"

She levels a serious look at him. "Of course I'm coming back." She kisses him. He accepts it with taut resignation. Then she gets out of the truck and he drives off without waving goodbye.

The flight is long. She hasn't brought anything to read. She didn't think she'd be able to concentrate. But she can't sleep, either. Everyone around her seems to have some kind of digital device they're using to entertain themselves. She wants one—it would be nice to watch television, something she hasn't done in earnest in twenty years. Though in all likelihood you couldn't get any stations on a plane. But then what are these people watching?

They land in Denver and she changes planes and then, hours later, they land again. The light in Los Angeles is very bright; the airport workers on the tarmac are orange blurs. It's as if her pupils can't contract enough. She's near the back of the plane. The man beside her stands up as soon as it's allowed, though it will be several minutes before he'll be able to move. He stands awkwardly at his seat, sighing impatiently at regular intervals.

Elisa expects to see bustle when she emerges into the terminal. People in sunglasses, on phones, men in African robes, strung-out rockers on tour. Instead, the concourse is nearly empty. Sam is supposed to have met her, but there's no sign of him. She stands in the middle of the broad worn carpet and squints in every direction. Then she sits down and rummages in her bag for her phone.

When he emerges from the men's room twenty yards down the concourse, she doesn't recognize him. Or rather she does—it must be him, she knows it as soon as she sees him—but tells herself she must be wrong. In truth, she has been preparing herself for this moment for weeks. She understood he would be different. She imagined him thinner than was healthy, unshaven, pale-skinned. Tired. This image frightened her at first, but she has gotten used to it. She is ready for it.

But Sam looks nothing like it. He's clean-shaven, tan, and overweight. He's wearing a pair of pleated khaki pants, running shoes, and a golf shirt. There's a cell phone holster on his belt and he walks with effort, as though sedated.

She stands. He acknowledges her with a nod. When he is standing before her, she cannot help herself—she throws her arms around his neck and pulls him close. "Sam!" she cries, and he's sweaty, he smells sour, she cannot believe this bloated creature is her son.

He stiffens and she feels his hands gingerly patting her back. His shoul-

ders are big, they're rounded, they feel like someone else's. But no, this is
Sam. He stumbles a bit, takes a step back; she releases him. His face is obscured by flesh, but the eyes are the same. They seem to search her face
for some kind of purchase.

She stands very still and lets him look at her. He sounds tired as he
says, "Hey, Mom."

"Sam."

"You seem different."

Her laugh is almost a sob. "I feel different."

Sam looks down at his feet. He says, "So . . . you know where you're
staying?"

"It's a chain hotel. Near your house."

She gives him the information and he nods. "Wanna go, then?" he
says, and they walk together down the concourse. He keeps his hands
shoved into his pockets, and his effortful walk now reveals itself as a slight
limp. One of his feet isn't quite straight, and he grunts, nearly inaudibly,
with every step. She wants to ask him what happened, but is certain that
she is either already supposed to know, or has deliberately been prevented
from knowing. (She remembers his fake limps from adolescence, his indulgence in others' pity.) A smell comes off him, like an office cubicle out
of which the custodian has not yet carried the remains of lunch. She gasps
a bit, holding back tears, but Sam doesn't seem to notice.

They say nothing to each other as they leave the airport. He offers
a questioning look at baggage claim, and when she shakes her head he
nods and continues through the automatic doors. The air is brutally hot
but dry, and she suddenly wishes she were in the sun. But in fact she's
in the parking garage, getting into Sam's car. It's quite new, an SUV, and
very large. He gets behind the wheel and puts on a pair of aviator sunglasses that match, almost perfectly, the curve of his face. He looks like
a giant insect.

Sam had a toy spaceman helmet, once, that Lorraine had given him.
It was yellow, like a hard hat, and covered his head entirely; a large hinged
visor of reflective translucent plastic obscured the face. For a time, he
wore this helmet almost all day long: he would sit on the sofa reading
picture books through it, he would sneak goldfish crackers or raisins up
under the visor. He wore it to dinner, wore it riding his scooter, when

they went to the store. He usually took it off to sleep, but occasionally she would find him in the morning still wearing it, the visor fogged, snores echoing out from under it.

He must have been five. He didn't seem to have any kind of fantastic identity that he associated with the helmet, no invented narrative. He just wore it. The helmet was an accessory to his personality.

Its only apparent power, real or imagined, was that his brother ignored him when he was wearing it. Occasionally Elisa would catch Silas staring at Sam, gazing at the reflective surface of the visor, perhaps at his own reflection, or perhaps just lost in thought about the impression the helmet made. But he didn't bother Sam in any way—didn't push or hit, didn't steal any toys or books or food. If anything, Silas redoubled his disruptive efforts elsewhere in the house, but it was a relief to Elisa not to have to pull them apart, to settle disputes.

The era was short-lived, of course. The helmet was always a little too small, and then Sam hit a growth spurt. Washing his hair one night, Elisa noticed twin wounds on either side of his scalp: scabbed and bloody tracks, as though he'd been scratched by some animal. She picked up the helmet, which lay on the floor behind her: its interior was filthy, greasy, crusted over with black deposits on two reinforcing ridges that matched Sam's scrapes.

It had to hurt him even to put it on. The ridges worrying at the wounds all day long, the cuts struggling and failing to heal themselves. Sam winced as she applied disinfectant to the cuts, and then, later, silently watched her clean the inside of the helmet with rubbing alcohol, apply strips of felt to the ridges with double-stick tape. Elisa dreaded the day he had to give it up; she thought he would cry for weeks.

But it didn't happen. For a little while Sam carried the thing under his arm, like an astronaut walking across the launchpad after a successful mission, and then at last he relegated it to his closet. Silas took up, once again, his efforts to torment his brother. Elisa tried to interest Sam in other helmets, none quite the same, but he shunned them.

On the one hand, it was as if he were determined to put it all behind him—not just the toy itself, but his need for its protection. He seemed, in this one small way, very adult.

On the other hand, there was something perverse about the totality of his resignation. Come on, she wanted to say—if a plastic helmet made Silas stop, then anything could make him stop. The helmet isn't *magical.* This last, she did say to Sam, while she sat on his bed trying to talk him to sleep. *It's not the helmet, it's you.* But the boy shook his head—she could hear it in the dark, his hair scraping the pillow—and she thought, but didn't say, *Come on, Sam, fight back. Fight back.*

Now they're on the freeway and her son exudes that same grim acceptance of circumstance. She doesn't even know what the circumstance is, but she can feel herself bristling in the presence of his capitulation to it. It's midafternoon, not yet rush hour, and their progress is swift. Sam says, "I guess you're not going to talk, then."

It is the same conversation she had hours ago with his father.

"Fine then," he says, without giving her a chance to reply. "So you're here, and in a while you'll go home, and I'll never know what this was all about. And yet here I am driving you around."

She says, "It isn't anything in particular."

He has no response to this. Minutes pass.

She says, "Things are changing at home."

Nothing. She is fixated on his heavy thigh, sunk into the driver's seat. Tears are pouring down her cheeks, though there is no tightness in her throat; she is able to keep her voice steady.

"Forgive me, Sam. I don't really know why I'm here."

Possibly he makes a small grunt of acknowledgment. His body shifts against the vinyl seat. She goes on: "There's something . . . wrong with me. It might be best if you—if you pretend I've got amnesia. That I don't remember anything about the past few years." She turns to him. "I know that your father and I apparently decided to—to put you behind us. I don't understand how we came to that decision. I accept that we did, but . . . do I owe you some kind of apology? I think I do. May I apologize to you?"

It takes him a few seconds to come out with, "What do you mean something's wrong with you."

She lets out a sigh. "I don't know. I don't even know. But I don't remember anything that happened. Not for years now."

There's a minute during which his breathing seems to quicken and deepen. He is so strange to her, bovine and implausible.

"You can do whatever you want," he says quietly.

"Do what?"

"You wanted to apologize, go ahead."

"I'm sorry," she says. It doesn't sound like she means it, but she does, she does.

He nods. She takes a tissue out of her bag and wipes her face.

The car pulls up in front of a motel, and Sam parks. "I have to go back to work," he says. "Silas is having you over for dinner. Some people are coming. You should be there at eight—it's just a couple of blocks." He pushes his sunglasses up the bridge of his nose; his entire face is slick and sweating. "I dunno. It's fucked up. It's fucked up that you're here."

She can't speak.

"I don't mean to be mean. You know. But I just . . . I really don't get it."

"I don't either."

"Okay, well . . ." He puts the car back in gear. "I really have to get back to work. Silas needs me to do some shit."

She can't stop herself—she says, "You still work with Silas."

He lets out breath and tips his head back. "Jesus. Yes. I still work with Silas. I do the books at Infinite."

"I'm sorry."

"Me too," he says, but she doesn't know what he means by this and he doesn't seem to either.

She gets out of the car, takes hold of her bags, and shuts the door. The tires bark on the pavement as Sam drives away.

37.

The neighborhood they live in is called Silverlake. She learns this from the motel clerk, who is a young black woman with pierced nose and tongue and an ostentatious straightened hairdo. When Elisa asks if there's a place nearby to get coffee, the girl points and says, "Five blocks."

But first she checks in. It's four thirty in the afternoon. Her room is cold and dry. She takes a nap, then wakes up shivering half an hour later, her skin pulled tight, wondering where on earth she is.

The café is staffed by people who look like the girl at the motel. She sits at a wobbly table sipping her coffee and examines the maps she printed from the internet. The boys live on a narrow winding street several blocks from the main drag; she memorizes the route to their house, then tucks the papers into her bag and walks there.

A Spanish-style bungalow in apparent disrepair, the white stucco cracked and falling off, the shrubbery unwatered and half-dead. She stares at it from across the street for a while. No cars pass, though she can hear, faintly, the noise from the main street, blocks away. She contemplates returning to her motel but instead walks across the street and climbs the steps onto the wide shaded porch. A table and chairs are set up, and on the table lies a half-full ashtray and a bottle opener. A wind chime hanging in the archway is silent and still.

The driveway is empty of cars and the broad front window lacks any curtain or shade. She walks up to it and peers inside.

Elisa is surprised—the living room is quite tidy, perhaps to a fault. The Swedish-style furniture is new; the jute rug is clean and lies on even bleached floorboards. There's a glass coffee table, an insectile aluminum floor lamp, and a sofa and two chairs draped in matching white slipcovers. Beyond this arrangement is an open door frame that leads to a bright kitchen, with black-and-white tile floor.

There appears at first to be a blanket wadded up on the sofa, partially covering a reddish-brown pillow. Elisa blinks, and the blanket and pillow rearrange themselves into the image of a naked red-haired girl.

The girl is asleep. She looks nineteen or twenty and is dangerously thin. Her flesh is pale and she has no breasts to speak of. One arm hangs down to the floor and the other is pinned under her body. Her legs are spread, her genitals in plain view. Elisa draws in breath and the girl opens her eyes.

At first, the girl appears not to have seen Elisa standing in the window. She makes no move to cover herself, and anyway there is nothing, no robe or towel nearby, for her to use. But the longer she lies there, eyes open, the clearer it becomes that she has seen Elisa and is staring at her. The eyes are bleary and the face freckled; the girl's lips are parted and between them lie small yellowish teeth. She is like a rare, damaged specimen of some endangered species, some strange rodent or bird.

Is the girl drugged? There is no expression on the face; the eyes blink with exaggerated slowness. Elisa doesn't move—she wants to leave, but this would somehow be worse, a greater invasion of privacy than remaining still. Her ankle itches and her bladder feels heavy.

Finally the girl closes her eyes and rolls over and returns, evidently, to sleep. Her legs are sinewy, her feet large. Elisa watches her draw and exhale breath.

What precisely does she think she is doing here on this porch, in this city, interfering in lives she has evidently forsaken? Muscling this world onto some path where perhaps it doesn't belong. She's doesn't have a plan, not really. She is still groping, still doesn't belong.

But she felt this way, often, in her real life, too, didn't she? It was the signature emotion of parenthood. There was no way to know what actions had which results, whether all of it was her fault, or none of it.

She has been assuming that her memories of life before the crash are valid here, but maybe they aren't. Is any memory valid, really? Has she ever remembered anything the way it really happened? Has anyone, ever?

Maybe none of this world belongs to her. None of it.

She climbs down from the porch and wanders the streets, sweating. The light glinting off car windshields is again too bright. A greasy haze of unreality coats everything. She suddenly feels sick, as if the coffee she drank has just changed its mind, and she sits down on a curb over a street grate, expecting to vomit. But the feeling passes and is replaced by exhaustion. She finds her way back to the motel and asks the clerk to call and wake her at seven fifteen, but the clerk shakes her head and says it's all computerized, just push the wake-up button on the phone.

Elisa's hand is trembling as she does this, sitting on the edge of the bed, on the slick synthetic-fiber comforter that will not allow her body to find any purchase. When the operation is finished, she throws back the bedclothes and climbs in, shivering and fully dressed. Falling asleep makes a sound in her mind like a steel marble circling the drain.

38.

Two hours later she stands on the sidewalk again looking up at the bungalow. The driveway is full now; Sam's SUV is here, a small sports car, an old Volvo, and a motorcycle. Long shadows of palm trees and phone poles rake the street. Her breathing is quick and shallow and she wants to run away. But she climbs the steps for the second time that day and knocks on the door.

Sam answers. His body fills the doorway. There's a large glass of something in his hand, whiskey she supposes, with a couple of half-melted ice cubes floating in it. He manages a small smile that quickly fades. "You don't have to do this," he says, and she can detect in him, for the first time, some small reservoir of compassion. She thinks, This is really happening. This is how things are.

She says, "I came all this way."

After a moment, he steps aside and lets her in.

People, young people, fill the living room. Each holds a drink in one hand—straight-sided glass tumblers of something—and a cigarette in the other. They embrace no recognizable style. One boy looks like the counterpart of the girl at the motel—black jeans and tee shirt, piercings and wild hair. Another wears suit pants and an untucked oxford shirt and tiny round glasses with lenses not much larger than his eyes. There are a couple of guys who look like members of a biker gang—she recognizes one of them from photos of the Infinite Games staff. A fat girl with big breasts stands alone by the wall. And the girl from earlier is here, wearing a simple, baggy linen dress that is too big for her. Its hem drags on the floor.

It isn't that any of them is particularly unusual, set against the strangeness of humanity; taken alone, any one would qualify, at first blush, as mildly eccentric. But there is something abstracted about them as a group; the party seems conceptual, like a movie set. It is as if none of them knows any of the others, as if they have all just met.

Sam comes up behind her and says, loudly, "Everyone, this is Lisa."

A few people turn and say hello. The fat girl actually appears frightened.

She is trying to decide, in the half-quiet that follows Sam's introduction, whether or not to reply when a figure appears in the kitchen doorway, holding its own drink and cigarette. It is unmistakably Silas. His eyes travel first to the red-haired girl, and then follow her gaze to Elisa.

In spite of everything, she wants to cross the room and embrace him. Oh, Silas—I know you so well. Every year, in that motel room in Wisconsin, she has lain on the bed, eyes closed, and imagined what he would look like if he were alive. She has invented a hundred scenarios for him—lives he could lead, experiences that might transform him. He has been rich, he has been imprisoned. He has been married, itinerant, famous, missing.

She never imagined this one, of course.

Silas is advancing toward her across the room. The party has lost interest in her, conversation has resumed, but she can't shake the feeling that everyone is watching, that they all know what she has done, what has happened to her, what is going through her head. That they are witnesses to an experiment of which she is the subject.

He is standing before her now. It's him. "Lisa," he says.

His body is strong—that's what strikes her. Always, as a child, he was smaller than his brother, slighter. He is wiry now, muscled. He looks like he could climb up a wall, jump from rooftop to rooftop.

And his face, it is so familiar: the expression of impassivity, the features flattened by indifference, as though pressed against bulletproof glass. His eyes are half-lidded, his small mouth opened slightly, the skin tanned and lightly coated with sweat. He is twenty-four years old. She flinches when he takes one of her hands in both of his, lifts it to his thin lips, touches it to them. They are warm and dry.

"Silas . . ."

His eyes open wider and meet hers. They seem to know that she isn't his real mother. He releases her hand and it falls to her side. "Would you like anything to drink?" he asks. She can't read his tone.

"All right," she says.

His eyes bore into her, then blink. He doesn't ask her what drink she wants. He just turns and walks back toward the kitchen, with a spring in his step. She remembers him as a toddler, the sight of his small hard back retreating through a doorway or around the corner of a room, the feeling that something just out of sight was about to happen, something would be . . . disrupted.

There is a presence beside her and she remembers that Sam is here. That Sam exists. He's breathing loudly again, loudly enough to hear against the background noise of the party. She turns to him and he is gazing at her with mild curiosity and apparent exhaustion. His glass is empty except for the ice cubes, which are little more than slivers now. His face is red and puffy and she realizes that he is an alcoholic. *Silas is doing this to you. I did this to you.*

Sam turns away and follows his brother, heaving himself across the room. Elisa is left alone at the door. She can see the boys moving in the kitchen. She doesn't want to be standing here when they come out.

Everyone in the room is half her age, but they seem older somehow. She stumbled into parties like this in college—disdainful or insecure people, trying to act cool. She liked the law students for their politeness, their confidence. They were invested in the system, they felt comfortable there. Elisa never thought of herself as a misfit—she didn't like misfits.

Having children changed that. The pitying way other parents looked at her when Silas pushed their kids or stole their toys. She understood the outsider mentality. It came in handy in her old life, her real life, where she painted paintings and had extramarital affairs. She feels compelled to let these people know—I've been loathed and pitied, too. I paint paintings.

Instead, she goes over to the red-haired girl in the long dress and says, "I owe you an apology."

The girl blinks.

"I came to the house today and looked in the window. I'm afraid I may have embarrassed you."

The girl looks frankly at her, taking in her clothes and shoes and face. She says, "You're their mother." Her voice is surprisingly low.

"Yes."

The girl shifts her insignificant weight from one foot to the other and her dress moves against her body. It's obvious that the dress is all she's wearing. It's so large and hangs down so far that the upper edge of an aureole is visible at the neckline. Her nipples show through the thin fabric and Elisa feels cold looking at her, though the room is warm.

Elisa hears more people entering behind her—a small crowd in fact. She smells cigarette smoke and hears bottles clanking together inside a paper bag. And then she realizes that she has seen this girl before. The perfect round arcs of the eyebrows are the same, and the oval chin. The oversized, not big, nose.

"You're the girl from the game," she says.

"What?"

"From Mindcrime. Silas's game. You're the waitress at the diner."

The girl appears confused for a moment; her eyes film over. Then she seems to remember, and just as suddenly to lose the thread again. Elisa feels bad for bringing it up. The waitress in the game was voluptuous, full-hipped and large-breasted, radiant with health. Whereas this girl is sick. Did she ever look like the waitress? She blinks, again meets Elisa's gaze.

"What do you do?" the girl asks.

"I work at a lab," she replies, then corrects: "A college, I mean." But the girl isn't listening.

"No. What do you *do?*"

"I don't understand."

The girl licks her chapped lips. The lip-licking continues. She's smiling, a strange distracted smile that could be left over from some other conversation. The teeth are small and sharp with tiny spaces in between them, and a hard look has come over her face, a desire to inflict hurt.

"When you're not at your lab. *At a college.*"

After a moment Elisa says what she fantasized saying moments before, she says, "I paint."

The girl says, "Waterfalls? Horses?"

"Abstracts." But she doesn't, of course. This Elisa doesn't. Her studio is an office now—Derek's office.

"Abstracts," the girl says.

"That's right."

"Do they match your shoes?"

There's a tug on her arm. It's Sam, rescuing her from the conversation. The girl looks at the floor and Elisa mutters goodbye. She is introduced to some new people, none of whom she notices. Suddenly she wants that drink. She detaches herself from her son and goes to the kitchen. Silas isn't there. It's small and dirtier than it appeared through the window, the stove burners lined with aluminum foil in which grease is pooling around bits of burned food. At least they're cooking, she thinks, that's a good sign. A bottle of bourbon is standing on the counter, and she helps herself to some, using a cracked tumbler from the drying rack. There's a jar beside it, a mason jar filled with some brown liquid that seems to be slowly swirling and glittering, and she stands there a moment, sipping the bourbon, trying to figure out what the jar contains.

Silas walks in from another room, running his hand through his hair. "Oh," he says, "that's right. Your drink." He brushes his hands together, as though he's just finished sawing some boards, and leans against the stove, arms crossed.

Elisa's heart is galloping. She takes a deep draught from her glass and says, "Silas, what is wrong with that girl?"

"What girl."

"The red-haired girl. The waitress from the game."

His eyebrows rise infinitesimally, but his expression remains otherwise unchanged. "Rachel? She has problems."

"She needs help."

"Going to unleash those crack mothering skills?" he says. "Worm your way into her heart? With all of your kindness and charm? All your experience helping people?"

She can't speak. He goes on.

"What with your life devoted to thinking about things besides yourself and your petty desires."

"You should talk," she says.

"I don't pretend it's any of my business. That girl is fucked up and she is dealing with it. It isn't my fault. Not everything is my fault. This will come as a surprise to you, Lisa. I'm not to blame for everything. Some stuff is even your fault."

39.

She feels it, the old helplessness. The feeling that she has run, suddenly, unexpectedly, out of options. This was the signature emotion of her years as a parent of small children, the feeling that at any moment the mother in her might simply expire, leaving her alone, in some private world of failure, with the parts of herself she had abandoned. There must have been some signal she gave off, some stale odor or subtle corporeal slump, that telegraphed this emotion, because Silas always seemed poised to exploit it, to see what he could accomplish inside the space it created: the time he learned the word *bitch,* and all day he said *bitch,* because he had heard her refer to another woman this way, and knew she disliked this woman, and knew the word would do something to her, would make her react. And so she didn't react, not at first. She turned the other cheek, like the pediatrician told them, like the child psychologist told them, like the piles of parenting and self-help books told them, she turned and walked out of the room.

But walking away was a reaction, ignoring was a reaction. It meant a real reaction was forthcoming. He followed her around all day, saying the word, until finally, the day nearly endured, her head aching and throat tight, she went into Sam's room to say goodnight, and *Sam* looked at her, his face quivering with uncertainty, and said, ". . . bitch?"

She slapped him, hard, across the cheek. And before he could react went into Silas's room where Silas lay on his bed beneath a galaxy of glow-in-the-dark stars laughing, and she slapped him too, harder, twice.

Silas screamed—not cried—as though she were sawing off his leg. She could feel through her feet the boy's body writhing in the bed as in an epileptic fit, and his head thumping against the wall beside it, something he had begun to do to drive them madder still (but there she goes, as-cribing motivation to this strange act, when who could know, really, why Silas, or anyone for that matter, did anything?)—there were marks there, visible in the daytime, stains and depressions left by his sweaty head. And by now Sam was crying too, and Derek's feet thundered on the stairs and she felt herself being pulled out of the dark August-hot bed-room, away from the stink of boyhood and the wailing and the thump-ing of Silas's head against the wall.

Derek led her down the stairs. He laid her on the sofa, pushed her down, held her arms down at her sides. "Stop it, stop it," she was telling him but he wouldn't let go, and soon she was struggling, like Silas, thrash-ing her own head, trying to knee him in the back.

Eventually she gave in. He wasn't going to let go unless she gave in. So she lay still listening to the children cry and she said, "I need to apol-ogize to Sam."

"What happened?" Derek said, and she could not stand the fucking sound of his fucking patronizing holier-than-thou voice, as though *she* was the only irrational person in the house. Fuck you, Derek, she thought, fuck you for eternity.

"*Sam* called me a bitch and I slapped him." *Not true,* a voice told her, he had *said* the word, he hadn't called her anything. He had said the word and she had assigned the intent. But she did not correct her story.

"Sam did?"

"Let go of me, Derek."

"And that's what he wanted," Derek said, almost to himself. "To make you slap Sam."

"Let go of my arms."

"Are you sure?"

Die, you fucking fuck. "I have to apologize to Sam."

"You won't go into Silas's room."

"Derek," she said between clenched teeth. *"Let fucking go of me."*

He did as she asked, slowly, as if she might spring up and attack him, and she climbed the stairs and apologized to her son. This would be the first time they almost decided to separate, she and Derek, the first of three. The second was right before Silas calmed down, right before he started doing well in school; and then there was the one right before his death.

They should have broken up sooner. Their love for each other was not important, but this wasn't clear to them at the time. They just wanted to be with the only other person who understood, whatever the consequences.

"He made me," Sam whispered to her that night, tears on his cheeks. "I know," she whispered back, "I'm sorry," and rocked him to sleep.

Two weeks later he turned seven.

40.

She tries to keep a steady voice, though her throat is tight and the words come out strained. "I see what you do, Silas. Online."

"Online?" She has caught him off guard. His face is long, bony, a man's face, not a boy's, and the word *massive* occurs to her, though he is not large. He is simply her son, a man.

"The forums you're on. You treat people badly. You invent new versions of yourself just so you can treat people badly."

Silas's eyes widen and he barks out a laugh. "You're *webstalking* me?"

She hears a noise behind her and in a moment feels a hand on her arm. It's Sam. "Mom."

"That is really something," Silas is saying. "I'm not nice enough to people. On the internet! Did you catch that? I'm a dick on the internet, and Lisa has flown out to LA to let me know."

"We ought to go," Sam is whispering.

"Listen to your good son, Lisa, he's right. You ought to go."

But I don't want to go, she's thinking. This is what I came for. Although it occurs to her that, ultimately, she doesn't really know what she came for. Except to see. Her eyes fall from her son's face to the counter, where the liquid in the jar is still swirling, though no one has touched it. The liquid is pearlescent. It appears to be illuminated from within. And she wonders, ludicrously, and for no clear reason at all, is this part of an experiment Silas is doing, part of his effort to create other universes? Perhaps it is in this kitchen's twin, in another universe, that he created this one. And now, from inside this universe, he is trying to create another. That's it, in the jar, that's the matter that will expand into it. *Ten pounds of matter*, Betsy told her, *packed into a really tiny space*. She wants to reach over and pick up the jar, see how heavy it is. She looks down at her glass and sees that it is nearly empty.

Silas is staring at her. If he has noticed her noticing the jar, he gives no sign. She allows Sam to lead her out of the room, through the crowd of people, out of the house. She'll come back. She needs to pick that thing up, to heft it and peer into its depths. The red-haired girl is nowhere to be seen. Elisa leaves her glass on the table on the porch, beside the ashtray and lighter.

Down the front steps and onto the sidewalk. Sam is marching her along the street, his fingers tight around her arm. She says, "Sam. Let go."

He releases her, tosses the arm back to her. It flops against her side. "I told you not to come." They're walking fast, toward her motel.

"That girl," Elisa says. "What's wrong with her?"

"She's Silas's." Dismissively, as though this makes speculation pointless.

When they reach the motel he follows her into her room. The curtains are open and the evening sun is blazing through the window, but the room still seems dark, and the air is clammy. Sam turns the air conditioner down. He has brought something with him, in his pocket, a bottle of whiskey the size of a beer. Elisa sits down on the bed and watches him unwrap the two tumblers from the tray on the nightstand and pour a few fingers of liquor into each. He still has great facility with his body, when he isn't around his brother. She remembers the towers of blocks he liked to make, such irresistible invitations to Silas. Even long after it became clear these projects would not survive his brother's attention, he continued to build and defend them. He would spend hours beside a tower of blocks, his body taut with attention as Silas walked by.

Sam takes the only chair in the room, facing her, and hands her one of the glasses. He says, "You have to tell me what you want."

She drinks. "I just wanted to see you."

"What did *he* think?"

His enunciation of the word *he*—an emphasis half mockery and half vestigial respect—tells her that he is referring to Derek. "I don't know."

"And the therapist guy. Who you hired to do all this to you."

"You know about all that?"

Sam doesn't respond.

"I didn't tell him I was coming, Sam. The therapist, I mean. I just came." Though she remembers, moments later, that she is lying. When he doesn't respond, she says, "I needed to see you."

"Is this amnesia thing a real thing, or is it just bullshit?"

She leans over to place the glass on the nightstand. She doesn't want it. She says, "It's real."

"You honestly have no memory of, what exactly?"

"I told you. The last . . . nine years. I do have memories. Some of them are . . . inaccurate."

The sun is sinking behind the line of buildings across the street. A car horn sounds, and somebody shouts. It's getting harder and harder to make out Sam's face. He doesn't speak; she thinks he's going to, for a moment, but then he doesn't. She remembers other hotel rooms at other times. A camping vacation that went to pieces: they ended up in a cheap roadway motel, sprung for an adjacent room for the kids so that she and Derek could quietly fuck with the TV on. Actually, that was a nice trip. Very nice. All four of them got along: united in failure. There was a trip to Derek's parents' place, the guest room under renovation (the guest room was always under renovation), the Best Western near the highway, with the indoor pool so overheated she fainted. They never seemed to plan to stay in hotels, they were only a substitute for real plans.

She says, "I remember Silas . . . dying. When he was fifteen. And then later, you're happy. You're not like this." She has to squint against the sun. She says, "None of this seems real to me, Sam. There was no shrink. You live near us. We share a car."

She says, "I want my Honda back, Sam."

He is staring at her.

Elisa can't stay upright anymore—it's as if Sam's gaze has released her. She lets herself lean toward the pillows, and then she's lying down and her eyes are closed.

"Tell me things," she says. "About yourself. Things I don't know."

He's quiet for a while. She thinks she's going to fall asleep, but her body is buzzing. Every now and then her fingers twitch, as if she's grabbing something in a dream.

When he speaks, it's with effort, as though he is forcing himself to play along. He says, "I don't know. I assume you don't remember the meeting."

She shakes her head no.

"The family meeting? The one where you told us?"

Now she doesn't want to hear it. But he has decided to tell her. He shifts his body on the chair, with effort, and when he speaks he is panting slightly.

"You scheduled it. Like it was a work meeting. It was at 5:00 p.m. on a weekday. Silas was off in his room coding or something. I was . . . I don't know what I was doing." He clears his throat, inhales through his nose like an old man. "You got us all around the dining room table and said basically you were kicking us out and were going to cut off contact for a while. And I said A while?, and Dad said Indefinitely. And Silas said, Who told you to do this, the shrink?, and you said, It's something we worked on with Amos."

"Oh, Sam . . ." she says.

"And Dad started rattling off the details, like we had two weeks to do this and a month to do that before you changed the locks, and Silas was just laughing and laughing. Because he had just heard about the job, like, that same day."

"This one? The one . . ."

"At Infinite. And he was like, You know what, how about we leave today? Like, right now? And he got up from the table and started carrying his shit out to the car. You guys just sat there like, what the fuck? And I could see your expressions just start to harden, like you must have promised yourselves you were going to do, and I sat there asking you if it was a joke, or what."

He has managed to drain his glass and pours himself another from the bottle on the floor.

"At some point Silas looked at me and said, Are you coming? And I looked at you and you just hung your head. Silas said, Can't you see, dude, they're done with you? Get up off your ass and pack. So I was like, fuck all this fucking shit, and I went with him."

"Where did you go?" Elisa asks him.

"Some motel. Silas called some girls. We got drunk. After a couple of days we flew out here. They paid for everything—they wanted him really bad. They gave me a job. We bought the house."

The room is quiet, but the air itself seems to be making a noise—a pink noise, a hiss with a low note in it somewhere. No, she realizes, it's just the air conditioner. And this is a disappointment to her, she wanted it to be the air, the sound the air made.

"Why did we do it?" she whispers, mostly to herself. But he answers.

"We were acting like assholes." And then, after a moment, "You were assholes. No, all of us are assholes, that's the problem." Sam is starting to sound drunk now, his teenage self is coming back, the self-pitying Sam, the whining Sam. She thinks, I'm an asshole for thinking that.

"Actually, that time, in the motel," he says, too loudly, "I cheated on Angie with some girl, Silas's girl's girlfriend or something. We made the girls go down on each other then I fucked the one, the other one. I called Angie and told her and she dumped me. Then we moved."

He wants to hurt her with this tableau of debauched sexuality. And she is hurt, but she is mostly confused. She says, "I don't know who Angie is."

There's a silence. Finally, "We were together for years. We were supposed to get married?"

"I'm sorry, Sam. Why—"

"Whatever."

She waits. He is panting, slumping in his chair. "Why did you call her? Tell her? Why were you . . . unfaithful?"

Sam doesn't answer. He closes his eyes and for a time he seems to be asleep. But he keeps his half-full glass upright and when he opens his eyes again he appears alert.

"You're not happy here. With Silas."

He doesn't respond.

"Surely it was about him, not you," she says, willing it to be so, begging him to agree. "What we were doing, it was about Silas, about breaking his . . . his hold on you."

The light in the room is lower now and illuminates the wall behind her. It reflects a green cast onto his face. He says, "I don't know. No."

"You could have been free of him."

He's quiet for a while. He says, "No. I came here. He . . . he got me a job. He took me in. Sort of like one of his girls."

"His girls?" Elisa asks.

"Yeah, he—well, you met one. He dates messed-up girls. He tries to, I dunno, fix them or something. Help them. It never works out, it ends in tears, you know."

"Maybe he's just taking advantage of them, Sam. Did you ever think of that?"

His eyes narrow. He appears puzzled. "No—I don't know what he's doing, to be honest. But taking advantage. No. He's not like that. With girls."

Elisa thinks, you don't know him like I do.

She consumes the contents of her glass in one gulp. There's something she wants to ask him. She can't. Then she does. "You . . . shared. Those girls. In the motel."

He's looking at the wall over her head.

"That girl," she says. "The red-haired girl. Do you share her?"

He shifts in his seat, drinks. "No."

"Sam, you don't like girls."

He's very still now. Quietly he says, "What do you mean?"

"You don't like girls. You're gay."

"I'm not *gay*."

"Yes," Elisa says, "you are. You came out. A few years after he died. You have a boyfriend. I think. You don't tell me everything."

The silence is much longer this time. She is in mourning now, mourning for the Sam she knows. Her friend, her only son.

His shoulders are hitching and his feet scrape against the floor. As if he's bound to the chair and is trying to get free. His empty glass falls from his hand onto the carpet.

"Sam?"

There are tears in his voice as he says, "I'm cooking the books!"

She waits.

"Silas is—we tried to start our own company. His games don't sell. You know—they're supposed to be arty. People hate him here . . . it's a fuckin' . . . it's a miracle we're not fired."

He draws a deep breath and his throat sounds a low and wandering note, a wheeze. When he speaks again, he has reined in his emotions.

"Silas is . . . he doesn't like working for somebody else. I mean, I can't blame him. He wanted to go independent. He found a partner, we were going to go in together on this space in La Puente . . . so we started . . . skimming off the top. I mean, Silas felt like—we both did—like we deserved it. They really are assholes, these people. But the guy, the partner . . . he fuckin' disappeared. We got robbed. It was so fuckin' stupid . . ."

They sit there in the darkening room, facing each other, Elisa on the bed and Sam on the chair. She reaches out and takes his thick pale hands in hers.

"Just come home," she says. "Leave it all behind."

He snorts. "Oh, for fuck's sake."

"I mean it."

"I can't just *leave*. I'm the accountant. It was all his idea but I'm the one. I could go to jail. I gotta try to make it right. We're living off of beans and rice."

"How much have you taken, Sam?"

He shakes his hung head.

"Your father and I . . . we could help you out. If you just quit now. Quit now and come home."

The shaking of his head, his shaggy head, slows and then stops. She has gazed at it, the whorls of fine hair, the hot slick skin, always a little oily, so many times in her life, every time she held him, comforted him. Whenever he was sick, whenever Silas hurt him. She wants to lean forward and kiss it, but holds back.

He says, "I still don't understand why you're here."

"You're my son. I love you."

"The things you said . . ."

"I don't remember!"

He withdraws his hands from hers, sits up straight, glares at her with his wet hard eyes. "That you couldn't help me. I was beyond help. I was weak to follow him. That I was ruining your life."

"No."

"That's what you said. You said I needed to break away. You'd be there if I decided to break away."

"That's what I'm saying now!" she cries.

"But you knew I wouldn't."

"Sam. I don't understand."

He's silent.

Her hands are tangled in her hair; her voice breaks: "It isn't supposed to be this way!"

But Sam is shaking his head again. "There's no way anything is supposed to be," he says. "Things can be as good or as bad as they want."

He gets up and heads for the door. But then he turns back, leans over her, and kisses her on the cheek. "This is so bizarre and fucked up," he whispers to her, "all of it." He picks up the whiskey bottle, holds it up to the light. He slides it into his pocket and walks out.

41.

In the morning, after dreamless unrestful sleep, she gets up, dresses without showering, and leaves her room. It's just after eight on a Saturday. Silas won't be out; she can rouse him from bed. She'll settle it with him. Come to some kind of agreement.

The air is cool, without a trace of moisture. Nothing is open but there's traffic anyway, as if people are driving for its own sake. She's walking briskly to combat the fatigue, her tennis shoes making no sound at all against the sidewalk, and it feels like the old life, tired and on the edge. She feels almost normal.

In the early light the house looks dumpier and more vulnerable. The gutters sag and the shingles are coming loose. She climbs the steps, tries the door, and when it proves to be locked she reaches for the bell. But she thinks better of it. Goes around to the back, lets herself into the yard through a low chain-link fence gate. A small screened back porch leads to another door, with a curtained window at eye level. She can make out a washer and dryer and part of the kitchen.

She tries this door, too, and it's also locked. But inside a rusted coffee can, on a bookcase slumped against the back wall of the house, she finds a key. It feels too heavy in her hand, and too cool, as if it has borrowed these properties from some other object, in some other place.

Silas used to lock his bedroom door, would lock her out, as early as age two. They found a way to jimmy it open—a tiny screwdriver or tweezers in the hole in the knob—but eventually Silas discovered this and stole everything in the house that could conceivably be used for unlocking. Derek began to keep a collapsible screwdriver on his key ring, but around the time he turned seven or eight, Silas managed to get his hands on a safety bolt, which he installed crudely on his side of the door, bypassing the knob entirely. They could have removed this, too, of course, when he was at school. If she remembers right, they may even have done so, once or twice. But the real answer was to give up.

This turned out to be the answer to a lot of things, with Silas.

Well, here are the results. They are cynical and unhappy here, on their own, and she and Derek are delusional and unhappy at home. She has created a family of miserable loners who seem incapable of helping one another.

Was there anything she could have done that would have resulted in a satisfactory outcome?

She needs to believe that the answer is no.

She slides the key into the lock, and a moment later she is standing in the messy kitchen, her heart pounding. Breaking and entering. But this isn't her real life, is it. This is where things are different. She is seeing if she can make things change. Hands shaking, she sets the key on the counter.

The house is quiet. She moves into the living room, which is as disorderly as the kitchen. The fingerprinted residue of cocaine smears the coffee table's filthy glass surface. Cut up plastic drinking straws and a razor blade. There's a wad of Kleenex stained by blood and an ashtray filled with cigarette butts and the twisted paper ends of joints.

A hallway leads away from here and she walks down it. The bathroom door is open, and three others are closed. No light is visible beneath one—a closet. She takes a breath and opens the next.

It is hard to imagine a sadder sight. Sam is lying asleep and fully clothed on an unmade bed, the sheets twisted together and trailing across the carpet, where movie and gaming magazines are spread within easy reach. The dresser drawers are all open and unfolded laundry spills out, mingling with the dirty shirts and pants that litter the floor. There's a smell of sweat and shit and come, and nothing hangs on the walls. The window shade is up. It looks out on an overgrown half-dead shrub and beyond it the back of another house.

She withdraws, pulls the door shut, then stands in the hallway drawing and releasing steady breaths. She remembers the game, Silas's game, a scene in which she walked through an empty apartment, with the intent of finding something, a handwritten letter, in a drawer. In her memory the experience seems real, no different from her memories of things she has actually done. If she stayed here, standing in the hallway, doing nothing, then nothing would happen, forever. This is how she feels. The world suddenly is very limited. So little seems possible—almost nothing, when you get down to it. She is struck suddenly by a powerful conviction, that she will exhaust this world's potentiality soon—that she will reach a city wall, or a high cliff, or a door that won't open, there will be nothing beyond this obstacle, and that will be the end. She can feel the membrane that separates this stunted universe from the next; for a moment it seems as though she can actually see it, the faint curvature of the circular world as it swallows its tail, closes in, sealing itself off from the horror of infinity. Her hand reaches out and finds the wall; the coarse unsanded surface feels very real. She walks to the end of the hall and opens the last door.

It is, by contrast, incredibly tidy. There are several computer screens set up on an angled desk, a case of reference books, an Oriental rug half covering a hardwood floor. The bed is made with bright red sheets, and the girl is curled underneath them, her red hair and cheek anemic-looking against the pillowcase. Beside her Silas is sitting up, his shirtless back against the headboard, with a paperback book in his hand. On his face is an expression of profound surprise.

Elisa feels a surge of excitement, almost joy. She stares at him. Then she turns and goes back to the kitchen and sits down at the table.

Silas appears a minute later, wearing boxer shorts and a clean white tee shirt. He has recovered from his astonishment. He says, "What the fuck."

"Sit down," she says, and the conviction in her voice surprises her; it does not match her emotions. "We have something to discuss."

He appears vulnerable here, without a drink in his hand. He's thin, she can see that he's unhealthy. But his eyes are alive with calculation.

After a moment he pulls out a chair and sits. On the counter behind him stands the object that preoccupied her yesterday, the mason jar filled with brown liquid. She intends to make demands, arrangements, to save his brother. Instead she says, "What is that?"

He frowns, turns, looks around. When he turns back to her, he's angry: she has surprised him again. "What's what?"

"That." She points. "In the jar."

Clearly he doesn't want to turn again, doesn't want to be tricked or thrown off balance. But he can't help it, he looks.

After a moment, he says, "I have no fucking idea."

"Really?"

"Some rotten shit from the fridge, I don't know. This is why you're here? You break into my house to ask me this?"

She says, "You have to let your brother go."

Silas squints at her. He drums his fingers on the tabletop; his other hand twitches on his bare knee. He looks like he should be smoking a cigarette and indeed glances around as if one might be there, freshly lit, waiting for his fingers.

"I don't get it," he says.

"Whatever you've done to him. Made him do. The money you stole. Let him go. Let him come home. Solve your own problems yourself."

Silas leans back, shaking his head. He holds out his palms. "What did he tell you—I made him do it? Steal?"

She waits.

"For what? My company?" He shakes his head. "No. I got problems, but I have a fucking *life*. *He's* the one with the real problems. Whatever he's stealing, it went up his nose or in his arm, it didn't go to me. And I'm risking my career to cover his ass. I would *love* for him to walk out that door," Silas says, pointing, leaning toward her across the table. "I'm sick of his shit. I share my house with him, my fucking work, everything, and he just fucks everything up. It's a good thing the startup fell apart, because he would have just fucked that up, too, right when it started getting good."

Elisa hesitates. Doubt is creeping in. To look at them, to look at both boys, the state of their rooms, she could believe him. But she doesn't.

"Your girl," she says. "Do you share her, too?"

Silas is shaking his head before she has even finished speaking. He throws his arm over the back of the chair. "Wow," he says. "Wow, that's awesome. Is that what he's telling you?

"Look," he goes on, "None of this is any of your business, Lisa, okay?" He's angry, his eyes are hard, but there is something strange in his voice, something she doesn't recognize, that is almost like sympathy. Was it always there? Even in the world she remembers? No, she tells herself, no, this world is different. It couldn't have been there. "You threw us over," he is saying. "That was your prerogative. But now it's mine to tell you to fuck off. If you want to take Sam with you when you do, more power to you. I would love it. Maybe then I wouldn't lose my job over him. But either do it, and leave me alone, or don't do it, and leave us both alone. My job is none of your business, my girlfriend is none of your business, the shit on my counter is none of your business. I could have predicted this," he says, looking tired and old. "That you would change your mind. What about Derek? Him too? Is he on board with this?"

She can't speak.

"That's what I thought. No, he makes too much fucking sense for that."

He stands up, pushes his chair in. She is surprised at how tall he is: he hadn't finished growing when he died. She wouldn't have predicted it. Again he gestures with his hand as though there's a cigarette in it. "You ought to go back to that shrink and have your head examined." He looks at the ceiling, then back at her. "I can't believe you did this. Came out here. Incredible."

"You should move your back door key," she says, and she is trying to sound defiant, but she just sounds like his mother telling him to put his things away. He is showing her his back, he is walking out of the room. "It took me ten seconds to find it."

Sitting there, illicitly, in her sons' kitchen, she is feeling her mind begin to rebel against it all: it would like to shut down now, reject everything, begin work on its own reality, some happy fantasy where it could exist in peace. But she has to resist: she has to consider whether or not Silas might be telling the truth. If perhaps she is wrong, and has always been wrong. About Silas and Sam and everything, in every possible world.

The answer can be found—Derek knows, Amos knows, Sam knows. Here, in this life, all the men have the information, and her role is to extract it, to wheedle it out of them, to beg them for it.

Silas is halfway down the hall now. She says, "Silas, wait!" And to her surprise he does, he stands there with his hand on the wall, close to where she touched it minutes ago. His back is to her. He's waiting.

"Where did you go? That time you ran away, when you were fifteen."

His hand drops from the wall and he half-turns toward her. He appears exhausted.

She says, "You remember—your lost weekend. You left school and didn't come back for days. Where were you? What did you do? We searched and searched." In her voice is real conviction, as if she actually remembers it, as if it actually happened.

But Silas is shaking his head. "I just wanted to be alone," he said. "That's all. I went off to be alone."

For a second he looks as though he's finished; he shifts his weight, he shows her his back. But then he turns back to face her. "And I didn't run away," he says. "I walked. It was easy. I just walked away and nobody followed me."

And now, as if in illustration, he does exactly that: walks down the hall, away from her, opens the bedroom door and passes through. The door closes, gently, and then everything is quiet again.

42.

She has one more day here. She has an idea about what to do, but isn't sure how to go about it. So she lies on her hotel bed, dozes for a short while, tries calling Sam several times. He doesn't answer.

Around noon she heads for the coffee shop she went to the previous day. There's a free internet connection—the first fifteen minutes are free, anyway. And her laptop battery is almost dead and she forgot to bring the power supply. But she works fast. Caltech, that's where Hugo Bonaventure teaches, and it's nearby. She tries to recall what he told her, the experiment his colleagues performed, and over her coffee finds the name of the man who heads the research team, and his office location. Buses go there: she plots a route. She is aware that it's Sunday, but sci- entists are in their labs on Sundays, she certainly remembers that much.

Of course this occurred to her before she left, though until now it hasn't coalesced into a plan of action. She has heard nothing from Hugo Bonaventure, and her offers to take Betsy out for coffee have gone unanswered. The plausible explanation she has been craving, the one that lies outside herself, has never seemed farther away. And now, in the wake of her conversations with Silas and Sam, she needs it.

This world is aberrant and wrong, and somebody needs to tell her this. Even if she can't go back. She will live in hell if she has to, if only somebody will please tell her that, yes, it's hell, and she does not belong here.

The buses are infrequent. She walks a long way to find the right stop, then is too late and she must wait in the heat for the next bus. She makes some transfers. She doesn't have the right change. She gets off, gets cash, buys some mints and asks for singles. It's an hour and a half before she reaches the campus, and she is exhausted and hot and feels like finding a tree to lie under and go to sleep. She wishes she'd taken the laptop out of her satchel, left it at the hotel. It's heavy.

Caltech is small, all of its buildings clustered within a single large city block. The buildings are dull and angular, sandlike, etched with strange patterns. She walks among them as if dazed, finds the one she wants, consults the directory board in the lobby. The air here is cool and almost nobody is around; she stands at the directory for a long time, listening to the sounds of her own breaths. Finally she climbs the stairs and finds the right office.

No one's there, of course; the door is locked. There is a schedule taped to it that refers to the spring semester already passed. She stands, thinking, for several minutes. Then she hears footsteps and looks up.

It's a tall young man, heavy and bearded, sweating, in a hurry. He moves past her and keys open a door a few offices down. When she reaches it, he is rummaging through a file cabinet, muttering under his breath.

"Excuse me?"

The boy looks up, startled—perhaps he passed her without even noticing she was there.

She says, "Where could I find Professor Simmons today?"

He blinks, stands up straight. "Uh. Lab?"

"Which building?"

"Or he might be at home. His wife's like nine months pregnant."

She waits.

"Downs? Like, right over there." He points. "I mean, it's the same building. Just, down the hall and through the double doors." She's about to thank him, but he says, "Wait, who are you?"

"He's working on something I'm involved in."

The boy blinks. He looks like the bass player from a seventies rock band. He says, "Hold on, I'll take you." He continues his search through the file drawer, seems to find what he wants in the form of a sheaf of heavily annotated, equation-covered papers. It is quaint, the idea that somebody would need to go somewhere to gather up some papers, in this electronic age. She likes it. The boy ushers her out into the hallway.

He walks a little too fast for her. She has to sort of run. They pass through the double doors, then another set, and then he stops and asks her to wait before turning to yet another door, this one protected by a proximity reader, in front of which the boy waves a lanyarded ID before entering.

She leans against a cinder-block wall with her eyes closed. The wall behind her is alive with some deep and thrumming energy. She doesn't fall asleep, or probably doesn't. When she opens her eyes a man is standing there. He is tall—are they all tall here?—and clean-shaven, with unkempt sandy hair just beginning to go gray. His cheeks are a bit sunken, his chin too long. He's dressed in jeans and a tee shirt that says, in a flowing script, *Choose Rudeness*. He says, not rudely, "You were looking for me?"

"Professor Simmons?"

"Yes."

Elisa licks her lips. "I'm Elisa Brown," she says. "A friend of yours sent you some things of mine. Some objects."

Puzzlement. "Who's your friend?"

"Hugo Bonaventure? He's at SUNY Reevesport for the semester. That's where I work."

The man's face is friendly, open, but she understands she doesn't have much time. The name Hugo Bonaventure does not seem to register with him.

"It's your experiment, correct, with the vibrating metal flange? That is also not vibrating?"

He appears surprised. "Yes, that's right."

"This man Bonaventure, he sent you some things of mine. To test. To see if . . . if . . ."

Simmons is waiting.

"He said you could determine . . . where they were from."

It takes a moment or two for his mind to churn through the possibilities, to decide that she is mistaken or not worth his time. She wishes there were something, anything, she could say to halt the process, go back in time by a minute or two, devise the perfect appeal to make him listen. But no, he's done with her, he is shaking his head, he is about to say goodbye.

Then he says, "Oh wait—that guy?"

She waits.

"Curly haired guy? From Belgium or something?"

"That's him."

Simmons sighs. There's a bit of sweat on his face, a light sheen, and he wipes it away with his hand. With the other he digs a phone from his pocket and glances at it, at the time.

He says, "Okay, follow me."

They trace her previous path through the building in reverse, and at equally high speed. At some point the phone in Simmons's hand rings and he begins talking into it about certain grocery items that need to be bought. "I got somebody here," he says, and pockets the phone, and then they're at his office door, which he opens with a key attached to a belt loop by a length of string.

It's a mess. Elisa is strangely gratified to see an academic office that adheres so completely to type. Books and papers are piled on every surface but two: a chair behind Simmons's desk, and a chair in front of it. He neither sits in the former nor offers her the latter. He is pawing through a giant pile of mail.

"He sent me some stuff. The guy."

She nods, though he isn't looking at her and can't see it. "He says you're colleagues," she says.

"No."

"But you know him?"

"He teaches here. He's not a scientist. He's more of a . . ." His elbow makes contact with a pile of mail, a different one, and it topples, spilling papers and packages onto the floor. "Fuck. He's more of a gadfly. He's in HPS."

"HPS?"

Simmons has found what he's been looking for: a brown padded envelope, torn open at one end. He sticks his hand in. "History and philosophy of science. Google him." He pulls the hand out, and there they are: her lipstick and list. The envelope is tossed back onto the desk. He offers her the objects.

"Guy thought I could test them or something. Or asked me to. Probably I'm just part of some little experiment."

She takes her things back. The envelope is lying there, still bulging slightly from Simmons's hand; it is addressed with a marker, in a bold near-scribble. There's a note inside, no doubt; she wants it. But she can't bring herself to ask for it. "Experiment?" she says.

"He pokes scientists, tries to make them react. You know."

She says, "So you can't test them."

And now Simmons seems to notice her for the first time. He looks directly into her eyes, scowling slightly, as if in order to figure out what precisely it is he's got here. She feels like a fool.

"You really think these things are from another world?" he asks.

Slowly, she slides the lipstick and list into her satchel. "I don't know what I think. Something happened to me. I'm just trying to figure it out."

He's nodding, nodding. Elisa is beginning to feel the full force of his concentration. She is attracted to him, to this intensity. It is akin to her own, she feels—or akin to what she once was. "I'm a scientist too," she blurts. "Or used to be."

But Simmons just shakes his head. "That guy isn't going to help you," he says, and shows her the door.

It's true, what Simmons told her—Hugo Bonaventure is a sociologist. She finds this out ten minutes later, in the computer lab on the first floor, after Googling him, like she was told to do. He is an eccentric, much beloved among undergraduates. He is interested in metaphysics, mass delusion, and the notion of science as religion.

His résumé is available on the HPS website. It's many pages long, listing dozens of papers and several co-authored books. Under the heading "Work In Progress" is a study titled "Science Faction: Why We Believe in Alien Abductions, Parallel Worlds, Superpowers, and More." The names of several collaborators are listed, and one of them happens to be printed on a business card Elisa already has in her satchel, along with a web address, the address of a physics blog she hasn't yet bothered to visit. She visits it now, and there he is, a collaborator himself. Hugo Bonaventure, collaborator on an ongoing study, "Science Faction," with Betsy Orosco.

43.

On the plane home she begins shaking. She feels no particular emotion; she's just shaking, as if she's very cold. But she isn't cold. The woman sitting beside her leans ostentatiously away and eventually presses the button to summon a flight attendant.

"Ma'am? Are you all right?"

Elisa's voice wavers as she says, "I'm fine."

"Do you need medical attention, ma'am?"

"No."

"Can I get you anything?"

"No, thank you."

A few minutes later her teeth are chattering and the hiss of the ventilation system is making her feel sick. The flight attendant comes back with a cup full of ice and a small bottle of gin. Elisa accepts it, pours it. Drinks it.

Only as she is falling asleep do the tremors subside. She wakes at landing with a desperate need to pee, and hobbles out of the airplane in actual pain. The feeling of release, when she reaches the women's room, is profound, and she presses her palm to her forehead and moans.

Derek isn't picking up his cell. It's Sunday, she doesn't know what he could be doing. She gets a cab. Out the window it's cloudy and cool and her body aches from sleeplessness and her bout of shaking.

At home, something's different, she isn't sure what. The truck is missing, but she calls out to Derek anyway. In the bedroom, she dumps her bags on the floor, then lies down on the bed. She falls asleep. When she wakes up it's dark and she notices that the closet door is open. It looks half empty.

She walks down the stairs. "Derek?" The only light is from the kitchen, where she finds a piece of paper folded into thirds with her name written on it in his handwriting. She picks it up, turns it over, unfolds it, and reads.

> Lisa,
>
> I had to leave for now. I need some time to think things over, and I think you do too. I'm staying with a colleague and will be in touch.
>
> Maybe you're right and we should revisit the past. But I don't know why you would go to California instead of telling me what's going on. I assume you had a bad trip. I hope I'm wrong.
>
> Sorry
> Derek

When she's finished reading it a second time she folds it back up and drops it on the table. Through the open kitchen window, from somewhere far off, she hears the sound of a girl screaming, then the scream trailing off into hysterical laughter. She goes to the refrigerator, pulls out a block of cheese, and eats the entire thing standing there with the door open. Then she goes to the living room and plays the game again.

PART THREE

44.

Time begins to accelerate.

Elisa spends the next two months attempting to restore her life to the one she lost. She throws out most of the clothes in her closet, then buys new clothes in her old size, as an incentive. She is almost there anyway, having eaten little over the past two weeks, and continues walking back and forth to work.

She gets an apartment. Derek is shocked; perhaps this is her intention. They have lunch together every week or two, and each time seems, to her, more pointless than the last. Derek's shock gives way to hurt and eventually to acceptance. She doesn't tell him anything, and doesn't ask him anything, about the past. (She does not go to see Amos, either, despite the voicemail messages he's been leaving.) Soon, she is certain, Derek will realize that there is no longer any real reason to meet, and they'll stop, and their separation will harden into established fact. Her new place is downtown, four blocks from the frame shop. It's a one-bedroom apartment, and she has decided to use the living room as an art studio. Through one of the windows it is possible to see a little wedge of lake, tucked up against the diagonal of a church steeple: a real lake view, without having to climb onto the roof.

Sam doesn't reply to her e-mails. She tries calling him at Infinite Games, but is told he isn't in. She doesn't leave a message.

The bearded man who has her old job at Killian Tech is still there in the corner office, plugging away. She looks at the company website and finds out that his name is Wayne Pratt. He has a personal website where he posts close-up photographs he has taken of various plants. His CV is available for download, as well. She downloads it: it now sits on the desktop of her computer.

She stops by the frame shop twice. Both times, he isn't there. In retrospect, she thinks she probably knew he wouldn't be, at those times. Desire seems very far away right now. She doesn't miss him; something about being in this body, being this Lisa, has undone her desperation. But she misses desire itself, she misses need.

After reading the classifieds every morning for a month, she sees an ad for a blue 1991 Honda Accord with 153,000 miles on it. She buys it, then sells the Intrepid. She spends some of the difference on beaded seat covers like her old ones. The first time she drives the car with the seat covers on, she cries. She considers, then abandons, the notion of trying to crack the windshield in the same pattern as the old one.

Her separation from Derek deepens her friendship with Judith. She resists this for a couple of weeks, as it wasn't part of the old life, and the woman is annoying. But it is nice to have a friend. After a time she begins to look forward to their lunches with nervous excitement, joy even, and she doesn't understand why. It is almost a cleansing ritual. They usually eat in the food court at the supermarket, where Judith can talk as loudly as she likes and Elisa can scream with laughter. Elisa never talks about herself, just listens to her friend natter on.

After one of these lunches, picking up a few groceries before returning to work, Elisa passes Betsy in the tea and coffee aisle. Their eyes meet and the younger woman looks away. Did she recognize her? She's thinner now, so perhaps not.

She begins to spend much of her free time online, on the MetaphysicsNet parallel worlds forum. She actually registers and chooses a screen name: CrackedLisa. She regrets the name a couple of weeks later, but by that time she's already begun to develop her identity.

The forum is carefully moderated. No apparent crazies. They divide into two main camps, people who philosophize and theorize about the concept, and people who think they have evidence of its real-world existence. It is not common for people to believe they are in a parallel world; at least no one says so. But she senses they are there, lurking. She reads back through the archives, three years' worth, digesting it all. People recommend books and she borrows them from the library. It becomes her hobby. She starts painting diptychs: nearly identical panels, save for slight differences. She doesn't tell anybody what she means by them. Of course there's nobody to tell except Judith, who wouldn't understand.

If there is pain from her separation, she is not conscious of it. She doesn't long for Derek. It's as though he's a food that spoiled and that made her sick, and now she never wants to eat it again. She is certain this will change, but so far nothing.

It's as though she's suspended between the two worlds. Or living in a world that is one subtracted from the other. Nothing at all seems real now.

45.

October. It's unseasonably warm, even under a dark gray sky. The orange and yellow boughs of maples whip in a hot wind but the leaves don't fall, not yet. The streets seem empty. The details don't match. It's fall break at school so she gets a couple of days off, and decides it's time. She goes to the frame shop. He's there. He has grown his winter beard already. She asks him to come to lunch.

They eat at the usual place, the Asian café. Elisa watches him carefully as he eats. He is so familiar: the careful way he has of keeping his beard free of food: he opens his mouth a little too wide, takes smaller bites. (Or is this, in fact, familiar? Is this a thing he used to do? It's suddenly unclear what is memory of their past together, what she has generated as part of her fantasy of him.) He has asked for an extra napkin and holds it under his chin every time he lifts the chopsticks to his lips. His movements aren't stiff, they're controlled. Fluid and hard. He talks about jazz. She doesn't want him to talk about jazz, he's not supposed to be interested in it. But she nods, listening.

She mentions her separation and his brow furrows as it does every time he must process new information. He makes a sound, a kind of clicking with his mouth, like a hard drive being accessed. The clicking isn't right—he didn't used to do that. She'd like to point it out to him, to make him self-conscious about it, but it's too soon for that kind of intimacy.

Elisa buys. She asks him if he really needs to go back right away. His mouth clicks.

They go to her apartment for sex and she gives him exactly what he wants when he wants it. He is taken by surprise and doesn't last very long. He's embarrassed, in fact he apologizes. "Don't apologize," she says. Her Larry wouldn't apologize. Or would he? The truth is, she doesn't know anymore. She didn't have these experiences with her Larry. Maybe he would have apologized. Maybe he would have come even sooner. While he dresses, he tells her she should come over and get a look at this new turntable he bought. He corrects himself: "New old turntable." It's got a belt drive, and he just installed a new belt. She doesn't understand what this is, or why she's being told, but okay. "Call me, then, we'll make a date." When he's gone she savors the taste of him before making coffee. That much is right, anyway. She's nervous, her hands tremble, but her heart is steady. It's not what she expected, none of it is.

She sees Derek at the supermarket. His shirt's tucked in and he has combed his hair. She can tell he's trying to make himself attractive to women. To a certain kind of woman—not the kind she has become. The kind Amos Finley and he—and she—tried to make her into. He turns and sees her and she expects him to pretend he didn't, to turn away, the way Betsy did. But instead he muscles his cart around and comes right up to her, and appears disappointed when he arrives.

Their pleasantries feel ridiculous. They have never engaged in them with each other before.

She says, "You were going to say something."

He is gripping the handle of his grocery cart and his knuckles stand out in sharp relief. "I don't know."

This is not something he often says. He won't look at her. He looks softer, as if he's been eating more without her there to stop him. This should make him look more like the Derek of the old life, but somehow he doesn't.

"It's kind of ridiculous," he says, finally. "That we're apart. And apart from the boys." Now he looks up. "I'm not asking you to come back, I'm just saying. The point of cutting off the boys was so we could stay together."

"And?" she says.

It's a mistake. It makes him angry. "Jesus, Lisa."

"I'm sorry."

But he's already turning away, hauling the cart behind him. "Nothing was ever easy with you," he tells her over his shoulder, and as she watches his broad back recede through the crowd she thinks, Easy? Are things supposed to be easy?

46.

One day she is walking past Killian Tech and sees that the little Zen sandbox and photo of the blond woman are missing from the corner office desk. So is the diploma that used to hang on the wall. Impulsively, she walks in. She asks for the head tech.

She is a bit surprised at the man who appears: gray-haired, in his sixties, he is lanky, stooped, confident in his demeanor. He's got a bandage on his elbow; something tells her he fell off a bicycle. She has never seen him before. The head tech she remembers was stocky, in his forties, a man named Ronnie. She introduces herself and asks if they need a lab manager.

"Yes, we do," he says, surprised. "How did you know that?"

She explains: waiting at the bus stop, she used to notice the man in the corner, hard at work. And then today his things were gone. "I'm detail oriented," she says.

But he appears puzzled. "How did you know Wayne was the lab manager?"

"I have some experience with this kind of work." Which is not really an answer.

When he doesn't reply, she says, "Listen—do you have a few minutes? Interview me for the job."

"Why don't you just drop off a CV?"

"I will, I will. But let's talk."

He opens his mouth to say no. Then he hesitates, says, "I know you. You work in the biology department, don't you."

This gives her pause—she didn't anticipate being recognized. But she says, "Right."

At last he shrugs, invites her to follow.

Elisa experiences a rising excitement. She was going to wait on this, she was going to bide her time. She's unprepared. It's late afternoon on a Thursday, her office closed early because a construction project snapped an underground power line. She is dressed like her old self, in jeans and a cardigan sweater. Non-Ronnie leads her down a hallway and it isn't quite right, it isn't what she has in her head. The floor plan was different. Is different. But it's close enough, with its drop ceiling and muted patterned wallpaper and faint buzz from overhead fluorescents. This is where she used to work—it has to be.

Ronnie's office wasn't a separate room; he just occupied the corner of the storeroom that lay at the end of the hallway. He didn't spend a lot of time there, he was usually out on the floor working. The room was lined with steel shelves packed with boxes, papers, glass items, chemicals in bottles. When occasionally he would summon her for a meeting, he would enter in front of her and squeeze into the small space behind his desk, and gesture toward a plastic patio chair, inviting her to sit.

But this hallway doesn't lead to the storeroom. Or if it does, they don't go there. Instead this manager, the new manager, opens a hollow-core door into a cramped office cheaply lined with wood paneling. There's a file cabinet in the corner. The lights here are buzzing even louder than in the hall. He points at a plywood waiting-room chair, upholstered in worn gray fabric. Then he folds himself into one himself, behind the desk.

"So what experience do you have?" he says, when she has descended, nervously, into her seat.

"I managed a lab for eight years. Very much like this one."

"You know what it is we do?"

She nods. "Outsourced research, genetic testing, forensic contract work, that kind of thing."

The man shrugs. "How many clients did your old lab have?"

Same as this one, she thinks. "It varied, depending on the size of the projects. Anywhere from three or four big jobs at a time to a couple dozen small ones . . . all told, there were thirty or forty clients we had regular contact with, maybe five or six we had work from regularly, that made up the bulk of the business."

He is looking steadily at her, his chin supported on his pointer fingers. "This was where?"

"Madison, Wisconsin," she says without thinking.

"You really should bring by your CV."

But she can't resist. She is looking around this office, thinking about the time Ronnie confessed an affair to her—a woman he'd met at a seminar in Rochester, they'd been seeing each other for a few months, and he was racked with guilt but couldn't stop. As he talked, her gaze was fixed on a poster over his right shoulder, some kind of parody of the New York subway map. The stops had labels like WEIRDOS and PIEROGIES. No posters are hung in this room. It appears that, like Ronnie, this man doesn't spend much time in his office. Suddenly she wishes she smoked, that she was smoking. She wants something to hold. She says, "A typical day here would probably go like this. Somebody, let's say you, or me, if you hired me, unlocks in the morning. You take a clipboard off the rack and do a walkthrough, turning on the machines and computers, flipping on the lights, checking on the petri dishes and so on. Then the techs would start rolling in around a quarter to eight to fire up the mice, check the cages, what have you."

He is scowling at her now, concentrating deeply, and she feels she is making a mistake, but can't stop talking. This isn't like her, she thinks—but it is, it is, it's like the old her, the missing one, who liked to stay up late in the lab at night, the one who loved men too much, the one who gave herself to Derek, to motherhood, and never looked back. And she remembers why she never looked back. It is embarrassing to be this person. She is exuberant and imprecise and makes a fool of herself. She breaks things, ruins things. Elisa tells herself Stop, don't blow it—but she keeps on. "For the rest of the day," she says, "they'll be logging results and crunching numbers. You'll have work to do for the city, I'd imagine, environmental stuff, a few nonconfidential police jobs, and by ten in the morning I'll have fielded calls from a couple of clients, handled some inquiries, and so on. The office manager, I mean. Afternoons we prepare portfolios for people, and I would compile those and send them off electronically, or if they want them hand-delivered with an explanation I will go do that. We also take care of small jobs in the afternoons—well water testing, drug testing, that kind of thing, usually this falls to whoever the intern is, a college kid generally. And then you usually leave by five thirty, stop in and see your mother or pick up something to eat—" And here of course she is thinking of Ronnie, Ronnie and his stern and handsome wife Gwen, and Ronnie's mother at the nursing home and the sandwiches he used to tell her he was going to order before he left, and did Elisa want one?, and she realizes that this will not do, this man isn't Ronnie and the lab is different. "I don't know what you do," she goes on, "but I double-check that everything that's supposed to be powered off is powered off, and everything that's supposed to be running is running, and lock the mouse lab and storeroom, and then I lock the front door and I go home."

She is panting and feels faintly nauseous. They're silent together for a moment. The head tech's face is taut, his eyes bright.

"Well, we don't have mice here," he says.

She can only muster an "Oh."

"Also, I don't . . ." He screws up his face, tilts his head, gazes at her with one eye half closed. "I'm not sure . . . my mother doesn't live around here."

"That was just a . . . an example."

"Is this some kind of joke?" the man asks. "Did Dean put you up to this? I don't understand the bit about my mother."

She keeps very still. Her sweater itches her and she clutches her bag to her lap.

"Something like that."

"You seem to have worked at a lab. And we do some of those things. Environmental testing, work for the city. Not the police. You've done this kind of thing, you say."

"Yes."

"But . . . this is a practical joke?"

"No, no," she says. "I just meant . . . I didn't mean . . ."

He is leaning forward now, palms flat on the desk. "I find this whole encounter very odd," he says.

"I'm sorry."

"You are the woman from the biology department, aren't you? Laura?"

"I was only—I'm only looking for another job."

He stares at her for a long time, and as he does, his face grows longer and harder, like something that has melted and then cooled.

He says, "I'm thinking it probably isn't going to be this one."

He says, "Do you want to explain yourself? Should I call the biology department?"

There's nothing she can say that will explain anything. She is afraid that he will get up and block the door. She doesn't think he would, but what does she know? About this man, or about anyone? People are who you think they are until they do the thing that proves you wrong. Her head has begun to pound.

She says, slowly, "It's not a joke, it's just . . . I thought it might impress you."

Silence. This is inadequate. But she doesn't have anything else.

"How about," she continues, "if I just get up and leave now, and never come back. This was a mistake. I'm sorry."

His expression does not change. She gets up. She leaves and doesn't go back.

47.

It's winter before she hears from Derek again. Or not quite, really: the week after Thanksgiving, snow falling and blowing in wild circles in the street, several inches already on the ground. It's a Saturday and she is watching this spectacle out the window and thinking what everybody else in Reevesport is thinking, which is that their hope for a prolonged autumn without scarves and gloves is now shattered. Of course there's a part of her that likes this weather very much, likes the feeling of forced indoorsness, the excuse to drink more hot coffee. She is glad to be alone. Thanksgiving she spent, for the first time in years, in Chicago, with her parents, and though she expected to be depressed by their advancing age and eccentricity, she found them almost charming. They didn't comment on her separation from Derek. They seemed genuinely glad to see her. They appeared very firmly in love with each other and in the idea of isolation from the rest of the world.

The first thing Derek says when he calls her is, "Crazy weather, huh?" and before she can stop herself it makes her laugh.

"I don't think we'll ever get good at that," she says. "Small talk."

"I suppose not."

There is a moment of awkward silence. It's strange to experience: they have shared so many hours of companionable silence in a quarter century—more—that the awkwardness seems to belong to someone else.

Derek says, "What are you doing right now? Can we meet?"

"Drinking coffee. Come on over."

She says this without thinking—he's never been here of course. To this apartment. His silence is answer enough; she corrects herself. "How about the Edge?" This is a café not far from here, though of course he'll have to drive. Though this only matters to her—he likes driving.

Fine, he says, he'll see her in an hour.

Like everyone on the street, she hasn't gotten the winter clothes out of storage yet, so she puts on a hooded sweatshirt and a canvas jacket on top of that, then walks to the café with her head down and her bare hands curled deep into her pockets. There are the sounds of wind and traffic, but no voices; people passing say nothing to each other, nor to their phones. Some crows somewhere are freaking out. It feels like the end of the world.

The café is warm and moist, the windows fogged and dripping, and the staff are playing loud music, as though to compete with the wind. She imagines that Derek will be annoyed by the music and she's right; though he says nothing, he can't resist training a sour expression in the direction of the counter. They both order black coffees—her inquiring look at Derek, a lifetime milk-and-sugar man, in both worlds as far as she can tell, goes unacknowledged—and take a table far from the window. On the bulletin board behind Derek is a pristine pull-tabbed ad for bass guitar lessons and a lost cat notice. She thinks, We are still married.

"I'll get right to the point," he says. "I've stopped going to Amos."

"Why?"

He levels an annoyed gaze at her. "We went to him to stay together. We're not together."

Her instinct tells her to apologize now, but her instincts are bad, so she says nothing. After a pause, during which his body jerks the chair, loudly, into a new position, he goes on.

"I don't know if you think this is permanent."

Is it a question? She says, "I have no idea what this is."

"Well, I think this is a trial separation."

"Okay."

He scowls, sighs. "Don't do that. Capitulate."

"I'm not capitulating. I'm just encouraging you to get to the point."

"Okay. Sorry."

She savors the sorry as he gathers himself to speak.

"Now that we've been apart for a while, it all seems so . . ."

She waits.

"It's not that I regret this. But it's hard to remember why I was so upset that you went to see the boys. It made me . . . it felt like the ultimate transgression. Given our arrangement. But now it seems more sensible." So far he has been staring into his untouched coffee mug, but now he looks at her face. "Maybe the arrangement wasn't sustainable. Maybe it was time to change. I still have no idea what happened to you at that conference, and if we get back together—"

They're both surprised to hear him say this and he appears, for a moment, to be choking back tears. He sips his coffee with a wince before he resumes speaking, now with his head down.

"All I'm saying is, it doesn't matter what happened. What the situation is now is all that matters. And I'm thinking we should apologize to the boys. And try to start over."

"With each other?" she asks him.

"With the boys."

Neither of them speaks for a minute. The girls behind the counter are laughing at something. They have turned the music down—Elisa realizes now that she and Derek are the only customers.

"It just isn't right," he says, and there is no danger now that he will choke up. His face is hard; his head looks heavy, like a boulder. He's showing his age: the cheeks a bit sunken, the lines deeper. He carries it well. He has always looked best under the weight of some burden.

He says, "It isn't right that we're all scattered like this. I don't know how it happened."

Elisa pats his hand where it is loosely clenched on the tabletop, then crosses her arms over her chest.

48.

They decide to write a letter, a paper letter, and mail it. To Derek, this makes things more official. Neither of them suggests doing it together, in person; instead each of them writes a draft and they compare them via e-mail.

Elisa's reads:

> Dear Boys,
>   Things have been changing in our lives and we wanted to talk
> to you about these changes. We have separated, but are in close
> touch with each other, and have come to realize that it was wrong to
> cut off contact with you years ago. We realize that it would be
> difficult for you to forgive, and don't expect you to. But we want to
> open the lines of communication. Will you talk with us about this?
>   We are so sorry. We hope that we can all be some kind of family
> again.
>
> With love,
> Elisa and Derek

It takes her ten minutes to write the letter and two hours to decide
whether or not to sign it "Mom and Dad." When it's settled, she opens
her e-mail to send the draft to Derek, and finds that he already has sent
his to her:

> Silas and Sam:
>
> It is probably a shock to find a letter from your parents in your
> mailbox, and I hope you have opened it and are reading it now. If
> you haven't—if you instead threw the letter away unopened—then
> we can hardly blame you, given our recent history. We are writing
> to tell you that we now believe our decision three years ago to cut
> off communication with you was wrong: it was extreme, insulting,
> and unnecessary, and the worst part is, it didn't even work. It may
> surprise you to learn that we are now separated and living apart,
> and we are separated from you as well. And in a sense perhaps you
> are, and maybe always have been, separated from each other. This
> last is also our fault, certainly as much as it has ever been yours.
> We are finally beginning to accept that we were not good parents;
> we did not deal with your troubles well, nor our own, either.
>
> This realization is particularly difficult for me, as I grew up, at
> first, without a good father, and later with no father at all. My

father was a bad man—he was domineering, belittling, violent, and sadistic, and he beat my mother and nearly drove her to madness when I was a boy. It was a relief when he finally left, and over the years of my late childhood I watched my mother transform herself from a tired, beaten-down victim to a self-sufficient, strong, loving parent. I admire her deeply, and cherish the relationship I have with her today. I am glad she has been a part of your lives, and I know that I hurt her terribly with the decision your mother and I made together. Maybe she has been in touch with you—I have not asked her.

I never talked much about my father to you, because I didn't want him to have any effect on my family, but now I fear that he has had all too powerful an effect, and I have allowed his influence to ruin our lives together. I am sorry. I have lived a life of fear and passivity, and look at where it has brought us.

We would like to ask you to please consider restoring communication with us.

This letter is not signed, and neither is the e-mail he sent it to her in. Derek has never said these things to her. He never said anything about being afraid, or feeling passive, never told her that his father beat his mother.

The loneliness she feels, sitting in her apartment in front of her laptop, is so profound that she wants to go to Derek's house, to go home, take him to bed. Beg him if necessary. Instead she sends him her version, and a few minutes later he agrees that it is the better choice.

They send the letter; the boys do not reply. Eventually Derek sends his version. They are still waiting.

49.

Now she returns to her apartment. Now she gives up trying to remake this life into the old. She drinks, heavily, every Friday night with Judith. This was Elisa's idea, and Judith seems delighted by it, though it isn't as if she doesn't have lots of other friends, with more in common than she has with Elisa. Elisa should be more grateful, she thinks. Indeed, this new ritual is a kind of penance, for the days, some months ago, when she thought she might become friends with Betsy, the physicist. But clearly the woman has decided that she is some kind of freak. In retrospect this attempt at friendship seems silly, and an insult to Judith, her actual confidante and reliable, if ill-matched, pal. One of the things they talk about is Larry, whom Elisa sees again, several times more, with a growing sense of futility and effort and unease. It just isn't him, he isn't the man she loved, and she isn't the woman who loved him. It isn't even close, really, and soon she stops returning his calls. She avoids walking past the frame shop now and doesn't eat at the Asian café. She artificially maintains the sense, in her own mind, that theirs is a relationship coming to an end, so that she can have something to talk about with Judith. But in truth it never really got off the ground.

She thinks about Derek all the time. She would like to make amends but isn't sure what she wants to do with them. So she does nothing. They, too, have stopped getting together for coffee.

Elisa no longer wants to go back. Indeed, she is increasingly frightened, throughout the month of January, by the possibility that she might now be sent back against her will, in an instant, the same way she got here. She begins to think in terms of cause and effect: What did I do to cause this? What should I do to prevent it from happening again? She once feared the apparent randomness of her situation. Now she fears that some intelligence might be behind it, after all. She lies awake at night in her apartment with her jaw clenched, imagining having to mourn Silas a second time.

And as for Silas, he has disappeared. The forums say that he has left Infinite Games, though no one knows why. Minefield hasn't posted for weeks. She doesn't know where Sam is, either.

The one thing she does with any regularity that gives her some satisfaction, or at least some relief from her boredom and anxiety: she spends several hours a night on MetaphysicsNet. This allows her to transition from eating to sleeping without drinking too heavily, though she does drink. There is an almost frenetic level of activity on the parallel worlds forum. She begins to wonder if what happened to her happened to many people, at the same time, all of them conspiring in anonymous silence, afraid to speak out. At times she feels as though the claim is on the verge of being made, by almost everyone. And then, at other times, she feels completely alone.

Every day somebody seems to have discovered a new book, or study, or TV program, or blog on the subject. Every day the full membership gathers in a thread devoted to the latest thing and discusses it frantically. Elisa begins to think of the other forum members as actual friends. Joereilly lives in Palo Alto and in his avatar is posed, fat and bearded, in front of a sports car. Misstake is a lesbian with bangle earrings. Rare Fern is from Vancouver, British Columbia, and is supposedly a twenty-five-year-old woman whom all the men on the forum constantly flirt with. Of course she might as well be a man, any of them might be anyone. She has exchanged several private messages, and more recently e-mails, with a woman who calls herself DippedInSunshine, but whose real name is Patricia. Patricia is a divorced mother of three adult children, the youngest now in college. She is unfailingly cheerful, both on the forum and in private correspondence, but not, Elisa senses, frivolously so. Her cheer is genuine and stems from an actual, if groundless, belief that things will turn out all right for Elisa.

Elisa has told her about the letters they sent to the boys. She has told her about her guilt, Silas's disappearance. She doesn't tell her that Silas is dead, in a parallel world. Patricia's responses have been perhaps the only kindnesses she has been done in many months that actually have had any effect. They are written in an evident rush, in a kind of rolling, opportunistic grammar, punctuated only with ellipses. *I know this is hard to accept . . . but you will love again . . . your wayward boy and romance as well . . . to be grieving . . . is good for the soul . . . you need to heal . . . it will take time . . . but believe me your life has just begun . . . .*

In this, anyway, Patricia is mistaken: Elisa turns forty-six in February and feels very much as though her life is mostly over. Derek actually takes her out to dinner. He gives her a handbag as a present. She is fairly certain a woman helped him pick it out—it's all wrong. She ought to be moved by this, by his sad effort, but she can't muster the proper emotion. Derek looks older; the planes of his face have shifted. All through dinner she thinks, We're going to die soon. Nothing is said about either divorcing or reuniting.

For some months Elisa has known that there is an annual conference of the MetaphysicsNet community. It is actually a combined event between MetaphysicsNet and a larger internet forum devoted to science fiction movies and television. There are presentations from cable TV networks, panels devoted to popular shows, and lectures from the more game or nerdy scientists and researchers in various cutting-edge topics—antigravity, rocket propulsion, theoretical physics, and the like. The scientists who actually populate the parallel worlds forum seem to regard the conference as a kind of vacation from their real lives—an opportunity to talk about the things their colleagues find strange or uninteresting.

Patricia tells her to come. *You will love it . . . it could be the beginning of a new life for you . . . restore your faith in others . . . the people are wonderful . . . you will meet lifelong friends and companions . . .* The conference is in July, in North Carolina. She buys a ticket and reserves a hotel room.

In March, Judith invites her to go out of town for the weekend. They drive together to Toronto and they do there the same thing they do in Reevesport—drink too much and talk about men. Or rather Judith talks about men while Elisa laughs. She finds it easier and easier to laugh with Judith, and this should make their time together restorative. But the laughter leaves her with a hangover—it feels fake, it hurts her throat and face, and in the morning, after Judith, she is prone to crying jags. She succumbs to one of these in their hotel room their second morning in the city and Judith climbs into her bed and holds Elisa in her arms. This is a fine gesture; nobody has touched her in months. But it just feels awkward. She stops crying, not because she's finished, but because she wants Judith to get out of her bed. Later they go to a museum, they go to a show. Then, on Monday, they listen to right-wing radio as they drive back to Reevesport.

In April, Elisa gets a lump at the back of her jaw. She thinks, This is the beginning of the end. The doctor says it's a swollen lymph gland and tells her it will go away. In May, it goes away.

In June she fucks a librarian who, when it's over, says to her, "You could have at least pretended to like it." Also she gets a call from Derek but the ringing stops before she can answer. Maybe he changed his mind. Maybe he dialed her by mistake.

Someone named highdigger appears on the parallel worlds forum. He seems to be a young man, with a young man's presumptions and confidence. He asks a lot of questions, and his sig line comes from Wilhelm Reich. He says he thinks maybe he'll go to the conference. When, in the last week of June, he calls somebody an idiot for assuming that a particular movie plot is scientifically plausible—*Your naïveté disgusts me*—the chill she feels reaches all the way to her toes. She is sure this is Silas. A wave of recrimination appears to drive him into hiding. Elisa sends a private message—*Who is this?*—that goes unanswered.

In July she takes a week off and drives to North Carolina for the conference.

50.

She's driving. A Thursday morning in July, hot outside, so the windows of her Honda are down and the highway air is rushing in. It's the third hour of a daylong trip from the town where she is living, barely, a life without apparent purpose, to the town where she will meet, for the first time, her imaginary friends.

Her name is Elisa Macalaster Brown. It has been a long time since she's driven alone on a highway for more than a few minutes, and she is surprised to find that she is frightened. Everyone is driving aggressively, coming up close behind her, flashing their brights, swerving into the passing lane and blowing by. Their cars are sleek, the windows closed, the engines making almost no sound. The big rigs, on the other hand, are extravagantly loud. Their trailers bounce and rumble and sway over her, and she hugs the wheel as they pass, terrified of being sucked into the slipstream. She regards this fear as good. It means she doesn't want to die.

She breaks for lunch at a truck stop outside Harrisburg. She orders a cheeseburger and a strawberry milkshake, but when they arrive she only wants the milkshake. Fat men in plaid shirts turn from the counter every few minutes and look at her. On the way out, she buys a bottle of Visine and a pair of aviator sunglasses. In the rearview mirror she looks like a character in a movie about the apocalypse.

Her satchel is open beside her on the passenger seat. Inside are magazines, books, her computer, and a folder of conference materials, including a schedule, some coupons, and an ID tag attached to a lanyard. The lanyard is printed over and over with the phrase *TIME COP Thursdays This Fall on SciFiTV.* Of this conference she has no expectations, no hopes. She is simply trusting Patricia. Judith is a bit jealous of this mysterious other friend from the internet—she seems to have been hoping she would be invited along. Not that she would have come if Elisa had asked.

Elisa has a picture in her mind of Patricia: a tiny woman, elfin, with big ears and an innocent, sprightly manner. In her imagination, Patricia wears red Keds, like a child, and speaks very slowly, in an even, breathy monotone.

Somewhere in Maryland, she has to stop and pee, but the rest stop she has chosen is entirely out of order. There are no signs, no caution tape, it's just abandoned. She does what many before her have apparently done: she follows a rough trail into the woods behind the restrooms and squats among the trees. The sound of the highway has nearly been swallowed up by the vegetation, even though she can still see the cars and trucks passing. Halfway through she thinks she hears a twig break and again is filled with mortal terror. But nobody is there. She again decides to regard her fear as good.

The conference is at the Holiday Inn in Chapel Hill. It is supposed to be a pretty town. But the hotel is just off the highway, and she doesn't know if there will be time to do anything else. She checks in at the desk and is given a key card, which she uses to let herself into a small room containing a large bed, television, end table, and upholstered chair. It is like every other hotel room in America: too lush. There are too many pillows, too many layers of curtains, patterns everywhere. Immediately she would like to strip everything away so that it is all simple. She does remove the comforter from the bed and stuffs it into the shallow closet, and this allows her to feel slightly calm.

It's time to venture down to the ballroom, where there will be an opening-night presentation.

Elisa puts on her lanyard (the tag reads *CrackedLisa*) and picks up her binder and rides downstairs in the elevator. No music: the elevator is a silent box. She listens to herself breathing. The doors open onto the lobby, where a sign marked METAPHYSICSNET/SCIFITV, with an arrow, stands on an easel. She follows it to the ballroom.

The room is enormous. In the center stand hundreds of folding chairs arranged into neat rows. Around the edge, buffet tables are covered with food. The front of the room is dominated by a low stage. A lectern stands in the center, with a giant screen behind it. There is a hum of loud conversation.

It's mostly white men, and most of the white men have beards. They are all holding plates of food and cans of soda. Nobody else seems to have brought down the binder. Elisa chooses a chair halfway back, along the inside aisle, and sets her binder down on the seat. Then she goes to the buffet and helps herself to a sandwich and a can of soda.

She wanders around the edges of the hall. More people keep coming in—there have to be 150 here now. Her arms are trembling a little bit: they are tired from the drive. Why did she come exactly? She wants to go back to her room and hook up her laptop and talk to these people on the internet. These aren't the people she knows—these people have faces and bodies, their personalities are manifest on their faces. A frizzy-haired woman, whip thin, cackles at a bearded man's joke. A chubby boy stands alone, wincing: he looks like a graduate student in some impractical subject. A pale man in a plaid shirt is swaying as if in a gentle breeze. Elisa keeps her smile carefully calibrated to deflect unwanted attention. And how is she supposed to eat her sandwich with this soda can in her hand?

She returns to her seat, balances the binder on her lap, and uses it as a table. She faces forward and waits. In spite of herself, she scans the room, in vain, for Silas.

Eventually the lights dim and grow bright again. People sit down. Somebody, a round-faced man, settles in beside her, wiggling his behind on the chair. She suppresses a wave of panic. The lights go dark and stage lights come on and people applaud. When a man walks onto the stage, they applaud again, louder this time.

He's lanky, easy, charismatic in a nerdy way. He wears khaki pants and a white shirt that looks like a tablecloth. He bought that shirt for himself, Elisa thinks.

"Good evening, and welcome to the seventh annual MetaphysicsNet-SciFiTV conference!" Applause. "I'm Peter Turner, founder of Metaphysics-Net, and I'm happy to say that this year's conference is our biggest and best yet!" More applause. Peter Turner describes what is in store, which is to say what is listed in the binder on Elisa's lap. We like things to be redundant, she thinks. It's a comfort to us to be told what we already know. Because we don't trust ourselves—we need to be reassured.

Indeed, Elisa feels reassured. She is grateful for the repetition. There is something mesmerizing about this experience: sitting in this large dark room with all these strangers, the carpeted floor and walls swallowing sound, so that there is no echo. The PA system on the verge of feedback but never reaching it. She can hear the hum of the air-conditioning and feel a faint vibration underfoot, as though powerful generators are operating directly below her. The man beside her is breathing evenly through his mouth, and every now and then the breaths give way to a chuckle, after which the breaths speed, then slow, then settle. The speaker begins, then ends, a sentence; when he's through he begins another.

All around her, the spectacle of humanity in control of its emotions and actions. All around her, calm anticipation. She tucks her unfinished meal underneath her seat and folds her hands together on her binder. She closes her eyes.

Peter Turner introduces the opening speaker, who receives a loud ovation. She hasn't heard of him—he works in Hollywood. He's the consultant for a famous TV series about UFOs. People laugh as he speaks but Elisa isn't hearing the words. She is thinking about the other Lisa, in the other world. She is convinced that this other iteration of her is also at this conference, that world's version of this conference, and that she is sitting in this same folding chair—that the two of them are still similar enough to have chosen the same seat. She feels that Lisa's hands on her own binder, feels them intertwined with her own. The other Lisa is thinking about her, too. Their hearts stutter against one another, then synchronize. Their breaths ease into phase. They have two sons and both are alive. They are married and they are separated. They work at a college and they work at a lab. They drive matching Hondas and are forty-six years old.

She is dimly aware that something has changed. There's noise. Somebody is touching her arm.

"Miss? Miss?"

It's the man beside her, the round-faced man. He's tapping her. She opens her eyes. The lights are on, and people are standing up. The man is younger than she is, but he is still calling her "miss." He says, "You're spilling your soda."

She looks down. Her soda can is leaning at a sharp angle in her hand, and a pool of liquid is flowing toward the edge of her conference binder. She stares at it in incomprehension. *I don't drink soda.* Maybe it was the other Lisa who chose it? Maybe she has switched—she's that Lisa now. She's back in the other world! Panic is rising in her chest; she gasps for breath.

"Uh . . . here," the man says, and he drops a paper napkin onto the spill. Then he takes the binder and can from her hands, brushing her thigh with his fingers in the process. "Sorry, sorry," he says. "You fell asleep?"

He sets the binder and soda on the carpet. She blinks at him. It's making sense now. She calms down. *I'm myself, not her.* His ID says *RueTheDay.*

"I don't think so," she says.

He's smiling at her now. He says, "Yes, you did. You're CrackedLisa!"

"Oh," she says. "I'm—yes, sorry." She holds out her hand. "I know you."

"What a pleasure!"

"Yes!"

"That talk was so awesome. Do you watch *Depths* on SciFiTV?"

"I—ah, no. I don't."

The man talks for a while. She remembers his avatar: it's a version of himself, rendered as a character from the cartoon *South Park.* The resemblance really is strong, uncanny even. He's very animated, around thirty. He wears a wedding ring and there are sweat stains under his armpits.

They stand up. He calls over a friend, an energetic woman it is clear he has a crush on, a crush that embarrasses him. She is curvy and pouty and also around thirty; her name is nottennis. Elisa knows her, too—she's the kitten wearing a jetpack.

Elisa listens to them talk. She answers a few questions. They seem excited to have an older person interested in the same things they are, although she hasn't recognized a single reference from either of them yet. She follows them out of the room and into the hotel bar, where she meets more people, shakes a lot of hands, and allows a tall, professorial type to flirt with her. His beard is prematurely white and there is a kind of flair to his personal awkwardness that she likes. She considers, then decides against, going to bed with him.

It occurs to her that she's wearing a wedding ring. She can't decide whether or not to take it off. If she leaves it on, maybe men will be less guarded with her, with less apparently at stake. But then again they might not even try. And is that what she wants, to hook up? Maybe a part of her does. She hasn't had much sex lately—why doesn't she want it more?

She leaves the ring on. She imagines that, in a parallel world, perhaps not the one she knows, she has taken it off and it has changed everything.

Several times throughout the evening a woman glances at her from across the room. She is around fifty, quite heavy, moon-faced. She wears round eyeglasses and a pink blouse with ruffled collar and sleeves and a capacious, coarse yellow skirt that reminds Elisa, in its thick folds, of the valance over the window in her hotel room. The woman isn't wearing a lanyard, and she seems to have a glow, like the moon itself. Her movements are slow and deliberate, as though they have been choreographed.

Elisa doesn't look for Patricia, because somehow she knows that this woman is her, though the woman is nothing like she imagined. They do not approach each other or introduce themselves: she isn't sure why. She feels disengaged in general from the conference, in fact—out of place and insufficiently interested. The bar is getting more crowded now and people keep jostling her from behind, reaching around her for their drinks. Bits of conversation intended for others are inadvertently shouted in her ear. *really sucked after season three. and boobs out to here. which isn't in the remake. lifetime of gastrointestinal whatever.* She looks around the room for Silas and could swear she sees Betsy Orosco exiting.

Betsy! Suddenly Elisa feels revitalized. She wants to talk to her, to get to the bottom of that whole thing. They really made a connection that day, last summer, didn't they? Surely Betsy doesn't think she's just some nut. Elisa doesn't mind, not really, what happened—she just wishes they'd been honest with her, that's all.

She gets up, mutters excuse me, pushes through the crowd. People keep staggering into her path carrying multiple drinks. Everyone's voice is loud, far louder than one might expect of nerds. Finally she's through and into the lobby, where the ambient temperature drops by five degrees, and where Muzak is drifting down from the ceiling. She looks around: there, down that hall. It must be her, the blue hair, the broad hips and purposeful stride. Elisa runs to catch up, sneakers squeaking on the fake marble floor.

It's not a hallway, actually, it's the foyer the elevators open onto, four sets of doors, four illuminated panels displaying the numbers of floors. One set is closing. Elisa hurries to it, peers inside as the strip of light narrows. There she is, the same rounded shoulders and cat-eye glasses. "Betsy!"

Betsy Orosco glances over Elisa's shoulder, looks right past as if she isn't there. Then the elevator doors close and she's gone.

51.

Sometime in the night she wakes up and tries to slide herself out of the big bed. She is bound up in the sheets, she feels them tugging out from under the mattress, and by the time one foot has hit the carpet the other has become stuck, and she flings her arms out for balance and finds the wall. She is standing there in the dark, in a frozen pirouette, her heart racing. She feels fully awake but knows she is not. The sheets release her foot. She collapses against the wall, pressing her face and both hands to it.

Elisa has no idea where she is. She doesn't know which direction to move in. She knows that she isn't at home: there is no sound from anywhere and no air is moving. She says Derek's name and then remembers she and Derek are no longer together, and then doubts that memory.

She thinks of the boys and experiences a moment of panic. In her mind they are five and six years old and in danger. This isn't right, she can't put her finger on how. She moves a step, then another, along this wall and suddenly fears moving further; she does not want to get closer to the boys. Whatever is the matter, she will make it worse. She says Derek's name again, and now it feels truly wrong: she's coming to. She's in a hotel. She went on a trip. Is she in Wisconsin? No—North Carolina. It's a Holiday Inn. The bathroom is just around the corner. She can move, now, in the dark.

Back on the bed she is sweating profusely. As if in response, the air-conditioning kicks on with a grunt. The clock reads 3:14. Then it reads 4:40. Then it's light and she is lying shivering with the sheets tugged off the bed and bundled in a heap beside it. She feels as though she hasn't slept at all.

She wears her lanyard to breakfast and sits with some people from the parallel worlds forum, including RueTheDay. They are mostly younger than she is, except for one very old man. His ID reads *CharlesSmith*. Elisa doesn't recognize the name. The group is animated and enthusiastic, and they are talking about the same things they talk about online, except that, in the absence of official moderation, they mention more television programs.

It's not quite what she was expecting. But she isn't certain what's missing. She finds herself peering across the banquet room, trying to identify other forum members, but she can't read their tags from here. She doesn't see Betsy anywhere. The woman she thinks is Patricia fills a bowl with scrambled eggs, then scans the room as though looking for a seat. She makes eye contact with Elisa, puts on a small demure smile, and walks in the opposite direction, to where there is an empty table. A few moments later a man walking on crutches sits down with her and the two sit facing each other in apparent silence.

The first major event of the day is a parallel worlds panel—it is one of the main reasons she is here. Her breakfast companions ask her if she is excited about it. Their attention takes her by surprise—it is strange that these unfamiliar people know something about her, about her preoccupations.

"I suppose I am," she tells them, and they all laugh.

A tired-looking man called part_human says, "You're just like you are on the board."

"What am I like on the board?"

"Reserved," says nottennis. She is clearly enjoying the attention of the men around her.

"Restrained," says PresumedInsane. He is her age, shockingly thin, Adam's apple, black beard spattered with gray.

RueTheDay says, "You're our resident grown-up."

"I'm not that much older than you."

"Not your *age*," says nottennis, "The way you *are*."

"Oh."

To her left, CharlesSmith silently works his jaw. He is alert but looks no one in the eye. After a time, he struggles to his feet and leaves.

Nottennis says, "Um, has anybody ever even heard of that guy?"

The parallel worlds panel is in a small conference room down the hall.

There's a dais with four microphones set up on it, facing about a hundred folding chairs. Elisa considers waiting for her breakfast companions, but doesn't want to sit near nottennis unless she absolutely has to. So she hangs back and sits on the aisle in an otherwise unoccupied row.

The panel consists of a TV producer, a science fiction writer, a blogger whom everyone but Elisa seems to have read, and Betsy Orosco. Betsy has come in late; she is in fact eating a piece of toast. The other panelists, all men, steal glances at her that Elisa interprets as appraising. Betsy seems confident, in her element. She finishes the toast and sits with her hands folded, waiting. When ten o'clock arrives, they begin.

There is no moderator; the four speakers introduce themselves and each offers some opening comments on the subject. None of the four seems particularly comfortable around the other three. To Elisa's dismay, the TV producer dominates—he shares stories about working with particular famous actors. The science fiction writer clearly dislikes him—he denigrates the narrative logic of the producer's most popular show. The blogger tells jokes that fall flat, and Betsy, at first, appears as though she regrets coming at all. She tries, gamely enough, to talk about the actual physics of the multiverse, in much the way she presented it to Elisa in her office the year before. But here, it isn't going over so well. She explains in detail, too much detail, the complex quantum requirements for a universe to be created, and the audience shifts in their seats. And when she tells them that travel among universes is largely impossible, several people actually groan.

"But you never know, right?" says the blogger.

"That's right," the TV producer says brightly, to mild laughter, "you never know!" By the time the audience begins raising questions, everyone seems exhausted, as if it's midafternoon and they have been conferencing all day.

At some point Elisa feels a presence beside her and turns to find that the presumptive Patricia has taken a seat two down from her. She is wearing a floral print dress, clean new running shoes, and a crucifix around her neck. She is staring straight ahead. Her hands are folded in her lap and she remains perfectly still. Elisa smells perfume.

Someone in the front of the room, she thinks it's RueTheDay, is asking

Betsy a question. "You say we can't travel back and forth between universes," he says. "But what about our consciousness? You know, our awareness?"

Betsy's answer, littered with finger quotes, is given with a wrinkled brow. Elisa is trying to concentrate on it. "I'm not sure if that's a question for physics. I mean, we'd need to define what 'consciousness' means, in terms of physics. If you want to get philosophical . . . in theory . . . I guess 'you' are already there, the iteration of you that is native to that universe."

"But is there . . . can you think of a mechanism . . . by which . . ."

"He's not taking no for an answer!" quips the blogger.

". . . by which the consciousness could travel . . . could be transferred . . ."

"Into the Matrix!" the blogger says.

". . . or I guess shared with that of the other you, or yous?"

Betsy leans forward. "Believe me, I want to say yes . . ."

"So say yes!" says the blogger.

". . . but physics is concerned with the kind of questions that we can support with mathematics or experimentation. 'Consciousness' is a psychological notion, a philosophical notion. It is interesting, but it isn't something we can apply freely to our work. I can't say that something like consciousness can be transferred because I don't know what it consists of. And neither does anyone else."

Yes. Yes, Elisa is thinking, nobody knows, nobody understands. And this ought to reassure her, because it means that whatever she wants to be true about this experience, whatever she would like to believe has happened to her, is possible. It doesn't matter what Betsy Orosco or Hugo Bonaventure thinks, it doesn't matter what the guy at Caltech thinks, it doesn't matter what Amos Finley thinks. They can't tell her otherwise, can they?—because they don't know. They can't know. The only person who can decide what it is that has happened to her is herself: the experience is hers to define, and hers to explain or not. Her life, her consciousness.

But instead of feeling reassured, she begins to feel panicked. Because it occurs to her that what she wants—what she has wanted all along—is not simply to know. It is to be believed. She has placed her greatest need in the hands of other people—strangers in an alien world.

They are all strangers here, even herself.

Elisa senses a movement to her right. It is Patricia. She is placing a twice-folded rectangle of paper on the seat between them.

52.

Elisa leaves the paper there. She knows it is for her but can't bring herself to pick it up. The room is decorated in various shades of beige and gray and the paper is the whitest thing in it. It lies slightly open, the four corners lined up sharply, pointed at her. She can see into its maw, where a few lines of text have been printed.

The science fiction writer is speaking now. Somebody has asked him how parallel worlds should be depicted in stories, if the concept is bound by rules. His response is impatient; he speaks as though it is beneath him to be asked such a thing.

"Every compelling concept is bound by rules. But I can't sit here and tell them to you. They're determined by the story."

But Elisa is still staring at the paper. She detects movement and looks up to find that Patricia has turned her head and is gazing at her with moist and beatific eyes, smiling faintly, pitying her. Patricia blinks—no, she bats her eyelashes. The smell of her perfume is stronger now.

And now Patricia stands up and walks, floats almost, out of the room. To Elisa this seems disruptive, drastic: isn't there a kind of hush in the room just now, a suspension of movement and sound? But nobody seems to notice it happening. All that is left is the paper on the chair and the voice of the science fiction novelist.

". . . for instance, in my last book, *Familiar,* which maybe some of you have read . . ."

"Very fine piece of work," says the TV producer.

"Why, thank you, Roland, have your people talk to my people. But in that book, the protagonist, a young man in search of his twin, enters parallel worlds through the pages of a book, a sort of enchanted book also called *Familiar . . .*"

The blogger says, "Everybody loves the po-mo," to scattered laughs.

Elisa is only half-listening. She reaches out and picks up the paper. Her dry hands make a sharp sound, sliding against it, unfolding it. She looks up to see if anyone has noticed. But nobody is paying attention.

The message has been printed on a computer. It reads:

> I know what you are going through . . . I can help you . . . I will come to you . . . we will talk . . . a better life awaits . . . don't worry. There is an answer to all your questions . . . a solution to your problems . . . don't worry . . . soon. Patricia.

Somehow the message reads like a code—it seems to say more than is printed here. She reads it again and again, straining against the possibility of hope. Could Patricia be the one? Why not? Someone just said something about the rules being determined by the story. This is her story, isn't it? She, Elisa, can make the rules.

The voices of the panelists fall silent. She looks up and catches Betsy frowning at her from the dais, as though trying to figure something out.

Elisa's fingers begin to twitch. The paper in her hand crackles and she rises to her feet. She's angry.

"Betsy!"

The room turns to her. There's a wildness in her voice, a raggedness that is almost sexual. Her breaths catch in her throat and suddenly her heart is pounding so frantically against her blouse that she thinks she can see, on the periphery of her vision, the fabric moving. She tries to calm herself, to tamp down the desperation in her voice, but it's hopeless. She says, "I wonder if you might talk about my experience of this phenomenon. What we talked about last year. And where you stand on that."

Someone coughs. The silence deepens. Betsy opens her mouth to speak, then closes it again and glances at the papers in front of her. She looks up and says, "I know that . . . I'm not sure . . ."

"You sent me to your friend Hugo. He was going to do tests . . . well, he was going to have his friends do them. Tests. On my things."

She doesn't sound like herself at all.

"A tube of lipstick. And a list. One from both worlds, one from this one alone!"

Betsy is frowning again. She says, "I don't think . . ." and then trails off. She's gripping a pen in her fist and is clicking the nib in and out with her thumb.

"I went there—to the lab. They gave me my things back. They didn't know you, or Hugo."

Into the eerie quiet of the room, Betsy says, "I'm sorry, I don't know anything about that."

Elisa says, too quietly to be heard, "Did you ever believe me?"

And by now someone else has raised a hand, asked the TV producer a question. Elisa is still standing, still staring at Betsy, who is still clicking her pen. Eventually Betsy looks away, and Elisa sits down. She is not entirely sure what specifically she just said. The folded note is still in her hand. Her heart is still racing.

And then the room is empty, or nearly so, the neat rows of folding chairs have been disrupted and young people wearing eyeglasses and ID tags are bustling about pushing them back into place. Some people are standing near her, it's nottennis and RueTheDay. There's an electric, frightened intensity about them: at first she assumes it's because they are attracted to one another, that RueTheDay is contemplating an affair. And maybe they are, maybe he is. But then she asks them what they're doing next, are they going to the movie premiere in the ballroom, and they are strangely evasive. Nottennis takes a step back, bumping into someone to whom she must apologize.

"Uh . . . yeah," says RueTheDay, "I think maybe we'll make our way there eventually."

"We have to do something else first," nottennis adds.

"Maybe we'll see you there?"

Elisa nods, folding the paper in her hand into a still smaller rectangle. "Sure. Sure."

The two of them retreat with evident relief, while Elisa stands blinking, wondering what just happened. She looks around the room. People are clustered in little groups, stealing glances at her. Betsy Orosco seems to have left, and the three male panelists are laughing about something at the dais.

She fears, is in fact quite certain, that she has made a fool of herself.

53.

That night she attends a talk on alien abductions and a panel on the possible alternate forms intelligent life might take. She meets a couple from the forum named Seth and Janet. These are their screen names. They tell her they just found the idea funny, giving themselves "normal" names to use online; they say they've taken to calling one another Seth and Janet around the house. Elisa didn't realize they were married. They don't seem to have been at the panel discussion this morning; they didn't witness her performance.

She goes with them to the hotel bar and the three of them drink. A lot. Seth announces at some point that he's going to kiss Elisa; Janet tells him to go ahead, in fact she dares him. He does it, and the two of them kiss for a while. He's only a few years younger than she is, and is quite attractive, with broad shoulders and a narrow waist and a bit of hair poking out of his collar from his back and chest. Janet whoops and laughs and then takes over, kissing Elisa with evidently equal enthusiasm. It isn't as unpleasant as she might have imagined, though it is indeed unpleasant. They invite her up to their room and Elisa says no at least twenty or thirty times. At some point they leave the bar. "But we've had such fun!" Elisa shouts after them. They are laughing too hard to hear.

Then she's with RueTheDay and nottennis, and they're laughing at her too. At times they whisper things to each other and then look at Elisa and crack up. She finds herself asking anyone who will listen that it is imperative that they wake up CharlesSmith and bring him down here immediately, and if they don't do it, by God, she's going to go do it herself. Then she is in the elevator and her hand is flapping uselessly against the glowing numbers. Somehow she manages to hit her floor and staggers back into the corner.

She hasn't been this drunk since . . . college? She can't remember very far back. The elevator heaves and sways. It stops, and the doors open, but she doesn't get out, she just remains pinned to the back wall, staring out at the hallway: a vase full of fake flowers on a round wooden table, a seascape hanging above it. There are voices. The doors close, and then, a moment later, open again. Three people get in, a man and two women; they are talking and laughing, the man looking over his shoulder.

". . . she was like, 'Okay, fine!' And I was like, 'Fine!'"

"Of course she's like that."

"Did you meet her mother?"

"Oh, God."

"And then that *coat*."

"She called it 'vintage.'"

"Well, we shouldn't make fun."

"Oh, yes we should!"

The doors open. The people get out. It's the lobby—the elevator has gone back down without Elisa noticing. She hits the button for her floor again. This time she'll do it—she'll get out of the elevator and go to her room. As the doors close and the elevator begins to rise, she studies an advertisement affixed to the wall above the buttons. It reads, "Good times, good friends. Your one-stop dinner solution on game day!" The phrase seems hilarious; she snorts and giggles. Then she sighs, loudly, and begins to feel as though something in the elevator is different.

It's a change in the light, a change in the space. She groans a little and it sounds wrong. For no reason that she can fathom, she says "Ow." She fixates on the spot where the horizontal crack between the doors and floor meets the vertical one between the doors. It's sort of sexual. The elevator stops. The doors open and the spot vanishes and she says "Whoa."

Three people get in, a man and two women; they are talking and laughing. The man is looking over his shoulder.

". . . she was like, 'Okay, fine!' And I was like, 'Fine!'"

"Of course she's like that."

"Did you meet her mother?"

"Oh, God."

"And then that *coat*."

"She called it 'vintage.'"

"Well, we shouldn't make fun."

"Oh, yes we should!"

Elisa tries not to move or make a sound. She has backed into a corner of the elevator, in an effort not to be seen. She is terrified. None of the people look at her. The door opens onto the lobby and they get out and Patricia gets in.

"Patricia?" she says, and her voice sounds very small and far away.

Patricia smiles that same beatific smile. She nods and presses the button for Elisa's floor. How does she know? Maybe she doesn't, maybe it's her floor too.

As the elevator rises, Elisa's breaths become shallower, faster. "Patricia," she says, "if they're out there . . ."

The elevator stops. The doors open. "Is there? Anyone there?"

Patricia shakes her head no, still smiling. She holds out a hand to Elisa and Elisa takes it, and allows Patricia to lead her into the vestibule.

But they're there. All three of them. And one of the women is saying, "And she said, 'Maybe you shouldn't come to the party after all.'"

"You have *got* to be kidding me," says the other.

"I am *not*. So I said, 'Fine, then,' and she was like, 'Okay, fine!' And I was like, 'Fine!'"

"Of course she's like that."

"Did you meet her mother?"

And as they enter the elevator the man looks over his shoulder, back at Elisa, who stares at him in horror. He blinks, and then the doors close and the people are gone.

There's a hand on her elbow. There's a smell of perfume. She is being guided down a hallway. She has had the presence of mind to dig her key card out of her pocket and now she is fumbling to slip it into the lock. But Patricia's soft hand is there to guide her. She is led into the room, to a chair, she is pressed down into the chair and then a soft shape is in the near-blackness of the room pulling back the comforter and sheets on the bed.

"Thankyou," Elisa is saying, "thankyou," and then her shoes are being removed, and her socks, and she's lying in the bed on the cool rough sheets and it feels so incredibly wonderful that she wants to cry.

"Is this real?" she wants to know, but no one answers.

Then she's awake again, the room is spinning, and she is kneeling in front of the toilet vomiting, with a warm hand, a hot hand actually, pressed into the middle of her back. "Gedditoff," she says and tries to brush it away, and the hand disappears.

She manages to brush her teeth and drink some water. Beside her, someone is cleaning the toilet with a wadded-up bit of toilet paper. She has the impression that it is perhaps Elisa, the other Elisa, come to visit this world. (Wouldn't that be nice, she thinks—we could be friends.) A peculiar sensation overcomes her—as she is nearly awake enough now, nearly sober enough now, to be disturbed by the presence of a stranger in her hotel room—of not quite being disturbed, or of contemplating being disturbed; she is aware that she can make, if she wishes, a *decision* about how she will feel. Her thoughts, though, are close and cluttered and bloated, jostling against each other in her head, and she can't keep them still enough to follow any one of them to its conclusion. She really just wants to get back into bed. She has taken her pants off, or somebody has, so she is standing here in the nightlit bathroom in her underwear and a linen blouse stained with flecks of her own sick, and the figure at the toilet rises, and the toilet flushes, and then she is led back to the bed and is asleep again.

54.

When Elisa wakes it is not yet morning, or it is morning and the heavy curtains have been closed, and Patricia is sitting in the chair, which she has moved to the side of the bed and in which she seems to be praying silently. The only light comes from the night-light in the bathroom, and the glowing alarm clock, which is blinking 12:00, and the strip at the base of the door. Elisa feels hollowed out and queasy; her mouth is filled with paste. She sits up. A glass of water stands on the end table, so she picks it up and drinks from it. Patricia is staring at her.

"I'm here to help you," Patricia says.

Her voice is unexpectedly rough and deep, like a heavy smoker's. Perhaps, in a previous life, that's what she was. She is holding something in her hands—a rosary? Elisa can't quite make it out, only the pale thick fingers working at it.

She is so tired—more tired, if this is even possible, than she was when she collapsed into bed. She wants this strange woman to leave so that she can go back to sleep. It would be simple enough to tell her so. To ask her to leave. Elisa draws a deep breath. She says, "I don't think you can."

"Take my hands."

"Patricia. You are Patricia, right? I'm sorry, I just need to sleep. I need to sleep."

The desk chair is positioned two feet from the edge of the bed. Elisa yawns. It is possible that she falls asleep again, sitting up with her head against the bedboard, for a few minutes, or maybe an hour. When she opens her eyes, Patricia is still waiting. Her hands are empty now and lying, palms up, fingers spread, against the floral print of her dress. Her glasses are hanging around her neck on a chain. The gloom makes her seem both more and less real.

That's it: Elisa must submit, or the woman will never leave. She drags herself to the edge of the bed, keeping the sheets twisted around her waist, covering her thighs. She drops her legs over the side, so that her knees are even with Patricia's; just an inch separates their bodies. Elisa reaches out and places her two hands, faceup, onto the other woman's palms.

"Okay," she says, "help me."

Patricia nods, once, and her heavy features rearrange themselves into a small, slow frown, a scowl of concentration. Her fingers close on Elisa's hands.

Elisa is so disappointed now: both in the conference, and in herself, for the way she has behaved. Why did she kiss those people in the bar? Everyone saw her do it. Why did she ask Betsy that question? It seems to her that she has run out of chances, not just here, but in her life. That this is the way it will be now: things will keep being left behind and never returned to, and life will take on a depressing, inevitable forward momentum, like a glacier's, slow and inexorable. And then it will end.

(She is wrong, of course. Things will change, they always do. There will be times when she looks back a few months, a week, even a day, and wonders at how innocent she was then, when the fabric of life felt so different. How could she be so oblivious to things that, in the here and now, are so obvious? Of course she will go back to Derek, eventually. He will, in fact, beg her to do so, going so far as to propose marriage to her a second time, though they won't have divorced.

It is true that the boys will stay disappeared, that she won't see them again for a long, long time. But they'll be in touch, after a fashion. She and Silas will seek each other out online. He will use his sig lines as signals to her. He will go by various names, on various forums; he will track her interests, her obsessions, hovering at the boundaries of her attention, moving out of view when she gets too close. He won't respond to messages. This will be their private game. They will follow one another's iterations, they will die off and respawn in unexpected places, and she won't tell Derek. And when at last he appears to her in the flesh, when he brings his brother to her as well, to forgive, it will be as sudden and inexplicable as everything else he's done, yet it will feel perfectly natural to her, familiar and unfamiliar at the same time, like everything else in the strange, enormous, echo-filled room that is her life.

There was only ever one Lisa, she'll tell herself then. There was only ever one life. It was just larger and more peculiar than she expected.)

But for now Patricia's fingernails are digging themselves into her flesh, and Elisa feels herself tugged forward, her elbows popping and cracking with the sudden strain, and out of Patricia's mouth comes a stream of loud, incomprehensible speech. Elisa cries out, tries to pull away from the other woman's grip, but it's too powerful, and Elisa is too tired and sick. "That hurts," she says between clenched teeth, but Patricia isn't listening, she's talking, it's all gibberish and Elisa can feel spittle landing on her bare arms.

And then Patricia's voice rises; she's shouting now. Surely this is waking up the other guests? Surely one of them is calling the front desk? The woman's hands are crushing Elisa's, she seems to be trembling; Elisa can feel it through the floor and can make out a glint of light from the dangling eyeglasses, shuddering in the air. Why doesn't she pull away? Why did she let the woman into her room in the first place? *It doesn't seem like something I would do. That just doesn't seem like me.* Here she is, though: Elisa has given up on escaping her, this woman called DippedInSunshine.

And now she tries to concentrate, she tries to listen. Because that was her problem, wasn't it—she didn't listen. The roaring in her head was always louder. So she concentrates on her fear and on the pain in her hands and on the torrent of sounds spewing from Patricia's mouth: these twisted vocalizations, the vowels elongated and shrill, the consonants clacking and popping in her face. It's language. It's saying something, something just for her, something that will help. She's so tired, but she digs in: she grips back, hard, and the two women sit there, trying to break each other's hands, one trying to understand, the other trying to make herself understood. Elisa wants to stop, but she can't, she knows that the second it ends will be the second right before it would have started making sense. And so she bears down, telling herself it will work, that in the end it's actually possible to believe in your dream so completely that you can drag the rest of the world into it with you.

Acknowledgments

For various kinds of assistance with this novel, the author would like to thank Tom Bissell, Jennifer Brice, Rhian Ellis, Brian Hall, Kristine Heiney, Fiona McCrae, Ethan Nosowsky, Jim Rutman, Ed Skoog, and Steve Strogatz.

A Graywolf Press Reading Group Guide

FAMILIAR

A Novel

J. Robert Lennon

DISCUSSION QUESTIONS

1. Do you think that Elisa really shifted into another world? If so, do you think she will ever return to her former life? How do you think her experience of the parallel world might affect her life in the former world?

2. Early in the novel, Elisa asks herself, "Is a breakdown a thing you feel, or a thing that changes your relationship to other people?" Do you think Elisa had a breakdown? If so, how did her breakdown change her, both as an individual and in relation to her family?

3. At one point, Elisa speculates that her shift was like a swap, and that the other Elisa is now living *her* life. Which Elisa do you think would have the harder time adjusting?

4. *Familiar* is just as focused on Elisa's possible parallel world as it is in the state of her dysfunctional family. In both of her lives, Elisa is deeply flawed and the family suffers because of it. What similarities did you see between the characters and their parallel selves? What differences?

5. Throughout the book, images of "cracked" things (windshields, skylights, elevator doors) appear frequently. What symbolic weight do these images hold? How does the user name "CrackedLisa" connect with these images?

6. There is a strong correlation throughout the book between Elisa's experience of her parallel world and the parallel world video games create

for us. Are video games a form of mindless entertainment or can they transform players the same way books transform readers? How can video games affect our understanding of and interaction with others in the world around us?

7. Elisa is able to track down Silas's numerous online identities by searching his signature tagline: "He saw himself in a strange city with his friend, except that the face of his friend was different." This is also the closing line of the book's epigraph. Why is this quote meaningful, for Silas and for the book as a whole?

8. By the end of the novel, Elisa's immersion in the parallel worlds online forum is so complete that she identifies with her user name, CrackedLisa. What does this identification suggest about how she acts in new situations, like the forum conference?

9. What do you make of the character of Patricia? Does she know something more than Elisa or is she a fraud? What do you think happens to Patricia and Elisa when they clasp hands in the hotel room?

10. On the last page, Elisa comes to the conclusion that "there was only ever one Lisa. . . . There was only ever one life. It was just larger and more peculiar than she expected." Do you think Elisa is speaking literally or figuratively?

ON WRITING *FAMILIAR*

J. Robert Lennon

On the morning of September 11, 2001, I was scheduled to fly from Syracuse, New York, to Cedar Rapids, Iowa, by way of Chicago, for the start of the promotional tour for my third book, *On the Night Plain.* I was supposed to be reading that night at Prairie Lights Books in Iowa City, and then continuing on to another week and a half of travel and readings.

By the time I landed in Chicago, though, the terrorist attacks on New York and Washington had already occurred, and every airport in America was closed. I managed to rent a car and make it to Iowa City, where I did indeed deliver a horribly lackluster reading to three depressed people.

Obviously the reading was lackluster—as was the case for most Americans that day, all of my personal preoccupations suddenly felt stupid and pointless in the light of national events, and it would be some time before I managed to write anything at all, let alone pick up the thread of projects I'd begun before the attacks. Clarity was in short supply among writers—none of us seemed to know anymore what was important about our work, or how we might write about the new political, moral, and emotional landscape of our country. I don't think I was alone that week in feeling less inspired than at almost any time in my life. The rest of my book tour was cancelled, of course, and I headed home in my rental car with my suitcase full of free *On the Night Plain* tee shirts.

Yet it was during that lonely drive back to upstate New York that I got the idea for *Familiar,* sort of. If you were on the roads during that time, you might remember the feeling of unreality that pervaded the country— the skies were clear and blue and free of airplanes, and the faces in the cars around me appeared hard and bewildered. I felt, like many did, I think, as though I were driving through a subtly altered world, one that was still familiar, but eerily so, as though remembered from a dream. It was uncertain, still, what had actually happened, and how things were about to change—a difference could be felt, sure, but when you tried to examine it, it slipped away from you.

I wasn't thinking directly of this experience when, a year later, I tried to write the opening chapters of what would eventually become this book. All I knew was that I wanted to write about a woman in a car who slips into a parallel universe. That's all I had. In those days, I was hoping I might someday be able to write novels without particular forethought— to just sit down and free-associate and come up with brilliant sloppy things that could be molded into shapely, metaphorically rich narratives. But I didn't have the chops. I abandoned the book after forty pages or so, then started taking notes for a different novel, one that I could plan out ahead of time, at least a little.

As it happens, I still don't have the skill to turn garbage into gold— who does? But not long ago, with another decade of experience under my belt, and a couple of novels that attempted, more directly, to address the aftereffects of September 11, I decided to revisit my abortive dramatization of my drive home from Iowa. I printed out the abandoned pages, then deleted the computer file. I opened a new file and rewrote the pages, to see if I could gather some momentum this time. And, lo and behold, I could.

Not that I knew any better what I was doing. But I did know that this book was not going to be about the terrorist attacks. Rather, it was going to be about the cognitive dissonance that traumatic events introduce into our minds—about the connections between the fragile construction of the self and the chaotic world outside.

The crazy thing is, I didn't want to write about parenthood. At all. I had realized early on that in the new world Elisa comes to inhabit, the son she is mourning never died. It seemed like a cool plot twist, that was all. I'd envisioned *Familiar* as an oblique, rather detached, bit of literary sci-fi, something spare and enigmatic. Indeed, the first draft of this book was brutally short. Everything went unsaid. The reviews, I imagined, would employ the words "restrained," "taut," and "edgy."

Instead, my wife, the writer Rhian Ellis—who, for a couple of decades, has served as my indispensable first-pass editor—called it what it really was: "unfinished."

It wasn't until draft three that I fully accepted that I was writing a novel about the psychological effects of parenthood—the transformations our personalities undergo in response to the utter impossibility of doing the right thing day in and day out for eighteen years and more. To survive being a parent is to fictionalize memory—to constantly re-create and re-contextualize the past, to invent a narrative that makes sense of the bizarre distortions introduced into one's life under the strain of responsibility, obligation, and love. This is a burden borne by even the happiest parents (and I do count myself among them), but it grows unbearably heavy when tragedy strikes. The death of a child crushes the self. It shatters all the illusions that keep our family lives intact. To the parent who experiences it, the loss of a child is like a bomb going off, a building collapsing, a world vanishing and another taking its place.

Unlike every thus-afflicted parent since the dawn of time, Elisa Brown is given a second chance, and her reaction, at least at first, is to long, terribly, for the tragic life she left behind. We are invested in our illusions—I wanted to explore what might happen if this particular one were stripped away.

J. ROBERT LENNON is the author of seven novels, including *Castle* and *Mailman,* and a story collection, *Pieces for the Left Hand.* His fiction has appeared in the *Paris Review, Granta, Harper's, Playboy,* and the *New Yorker.* He lives in Ithaca, New York, where he teaches writing at Cornell University.

The text of *Familiar* is set in Adobe Garamond Pro, drawn by Robert Slimbach and based on type cut by Claude Garamond in the sixteenth century. This book was designed by Ann Sudmeier. Composition by BookMobile Design and Digital Publisher Services, Minneapolis, Minnesota. Manufactured by Versa Press on acid-free 30 percent post-consumer wastepaper.